SHARPSTER

by

Elinor Hunter

A Kinord Book

Published by Kinord Books

Edinburgh

www.kinordbooks.com

ISBN: 978-0-9928080-6-8

For Jim, my love, my life

Chapter 1

'To succeed in life, you need two things: ignorance and confidence.' – Mark Twain

St Louis, Missouri, April 1968

HE WAS KING OF THE ROAD. Even after half a dozen beers, Kelton MacLeod was totally in control; knew this stretch like the back of his hand, could drive it blindfolded. But April rain had left an oily film on the surface and the left bend was sharper than he remembered. When his foot touched the brake, the vehicle careered towards the opposite grass verge. With a sickening thud his shiny new Ford Mustang hit something, became airborne then plunged nose-down into a ditch. In a split second of clarity he expected to go hurtling through the windscreen, but the grinding impact threw him forward and sideways against the driver's door. His ribs struck the steering wheel and he heard the crack of his skull on glass. Everything went blank and time stopped.

Inside his head, occasional pinpoints of light flickered like fireflies in the blackness. As consciousness gradually returned, Kelton opened his eyes. Through a fog of pain, the circumstances of the previous hour came back to him. What had he hit? A deer, or perhaps a dog? Whatever! He wanted to take a deep breath, but it hurt too much. He grunted with the effort of pushing himself back up into his seat to brace a knee on the dashboard. Lunging to the passenger side, he grabbed the handle and released the door catch. In slow, painful desperation he eased himself across and upwards till eventually he could clamber out of the wreck.

Disoriented, he stood quiet and still, before staggering towards a clump of trees for cover and almost tripped. Bending over to peer through the darkness, he made out a figure sprawled on the ground. *Geez!* he muttered to himself. Aloud he said, 'You okay? Hey, buddy, you okay?'

Getting no response, he gave a gentle nudge with his shoe, and knelt down to slap at the guy's cheeks. 'Come on, man, don't do this to me,' he pleaded. 'Wake up, huh?'

Kelton leaned in closer to press his thumb and middle finger at each side of the scrawny neck, feeling for a pulse, but detected no life, only the foul, unwashed smell of homelessness. Nauseated, he stood up, and rubbed his fingers down the side of his pants.

The sound of a distant siren gave him a jolt. The last thing he wanted was to be caught at the scene, but he could not resist a final look at the corpse. It most definitely was one for the record books, in a different league from the neighbour's cat and his mother's yappy little dog! He reached into his pocket for the knife he always carried, opened its blade and crouched down. Holding up a handful of the vagrant's greasy, matted hair, Kelton performed his gruesome ritual and tenderly wrapped the trophy in his clean, white cotton handkerchief.

*

She had just dropped off to sleep. The intercom buzzed. Alarmed, she leapt out of bed and went to lift the receiver.

'It's me,' said Kelton's voice. 'Let me in, will you? I'm hurt, had an accident.'

Amy tied the belt of her dressing-gown and waited for him at her door, scarcely recognising the bleeding, dishevelled character that limped stiffly along the corridor towards her. 'What happened?' She reached for his arm.

He recoiled. 'Don't touch me, let me sit down,' he groaned. His face was grey, his skin clammy and his breathing fast. He collapsed on to the sofa. For the next ten minutes, she stood gazing down at him, unsure what to do. Her panic increased when his teeth began to chatter, and his whole body shook.

'I think I should call an ambulance.'

Kelton opened his eyes. '*No!*' The strength of his protest startled her.

'You should at least be checked out at the hospital, in case something's broken. You could have internal bleeding, maybe you need X-rays ...'

'I'll be fine,' he interrupted. Slowly his tremors subsided and colour returned to his cheeks. He eased himself into a sitting position. 'I could murder a cup of coffee!'

'Was any other car involved?' she asked, setting a steaming mug on the table beside him.

He shook his head. 'No. I really got lucky. The road was deserted, I skidded and landed in a ditch. I'm a bit banged up ... nothing some peace and quiet won't cure. Just need to lie low for a few hours, get the alcohol out of my system, you know?'

'Sure,' Amy replied uncertainly.

'I can't tell you how much I appreciate this. Don't want a DUI on my record.' He gave a feeble attempt at a smile.

She stroked his brow. 'No problem.'

A glow of satisfaction spread through her. He'd knocked on her door instead of heading home, a flattering confirmation of the bond between them. His eyelids grew heavy and he nodded off to sleep. Amy crept back to bed. It was hard to credit how quickly things had moved along. Kelton was different from anyone she'd met before, regarded by her friends as quite a catch. Bright, good-looking and from a wealthy family – what was not to like?

Earlier that night, they had eaten at a fancy restaurant on their first proper date, instead of hanging out over burgers and Coke. Unaccustomed to alcohol, she'd found the wine pleasant enough after the first few mouthfuls, and he'd encouraged her to finish the rest of the bottle while he switched to beer.

'Since I'm driving,' he'd explained. 'This is a trick I learned a while back. Beer helps keep you sober.'

She loved his way of focusing exclusively on her. Looking intently at her with his big brown eyes, he'd leaned across the table to tell her she was the most beautiful girl he'd ever seen. Amy had raised her glass with a smile, and wanted to believe him. On the way home, they'd parked in a shady side-street. He reached across to run a forefinger down her cheek and she snuggled into the crook of his arm. The kisses began, softly at first then ever deeper and more insistent while his hands wandered to places no other guy's had gone. Abruptly she pulled away when they were caught in the headlights of an oncoming car.

'Something wrong?' Gently he drew her towards him again and smoothed her long blonde hair.

'Don't want people seeing us, that's all.'

He smiled. 'You're right. Why don't we move into the back?'

This was it. *The crunch.* She'd wanted him to desire her. Now he did, and she was scared. It was clear what he had in mind. She could turn him down, but that would be the end: a guy like Kelton could have any girl he chose. What she refused, he'd seek elsewhere.

Sensing her inner turmoil, he murmured, 'I never felt this way about anyone before, Amy. You and me, we're just right together ... please, I want you so much, it hurts. *I need you.* Please, honey.' His begging melted her resistance.

Thrilled by her own power, she would do anything rather than disappoint him. 'You poor baby,' she crooned.

For years she had anticipated this special moment, dreaming of candles, soft music and rose petals, but losing her virginity was far from the earth-shattering, life-changing event she had expected. The smell of a new car became linked with the embarrassment of that evening: a horrible tangle of legs and arms, where she'd lain trapped in the cramped rear seat, her bare skin sticking to the leather upholstery while Kelton's hot beery breath fogged up the windows. Again and again he'd thrust himself inside her until he was done, leaving her with a gooey mess between her legs and a crick in her neck.

Neither one spoke as they collected themselves. Then he'd taken her hand and squeezed it. 'I'm sorry if it hurt a little ... first time's always the worst.'

It was liberating to have her initiation over with, she consoled herself, even if the reality had not matched expectations. 'Yeah,' she'd replied shakily. 'I guess.'

As he dropped her off at her studio apartment, she'd little suspected he would be back at her door less than two hours later. It had been a strange night!

*

At sunrise, a passing truck driver reported the wreck. Initially, the St Louis County police found no casualties as they sniffed around the scene of the accident. Their cameras clicked, gathering evidence. On the trunk of the vehicle, the chrome logo of a car dealership had survived unscathed, a faster route to identifying the Mustang's owner than ploughing through official paper records.

Festooned with gaudy flags, Paterson Ford occupied a prime site on St Louis's Manchester Road, a twenty-mile-long artery of automobile showrooms and strip malls. At 10 am Jake Wright glanced uneasily at the squad car as it pulled into the parking lot. He buttoned his suit jacket, straightened his tie and stubbed out his cigarette.

Confidently he strode forward. 'Hey, how can I help you guys today?' The salesman's eyes darted nervously from one cop to the other.

'We're looking for the owner of a red Mustang convertible, V8, purchased here in the last month or so. Does it ring any bells?'

'Sure does,' came the reply. 'That was the kinda deal you get once in a lifetime. Rich kid's birthday, brings in his mother to see the only thing that'll make him happy: she writes a cheque for three grand, just like that! Wish they were all that easy!'

'Yeah, no doubt you do,' said Officer Joe Jasko dryly. 'We need the name and address of the buyer.'

'If you'll step this way through to my office, I'll find 'em for you. Could I bring you guys some coffee or anything?'

'A look at your records, that's all we want.'

'You betcha. Happy to oblige.'

*

Identification of the owner had been the easy part: tracking him down took longer. A watch was put on Kelton's home. From noon till dusk, a police car sat in the shade of a huge locust tree outside the MacLeod residence. Close to 8:30 pm, Joe Jasko made out a figure trudging up the dark street towards them, and stuck an elbow in the ribs of his sleeping partner.

'Here we go. Showtime. Our boy's made it back to Momma!' They watched him go inside.

Twice they had to ring the doorbell before Angie MacLeod answered. Her manner was hostile. Yes, her son was now home, but he was taking a shower. All right, she conceded, the officers could take a seat in the hallway while they waited. They'd have to excuse her; she had a phone call to make.

The atmosphere warmed when Kelton ultimately made his appearance, newly shaved and smelling of expensive cologne. Unlike his mother, he was respectful, if evasive. They questioned him about his movements the previous evening, and Kelton seemed eager to cooperate. Trouble was, he had no recollection of anything beyond ten o'clock, when he was driving home in the rain. How his car ended up in a ditch was a total mystery to him. At most he'd had a couple of beers, and like 99 percent of the population in 1968, he never used a seatbelt. 'I mean, does anyone?' he asked with a grin.

He guessed he must have been unconscious for quite a while, wandered aimlessly till miraculously he'd found his way home. It was as if his recent memory had been wiped clean. He hoped it was only temporary, otherwise he'd have to see a doctor.

At the cops' mention of a body discovered twenty yards from the Mustang, Kelton remained impassive, but Joe Jasko observed the twitch of a muscle by the side of his mouth. The silence was broken by the slam of a car door in the driveway. His mother's lawyer had arrived.

Under her breath, Angie MacLeod muttered, 'Thank God!'

*

Unconvinced by Kelton MacLeod's display of selective amnesia, Officer Jasko tried to build a case, but his efforts were thwarted.

'Listen to me,' growled the station commander, 'with no witnesses and no rock-solid evidence we can't pin anything on the kid. If he was drunk, he was smart enough to steer clear of us until he'd sobered up. Money's no object – his mother hired one of the best lawyers in town. On the plus side, we got one less down-and-out littering our neighbourhood.'

'And we forget the missing ear? I tell you, MacLeod's as twisted as a corkscrew.'

'Just lay off him, is all I'm saying. We ain't fighting a battle we can't win.'

Though his chief's callousness rankled, Joe had no choice but to obey. Deep in the recesses of his brain he filed away the accident dossier. Knowledge was power. It might not be this year or next, but sometime he'd nail that lying son of a bitch.

*

A short item appeared in the *St Louis Post-Dispatch*, reporting the discovery of a body on Ladue Road. The victim had been homeless and drunk. Despite being near the scene of an automobile crash, the authorities had established no connection between the two incidents and police did not regard the death as suspicious.

Amy laid down the newspaper and pushed her cereal plate to one side. Suddenly she'd lost her appetite for breakfast. Kelton had claimed no one else was involved in the smash, and yet she wondered.

At that very instant, a delivery man knocked on her door, bearing the most extravagant, expensive bouquet of red roses she had ever seen. The message on the card read:

Thank you so much for everything – you're the best! K.

In her excitement, all doubts about Kelton's honesty vanished. He could say the moon was made of green cheese, and she would believe him. She was in love.

Chapter 2

'They always say time changes things, but you actually have to change them yourself.' – Andy Warhol

SHE HAD SHELTERED HIM that first night, and kept her mouth shut. Kelton had appreciated her help, but within a few short months, that gratitude had waned.

Amy worked hard to persuade him to be a groomsman in her sister's wedding, saying, 'You'll enjoy it, and it's a perfect opportunity for you to meet all the family.' (And with luck, she too would soon be flashing a diamond engagement ring like her sister's.)

He felt cornered. Clearly she thought she *had* him, and could tighten the choke chain around his neck whenever she felt like it! It had been foolish to place himself at any woman's mercy, but he'd had no alternative. Now he was paying the price.

*

The sun beat down mercilessly. In the sweltering heat of a July day, the bride and groom posed for pictures by a rustic bridge. Close by, Kelton stood with Amy. He wished he could be somewhere cool, quiet and shady: the Missouri Botanical Garden in St Louis was not the best spot to recover from a hangover.

Consciously pretty in a coral chiffon dress, Amy whispered, 'You okay, honey?'

'Yeah, great.' His lip curled sarcastically. 'A penguin suit and goddamned patent shoes are just the ticket with the temperature in the nineties!'

She squeezed his arm in sympathy. 'We'll soon be inside, in the air conditioning.'

Slowly the wedding party moved towards the limos.

'About fucking time,' Kelton muttered.

*

The champagne instantly sweetened him up. He grabbed a second glass from the tray of a passing waiter as they wove through the crowd towards the top table.

'Isn't this fun?' Amy gushed. 'There are relatives here we don't see from one year's end to the next.'

He managed a tight little smile, and she relaxed. Kelton could be so charming when it suited him, yet life had become a roller-coaster since they'd begun dating. One minute they could laugh together, with not a care: the next, his abrupt mood change plunged her into a black hole. But he was drop-dead gorgeous, and intelligent with it: he dazzled her. They had more good times than bad. That was love for you, she supposed.

Once the meal and speeches were over, the band struck up, launching into *Baby Now That I've Found You*. Amy smiled, singing along as they danced, willing Kelton to realise that she really *was* building her world around him and couldn't let him go, as the lyrics said. He pretended not to notice. Towards the end they slow-danced to *What a Wonderful World*. The bride moved to stand in the middle of the room and young women gathered round her, shrieking in delight as she prepared to toss her bouquet into the air.

Kelton headed for the bar. The groom touched his sleeve.

'Hey, man, you're in big trouble,' he gloated. 'Amy caught the bouquet. Know what that means, don't you? You're up next!'

'Don't bet on it,' Kelton responded. He felt a friendly drunken arm on his shoulder.

'Let me tell you something, kid,' said Amy's father through a stinking cloud of whisky vapour. 'Marriage is a great institution. Yes sir, a great institution ... but you need to go for it early, before you're too set in your ways.'

The notion of being railroaded into this old goat's family made Kelton want to throw up. His feet ached and he was sick of these attempts to draw him into a web from which there was no escape. Amy was about to become history.

*

They'd been to see *Rosemary's Baby* at the Hi-Pointe and now they sat opposite each other in McDonald's. Sullenly Kelton picked at the French fries on their tray.

'So I guess you didn't enjoy the movie?' she asked, unable to stand the silence.

'It was OK,' he replied with a shrug.

'Hey, did you hear on the radio that Jane Asher and Paul McCartney broke off their engagement? It's hard to believe. They seemed like the perfect couple.'

'Yeah, but appearances are deceiving.'

He'd waited all evening to tell her his news, and this was as good an opportunity as any. He reached into his breast pocket. 'See what came in the mail today.' He shoved an envelope across the table. 'I'm going to Scotland on a twelve-month scholarship.' He looked her straight in the eye as he spoke. She would be upset. Too bad.

Shocked, Amy remained absolutely still. She hadn't seen this coming, but she never quite knew what to expect next with Kelton. 'Scotland?' was all she said.

He chuckled. 'Yup. University of Aberdeen.'

It was as if a thunderbolt had dropped from the heavens and smacked her upside the head. She was in a daze, yet everything around continued exactly as it had been thirty seconds earlier. She heard the sizzle of a new batch of fries, their smell wafted through the air, and there was the *ka-ching* of the cash register drawer opening and closing. A server clattered red plastic trays down on the counter then busily wiped the formica-topped tables, while the group of teens in the booth behind them noisily yakked and laughed. Yet nothing would ever be the same again for her.

'Why didn't you mention it to me before?'

He shrugged. 'I forgot – it's a while since I sent in the application.'

Tears welled up in her eyes. 'I wish you'd stay. I thought we were serious.'

'Serious? How do you mean?' he said, in fake innocence.

'You know, I believed you loved me, after the way things have been between us!'

His scalp tingled with annoyance. 'Listen, babe, nobody ever mentioned love.'

'Maybe not in so many words, but it was kind of understood ... I just assumed we'd soon get engaged, and so did my folks.'

Assume nothing, he wanted to reply.

'There was no one until I met you! I'd never have slept with you, if we weren't in it for the long term!'

He stared at her coldly. 'Nobody forced you into a situation you didn't want.' Languidly he draped one arm along the top of the plastic bench seat. His gaze was unblinking, his eyebrows defiantly raised. A piece of meat was wedged in his back teeth: he worked at dislodging it with his tongue. 'It's only a year.'

'That's an eternity! You'll swan off and leave me here on my own?'

'No. You're a free agent. No ties, right? Once I'm back, we'll see how things stand and take it from there.'

'So you're breaking up with me?'

He shrugged. 'Your words, not mine.' She'd paraded him like a trophy at the wedding. Now she'd learn not to take him for granted.

'You *used* me, let me save your ass after the accident, and took what you wanted!' She snatched her purse, its handle catching the tray and tipping the remains of the meal on to the floor as she slid out of the seat. 'You're a total bastard,' she said before running outside into the warm darkness.

Takes one to know one, he thought. Calmly he bent to pick up the napkins, cups, cutlery and every last scrap of food she had scattered. He stepped over the puddle of ice and spilled soda to place their tray in the bin, smiling to himself as he sauntered casually out to his car. It was fine to get that little bit of unpleasantness over with. Pity things had to end that way, but what was a guy to do? Sure, she'd helped him out of a tight spot, but a night's shelter didn't warrant a lifetime commitment.

On the drive home, news of the latest carnage in Vietnam came on the radio. Quickly he switched stations and turned the volume up to enjoy *Can't Buy Me Love* by The Beatles. It was exhilarating, the prospect of this new phase in his life! Fresh pastures beckoned. And he'd be well out of reach of Amy or the Draft Board.

Chapter 3

'Stepping onto a brand-new path is difficult, but not more difficult than remaining in a situation which is not nurturing to the whole woman.' – Maya Angelou

Aberdeen, Scotland, November 1968

WITH ITS FLOOR-TO-CEILING SHELVES of musty books, King's College library was a place for serious study. Carol Cooper had been engrossed in her work until the stray locks curling over his shirt collar drew her attention. For two hours, he remained almost motionless at the next table, his back to her, hunched over a thick textbook. Occasionally he ran his hand through his shiny black hair. She noted his every movement, liking what she could see of his profile when he turned his head to look up at the clock. He was tall, better-looking than Alex, she thought. She glanced at the engagement ring she'd foolishly accepted at the tender age of eighteen. Suddenly Kelton snapped shut his briefcase, and strode past her to the exit, unaware of the interest he had aroused.

Stepping outside to head up the High Street towards his flat, he met the cold blast of a windy, wet evening. He drew up his coat collar against the icy chill. Water gurgled noisily down the gutters of narrow stone houses that stood gable end to the pavement. In the glow of the streetlights, raindrops bounced crazily on the cobbles. It had seemed like a great opportunity, this scholarship in the land of antiquity, birthplace of the ancestors he'd heard so much about. But never in his pampered life had Kelton envisaged the degree of misery and inconvenience this world would hold, where he'd to walk miles each day, or wait an eternity for a bus. There was no McDonald's, only a Wimpy

Bar on Bridge Street. It was impossible to find a decent cup of coffee anywhere, let alone the free refills at Bob Evans restaurants back home! When the fog rolled in off the North Sea, it reeked of fish, shrouding everything in a damp greyness that made him nostalgic. He missed the blue winter skies of the Midwest: skies so clear that even during the bitterest of weather, with the St Louis temperatures below freezing, sunglasses were essential. Fat chance of that in Aberdeen!

Fed up and soaking wet, he ducked into the doorway of the St Machar Bar. A pimply youth beside him at the counter told a joke in the broad local dialect. Mellowing after a pint of heavy, Kelton joined in the raucous laughter that followed. He missed the punch line, but a warmth had settled over him. Great beer and mini-skirted girls just ripe for the picking could cheer things up a lot.

Back in the library, Carol reluctantly gathered up her books. For two years she'd stuck it out in her digs, at the mercy of a thrifty, unimaginative woman who shamelessly served the cheapest of fish and potatoes for almost every meal. The house was clean enough but unwelcoming, its carpeting threadbare, its ancient light fixtures fitted with dim sixty watt bulbs. A gas fire brought temporary warmth to the drabness of Carol's room, but the flame would abruptly sputter and die once each shilling's worth of heat was used up.

It was pointless to think of moving. Mrs Milne's had been highly recommended to her parents, its appeal enhanced by the landlady's insistence that guests had to vacate the premises at weekends. And Dad always knew best: liked having his daughter in safe hands, until she returned to the fold on a Friday night.

City living had come as a shock to Carol. Such hustle and bustle, limitless choices and distractions were intimidating to a country girl embarking on her university course. Initially she had hated it all, but gradually the scale tipped in the other direction: her new-found freedom became more precious than reassuring familiarity. Home loomed like a dark cloud waiting to smother her, forcing her to sacrifice her individuality, and become the Carol others wanted her to be.

She tried to think about Alex, but images of the guy in the library kept popping into her head as she dropped off to sleep. She could not foresee that the steady rhythm of her life was about to be shattered forever. It all started the very next morning.

*

With her lodgers out for the day, Mrs Milne went upstairs to make their beds, while Mr Milne dozed in his usual seat by the kitchen fire. An hour later, his chin still rested on his chest, and a trickle of saliva dribbled from one corner of his mouth.

Lazy old bugger, sleeping off his breakfast while I work my fingers to the bone, thought his wife.

'You ready for your coffee?' she called out at 11 am precisely but got no response. Shaking her head, she muttered while she toiled at the sink. She cored out the eyes of a large potato with her paring knife, then cut the chips for that night's meal and dropped them into a bowl of cold water.

'I said, do you *want* coffee or not?' she called more sharply. 'Here ye are, anyway!'

Roughly she plunked her husband's mug of Nescafe and a couple of custard creams on the table beside him. She touched his shoulder.

'What's wrong, Donnie? Speak to me. Are ye all right?'

But Donnie was far from all right. Mrs Milne took off her glasses and cleaned them on her apron. She stared closely at the man with whom she'd spent the last forty years. From her bag, she grabbed her powder compact to hold its mirror in front of his mouth: held her breath, half afraid that he was gone, yet oddly fearful that he would wake up suddenly.

'Good God, ye're deid!' she exclaimed finally.

Drawing her lips together, she delicately patted her permed hair with both hands and went over to the sideboard to pour

20

herself a stiff drink, though it was only 11:15 in the day. Trust him to pick a Thursday, her Bingo night! By supper time, everything was under control. The body was safely in cold storage at the undertaker's, a funeral arranged, the insurance company notified and a death notice submitted for the *Press and Journal*.

Never given to hysterics, the landlady calmly served her lodgers their evening meal, and waited till she had cleared the table to inform them of the sad passing of her husband. Her tenants received one week's notice to move out.

Carol felt she'd suddenly been granted parole from a long prison sentence.

*

When she stepped off the bus in the village square the following night, Alex was waiting to drive her the two miles home. As they entered the farmhouse kitchen Mrs Cooper immediately laid down her knitting and rose to welcome them.

'Come away in, you must be frozen! I'll fetch your dinner, Carol, it's in the oven. Will you have something, Alex?'

'We can help ourselves, Mam,' said Carol, laying down her bag in the hallway.

The father nodded to them and switched off the television, since the nine o'clock news was finished. 'Well, what like?' It was as cordial a greeting as he ever gave.

Alex nodded. 'Not bad, thanks.'

'And what's been happening with you this week, Carol?'

'Mrs Milne's husband died.'

'*Died*, did you say?' His habitually angry tone made even his own family uncomfortable around him.

'She gave us all notice to find somewhere else. I'm moving into a flat with Jill from my French class.'

Mr Cooper fingered his moustache and harrumphed. 'You'd be far better in lodgings where your meals are cooked and everybody has to be in at a decent hour o' the night! Isn't that right, Alex?'

Alex looked embarrassed. 'Och, I dunno. Depends on how Carol feels.' He moved towards the door. 'I'll leave you all in peace, let you get your tea. Pick you up tomorrow about seven, okay?'

'Fine,' said Carol, 'see you then.' The door closed behind him.

'Are you not going out to say goodnight to him?' asked the mother. 'You take that laddie too much for granted. I don't know how he puts up with you.'

The girl shrugged and her father took a draw of his pipe. 'You've got another think coming if you think we're letting you move into a flat. Between that and these short skirts you wear, there's no telling where all this could end.'

'I'm twenty, Dad! I'll make up my own mind.'

Mrs Cooper quietly set Carol's meal on the table. She had learned years ago to avoid confrontations. When Father spoke he expected no arguments. The silence that followed was broken only by the insistent click of her four little knitting needles as she worked on yet another pair of thick wool socks for her husband, because it was a sin to sit with idle hands.

Mr Cooper sat scowling and puffed at his pipe. He coughed, hawking up a glob of green phlegm that sizzled on the burning coals. 'You'll stay in lodgings till you graduate, or you'll get no more money from me.'

'Really?' Carol laid down her fork and knife, cleared away her dishes and slammed the door as she left the room to go upstairs. For once, she would do what *she* chose. She'd call their bluff and move into the flat with Jill, whatever the consequences. Unless she took a stand, they'd forever keep her pinned, like one of the butterflies in the glass display case on the parlour wall.

At the fireside, the father grumbled, 'The quicker Alex Murray puts a wedding ring on her finger, the better I'll sleep at night. She'll have a degree, but I want her settled with a man, a few bairns and a house to keep.'

Mrs Cooper concentrated on her knitting, and said not a word.

*

Two weeks after first seeing him, Carol found herself sitting diagonally opposite Kelton in the library. She coughed, and their eyes met for a second before she quickly looked away. She sneezed, and he gave her a little smile, mouthing the words, 'Bless you,' across the table. He had noted the engagement ring on her left hand. As she walked towards the exit, he came up behind her, and rushed to hold the door open.

'Thanks,' she mumbled, sniffling into a tissue.

Kelton gave one of his wide grins he knew the girls all liked, and looked down into her eyes with concern. 'Hey, you'd better take care of that cold with some chicken soup!' he said, and then he was gone.

His American accent oozed easy confidence. He sounded like they did on television or the movies. Snuggled up in bed that night, Carol relived the scene. It was irrational, but she just couldn't get him out of her head. Chicken soup indeed!

'Flat' was a grandiose title for the squalid room and kitchen she shared with Jill at the top of a grim old tenement building. The wood stairs creaked, the cracked linoleum squeaked and on each mezzanine was a communal toilet. But for Carol the place represented liberty, and she was happy. She and Jill made an unlikely pair yet they complemented each other. Life for Jill was one long party where classes, tutorials and exams were mere incidentals. Constantly aspiring to new heights of outrageous behaviour – it was the late sixties, for goodness sake! – she nevertheless appreciated Carol's dependability. Hung over from liquor or smoking pot, Jill could rely on Carol's notes for missed lectures. Having kicked her dirty knickers under her bed for the previous month, she knew she could borrow a fresh pair from her flat-mate. That was friendship.

*

It seemed natural that Kelton would say, 'Hi, how's the cold?' when they next ran into each other. Over coffee Carol learned that his year's study in Aberdeen would complete his doctorate. They talked about everything under the sun – music, books, movies, and America – and every now and then he made her laugh in a way that Alex never could. His pronunciation of St Louis, as if it were spelled 'Lewis' was quite a surprise, as was the drawl of his 'Mizzooruh'. For Carol, it added to his mystique.

As he spoke, she thrilled to his every word: something in her that had lain dormant suddenly came alive. He excited her, this sophisticated guy who had already travelled more than she would if she lived to be a hundred. One of life's winners, he was unafraid to try new things. He was articulate, charming and would be able to fit in anywhere: he was everything Alex was not.

Just half an hour with Kelton inspired her to be bolder than ever before, and Carol shocked herself by agreeing to a date with him the following Saturday evening.

Chapter 4

'"Oh," I said, "I'm so happy, I could die."
She said, "Drop dead," then left with another guy.'
– Elvis Costello

H ER MESSAGE THAT SHE'D BE STAYING in the city that weekend was received coolly.

'What about Alex?' her mother inquired in a hurt tone.

'What about him? It's no big deal for one week.'

'I don't know what's got into you.'

Carol cut the call short. 'Got to go, Mam, I'm out of coins. Talk to you soon. Bye!' She banged down the payphone, glad to have got that task over with. To hell with them all, it was time she had fun before it was too late. She would start with some retail therapy.

In the store she tried on several pairs of shoes – all low-heeled and eminently sensible, the kind she normally wore. As the shop assistant's patience began to wear thin, she reached up high on a shelf, and placed a box on the leather stool in front of Carol.

'You'd look fabulous in these. They just came in,' she said, unwrapping pair of black stilettos from their crisp, white tissue paper.

Carol walked unsteadily across to the full-length mirror, and liked what she saw. Were her legs really that slim? She twirled this way and that, while the assistant rolled her eyes and looked apologetically at another customer waiting for service. Carol caught her glance, and on an impulse said, 'Right, I'll take them.' Were they a bit too daring? She gave a shrug: so what if Dad

"

disapproved, and if they made her taller than Alex? She was buying these shoes for herself, not to please others.

*

Putting on an extra splash of aftershave, Kelton checked his hair in the mirror once more, then headed out to meet Carol. He approved of her looks: not stunningly beautiful, nor artificial and heavily made-up like others he had been with, but not homely either. Where Amy possessed a petite blonde prettiness, Carol's attraction was her wholesomeness. She had high cheekbones and good teeth, a natural sheen on her fair hair, and the long slender legs he always admired in a woman. Her air of innocence convinced Kelton she was a virgin, something he prided himself on discerning.

Exhilaration and guilt churned in Carol's stomach as she teetered along the street in her heels. She kept thinking about Alex, the only boyfriend she'd ever had – or wanted, up till then. Whenever she stepped off the bus in the village square each Friday night, he'd be waiting to take her home: dependable, kind, honest and hardworking – and boring as hell! His utter predictability had recently begun to grate on her ... and that, she told herself, was justification enough for tonight's date. Time spent with another guy would make her more appreciative, help her realise how well-matched she and Alex actually were ... or not.

She spotted Kelton in the distance, took a deep breath to steady her nerves, and hurried towards him.

'So, what's it gonna be?' he asked once they were seated opposite each other at a little table for two.

'I'll have what you're having.'

Kelton fought his way through to the bar, and Carol almost had to pinch herself to be sure this was really happening, that she was really here with the big, handsome American. She looked down, removed her engagement ring, and tucked it carefully inside her purse.

The Blue Lamp was seedy, dark and smoky, filled with the hubbub of laughter and loud voices struggling to be heard above the volume of the music. Kelton deposited two Moscow Mules and two bags of KP nuts on their table.

With the second drink, he moved his chair closer to hers.

'Wanna go to the dance in the Union later?' he asked, but Carol couldn't hear above the din. He stroked her face and lifted her hair, placing his mouth on her ear to repeat the question. His lips brushed the side of her cheek, and the sudden, intimate gesture took her by surprise. She blushed and nodded, relishing the unfamiliar smell of his aftershave.

He pushed his way through the noisy crowd, her hand firmly in his. With the buzz from the vodka, she scarcely felt her feet touch the ground, but that was fine. All she had to do was follow. Kelton was the type of guy who would forge ahead and take charge.

As the night wore on, the dance hall lights dimmed, the music from The Facells slowed and Carol wished she could forever keep his arms around her. They clung to each other in the darkness, the air heavy with hairspray, cheap perfume and unfulfilled desire. The final set ended with a da-DA, da-DA, da-BOOM from the drummer, and the spell was abruptly broken. The lights were snapped on.

He walked her home, occasionally pulling her into a shady doorway to kiss her, tenderly at first, then with increasing urgency once they were in the dingy lobby outside her flat. When his tongue circled hers, she grasped the dark curls at the back of his head. He was nuzzling the side of her neck, his body pressed against hers. His fingers slid under her coat, dangerously close to her breast, and Carol broke away.

'I have to go,' she whispered breathlessly. 'Just look at the time!'

He gazed dolefully into her eyes, as though he would give his life for only a few seconds more with her. He kissed her gently on the lips. 'Aw, honey, don't go yet!' But already she was fumbling in her bag for her key. 'Can I see you next week?' he breathed. 'Will you be in the library?'

'Yes, I'll be there,' said Carol, 'but I've got to go in now.' Quickly she shut the door, her heart racing, afraid of the impulses that had risen in her. The steamy sessions she and Alex had shared in the darkness of his car never made her feel anything like this. Nor did Alex ever call her honey.

*

The euphoria of the previous evening gave way to a sick head that made her want to crawl into a corner and die. Her insides quaked and quivered like jelly. The bright morning light competed with the transistor's jangling music to torture her senses. She closed her eyes, unable to face the fizzy orange drink on the table in front of her.

'Swallow it down,' insisted Jill. 'You'll be good as new in ten minutes.'

The Redoxon steadied her a bit, but nothing could get rid of her remorse. What had she been thinking, carrying on as she'd done last night, with Alex waiting for her at home? How could she ever hurt him? He was kind, gentle, considerate, and would be a wealthy man one day. He said he loved her, but that did not oblige her to sacrifice her entire future for him, did it? He'd give her the world, if he could, but his world was dull and she craved excitement. He deserved someone who would appreciate what he had to offer, just as she deserved ... well, she didn't know quite what she deserved, that was the problem. She knew this much: marriage to Alex would turn her into her mother, tied to a man and a farm she didn't love. She could not bear to settle for knitting and listening to *The Archers* as the highlights of her days.

*

She left her last lecture on Monday morning to find Kelton hanging around outside, waiting for her.

'Fancy seeing you here!' exclaimed Carol in surprise.

He grinned. 'Thought we might grab lunch, or have you other plans?'

'Not really,' she replied. 'Let me tell Jill and the others that I'll catch up with them later.' If he wanted to eat with her, she would be available.

By the end of the week, the pattern was established: lunch together for an hour, study sessions opposite each other in the library. The more they talked and laughed, exchanging glances surrounded by towering shelves of books, and sharing kisses outside her door at night, the more sure Carol became that she had to break off her engagement.

*

'I missed you last weekend,' said Alex as she got into the Land Rover the following Friday evening. 'D'you fancy going out for a bar supper tomorrow night?'

Carol looked out of the passenger window at the chilly darkness. 'Alex,' she began, 'there's something I need to tell you ...'

But the engine revved up, drowning out her voice, and she sat quiet and miserable. She hated herself for what she was about to do. They pulled up outside her parents' home, and she put a hand on his arm.

'Wait,' she said, 'I can't go in yet. We have to talk.' An awkward silence descended. She sighed. 'It's not going to work out – us, I mean.'

'Of course it will! We get on all right, don't we? And we've known each other all our lives! You're stressed with your exams coming up.'

'Listen to me, would you? It's not the exams, I can handle that. It's you and me!' She had to be brutal: there was no other way. 'I don't want to marry you, maybe I never did. I'm sorry, but it's better to come clean.' As she spoke, she held out her diamond ring.

His face changed, and for an awful moment, she thought he was about to cry. 'Why the sudden change of heart? Is it something I said or did?'

She had to finish what she'd started. There was no going back now. 'This isn't the kind of life I want.'

'You're tired. We should talk tomorrow.'

In response she mutely shook her head.

'I'm sorry that's how you feel. I always loved you.' The disappointment was almost more than he could bear. She didn't mention what she did want, only what she didn't. Her father was not wrong. Carol's moving into a flat had been bad news, the beginning of the end for them. Maybe she'd found someone else, but his pride prevented him from asking.

She collected her odds and ends, despising his vulnerability. A *real man* like Kelton would show more of a reaction, would fight for what he wanted! No sooner had she stepped out of the van than Alex slammed into gear and the Land Rover took off down the rough farm road, indignantly bumping and splashing its way through the potholes.

*

'I don't understand you, Carol,' whined the mother. 'This is no way to go on, taking a ring from Alex, then suddenly throwing it back at him.'

'I didn't throw it back at him, Mam. I just told him I can't marry him.'

'He would have been a good man to you.'

Mr Cooper glared at her suspiciously. 'What's behind all this, eh? You're not messing around with drink and drugs, are you?'

Carol laughed out loud. 'Do you think I'm stupid?'

'I think you're a damn fool, to treat Alex like this. The two of you would be fine together. You'd better come to your senses. This nonsense has gone too far already. Go on, pick up the phone and apologise to him.'

'Huh!' puffed Carol. 'I've nothing to apologise for. It would be far worse to marry him when I didn't really want to. Better to be an old maid than that.'

The father shook his head. 'Aye, and the rate you're going, that's how you'll wind up.'

Carol knew she had done the right thing.

*

She wished she could invite Kelton to spend Christmas Day at home with her family but it was too soon. Unthinkable, given her parents' disappointment at her broken engagement. Instead they were reunited in Aberdeen on Hogmanay, the last day of December. At the station, he swept her up into his arms the minute she stepped off the bus.

'Hey, it's great to see you again! You've no idea how much I've missed you!' He lifted her off her feet, and twirled her around. She laughed in embarrassment at his public display of affection. 'And tonight we celebrate. I've got tickets for a dinner-dance, so you've two hours to get ready. Okay?'

'Oh, I couldn't! I've nothing to wear,' she protested.

Beside him lay a department store bag. He handed it to her. 'You have now,' he said. 'Happy Christmas. I thought it would look stunning with your black stilettos.'

'You bought this for *me*?' she said incredulously, peeking inside the E&M's carrier. The scarf she had for him would seem silly alongside a gift of this magnitude. 'But how did you guess my size? Kelton, really you shouldn't have ... I don't know how to thank you!'

'My pleasure,' he replied, lifting her suitcase. 'Let's go. You can thank me afterwards.'

She had been taught that it was indecent for a girl to accept gifts of clothing from a man; it implied an improper familiarity. 'Anything you need, we can buy for you until you're married or able to support yourself!' Mr Cooper always said. 'And if we can't afford it, you don't need it.'

Inside her head, she heard her mother's nagging: *you're not for sale, nor should any man ever think you are.* She should politely decline this gift, yet wouldn't Kelton be hurt? That was the last thing she wanted. Then she heard Jill's voice: *don't be so bloody stupid. You're only young once and you should enjoy yourself, so FTLOT – fuck the lot of them.*

Carefully Carol drew the black cocktail dress from its tissue wrapping and laid it on her bed. Slipping off her dowdy winter clothes, she freshened up, and wriggled into the priciest garment she'd ever owned. She felt like a child playing dress-up, yet looking back at her from the mirror was a sophisticated, sexy woman. Putting the final touches to her lipstick, she smiled at her reflection and began humming *If My Friends Could See Me Now* from the musical *Sweet Charity*.

Chapter 5

'I generally avoid temptation unless I can't resist it.'
– Mae West

With a flourish, the bottle of wine was uncorked and a sample poured. Kelton swirled the dark red liquid around the glass, sniffed and swirled again. He took a sip and frowned.

'You know what?' he said, 'there's a tartness here that's just not normal. Could you bring another bottle?'

The waiter was startled. 'I'm sorry about that, sir. I'll be right back.'

Carol looked at him, wide-eyed. 'You're a wine connoisseur?'

'Git outta here!' he grinned, flashing his white, even teeth. 'That stuff was okay, but it pays to keep them on their toes. They respect you more.' He judged the next bottle to be much better.

They ate, drank and danced in a style she had never before experienced. The manager sent over two complimentary Drambuies with their coffee, and bowed as they left, in acknowledgement of Kelton's ridiculously large tip. Carol felt like a queen.

In her flat they snuggled on the sofa, and listened to the record player. After her favourite new single, *I'm Gonna Make You Love Me* by The Supremes and The Temptations, she put on a Rolling Stones album.

'That was a lovely way to finish the year, the best Hogmanay ever,' she said, sitting down once more. 'And thanks for this dress – I love it.'

'You're welcome. But Hogmanay ain't over till it's over!' he replied, leaning across to kiss her.

'Wait! You're catching my hem, don't tear it!'

He moved away and simultaneously slid his hand up her back to undo her zip. 'Might be easier if you took it off. Why don't I help you?'

The dress went slithering down on to the grubby carpet, and lay in a puddle of black silk. With his arms around her and his mouth on hers, he slowly backed her towards the bedroom, undoing her bra strap. Carol remembered tearing off his shirt. They ended up naked on her bed, and Kelton was on top of her. Something ripped inside her, before intense, tingling darts of pleasure shot through her entire body. Afterwards in the darkness, they lay laughing and breathless. In the distance, a clock chimed midnight, heralding the start of 1969, while in the next room Mick Jagger belted out *Let's Spend the Night Together*.

*

Jill returned and classes resumed. Carol frequently slept at Kelton's flat, where they could luxuriate for ages in the jets of unlimited hot water that rained down from his shower. With soapy hands sliding over each other's wet bodies, they laughed and kissed and breathed the same steamy air. Was it only a month earlier that she'd been content with her twice-daily wash up and a weekly bath at home, unfailingly preceded by a stern warning from her father?

'Don't run away all the hot water, mind! I'm not made of money!' he would call as she filled the tub.

With Kelton she discovered freedom and delicious decadence. Defiant now, she spent every second weekend at home. With her increasing self-confidence, her boundaries stretched: everything had become possible. Under his influence, her eyes had been opened and Carol adopted a different – if not always accurate – perspective.

From their first night together, he had come prepared with a condom in his pocket, leaving her confident that the business of birth control was safely taken care of. Then she began throwing up each morning. Over lunch one day in the Elphinstone Hall she toyed with her cottage pie, and pushed her plate aside.

'What's wrong, hon?' Kelton asked, because normally she had a healthy appetite.

'I'm pregnant.'

'You're kidding, right?' he replied. 'That's not a joke, by the way!'

'I'm serious, I've had a test at the doctor's. I'm due at the end of November.'

He laid down his fork. 'What a bummer! Why weren't you on the Pill like everybody else, huh?'

She couldn't believe his reaction, that he'd actually blame *her*, when he'd supposedly been taking the necessary precautions! She avoided his dark, angry glare. His mouth was distorted in disbelief ... or was it petulance? It was his first display of real temper. He sat seething for a few seconds, running his hand through the luxuriant black curls that she'd always loved.

Abruptly he stood up. 'I'm outta here,' he said. Grabbing his books, he pushed his way through the crowd to the exit.

Carol wondered what on earth she should do next. Would she even see him again?

Kelton strode up the High Street, heading for his flat. What a fuck-up to make of his life, just as he was about to be awarded his doctorate, too! The news had come as a shock, and the timing was bad. Gradually his rage abated: it should be easy enough to get rid of it. He wished he hadn't lost his cool.

Carol had started off as a pleasant distraction for him, and he'd enjoyed the challenge of taking her away from Alex. Then he'd got used to having her around: it took the sting out of being in a strange place, away from home. She wasn't a skank, like some he'd known. He was the first man she'd been with, but to marry was a huge undertaking. Certainly not one he was ready for.

He debated the pros and cons. Hell, he had to admit she wasn't bad, really. Marriage was not something he had seriously contemplated, but it might have its advantages. Going home with a wife and child would put paid to the possibility of being drafted to Vietnam! For sure, he needed someone pliable, willing to let him make the decisions: on that count Carol fitted the bill. Yeah, he told himself, he probably could do a lot worse, and it would shut his mother up about settling down. It was worth a shot. Nobody said it had to be forever, did they?

*

Sick with despair, Carol trudged up the dark stairs to the flat, swallowing back her nausea at the stale cooking smells on each landing. She'd messed up big-time!

Perhaps it was her fault that things had turned out the way they did. If only she'd acted with more sensitivity, used a little diplomacy, he might not have stormed out on her! She'd been an idiot to get herself into this predicament. How would she ever explain to her parents? The very prospect made her feel ill.

Weighed down with despair, she had almost reached her floor. Not till she stopped on the top step to fumble in her bag for her key did she raise her eyes to look along the passage at her door.

She almost cried with relief. Lying on the mat was a huge bouquet of red roses wrapped in cellophane! Her heart leapt as she read the attached card:

'Forgive me. Let's get married. Kelton.'

He wouldn't let her down! She assumed he loved her; some people just found it hard to say. Ecstatically grateful, she headed straight down the stairs again, to set off running along the street. From the nearest phone box, she called to thank him.

36

Chapter 6

*'Age is an issue of mind over matter. If you don't mind, it
doesn't matter.' – Mark Twain*

ALL THROUGH THE WINTER, Amy found it hard to trust any guy. Too often they were like Kelton, arrogant jerks interested in one thing ... until Jack appeared on the scene.

He was a client at the office where she worked as a receptionist. Tall and silver-haired, he charmed her with his courtly demeanour. Widowed three years previously, he had no children, and drove the biggest Cadillac around. He proposed twelve weeks after their first date, and Amy quickly accepted. She foresaw a country-club lifestyle that she might never otherwise attain: designer clothes and accessories, trips abroad to exotic places she'd never even heard of, and a home filled with all the trappings of luxury. Her parents called it disgusting to marry a man older than her father. Age is only a number, she retorted. It was a quiet wedding.

Returning from a month's honeymoon in the Bahamas, Amy longed for the company of younger people. She invited a couple of girlfriends and their husbands round for dinner, but once was enough. They were all joking around over drinks till Jack came into the room, then somehow his presence threw an immediate damper on the atmosphere. No matter how hard he tried to be one of them, his seniority set him apart: his attempts to be hip left him looking pathetic, and embarrassed the hell out of everyone else.

Social occasions at the club, which at the start seemed smart and sophisticated, quickly became marathons of tedium. Amy groaned inwardly, but laughed dutifully with the other wives while Jack and his senior buddies told the same stories for a second or third time. He treated her like a queen, yet she felt as irrelevant as a tiny tot permitted to sit at the adults' table.

Having believed she would reap the benefit of his years of experience as a lover, Amy was sorely disappointed. In the marriage bed, Jack had nothing more to offer than gentle caresses. Sometimes they snuggled really close under the comforter, but she was unable to tease him to more than a vague firmness in his penis. Try though she did to cajole him into action, coyly using her fingers and her tongue to encourage him, he would not be aroused. Infrequently she imagined something was building with each rhythmic stroke, but always the flame would flicker and die. Gently he would kiss her before turning over to sleep, apparently content. And Amy was left awake in the darkness, to resent the outline of his big muscular back that once had seemed so mature and virile.

Her rage at her husband's impotence increased as she thought of Kelton's lovemaking; memories of the dark nights in his car with his young, hard body against hers almost satisfied the longing that burned inside her. Not that Kelton been a particularly skilled lover, but he had been her first taste of forbidden fruit. His raw directness had both repulsed her and left her craving more. Time erased his faults, allowing her to recall only how good the sex had been. Her dreams plunged her into wild erotic fantasies, which lessened her frustration.

Jack was all right, really, just old! He provided her with every material comfort, and in exchange had stolen her youth. She was marooned on an island of luxury, frittering away her life with a boatload of old farts.

Chapter 7

'The boughs, without becoming detached from the trunk grow
away from it.' – Victor Hugo

FOUR THOUSAND MILES AWAY in Scotland, Carol called her parents to ask if she could bring her new boyfriend to visit. On the day itself, she stood by the window, anxiously watching for Kelton since they'd planned to go together to the bus station. There was the toot of a horn, someone emerged from a parked vehicle, and he was waving up at her from the street.

'Where did you get the car?' she asked, climbing in beside him.

He tapped one side of his nose. 'Avis rental. I don't want you spending hours sitting on draughty public transport. This way we make our own schedule.'

She appreciated his consideration, unaware that her comfort was not uppermost in his mind. Rather, he was reluctant to place himself at the mercy of her parents. Who knew how they'd react to the news of their daughter's pregnancy? He would visit on his own terms, and be able to make a fast getaway if necessary.

Her mother was first to greet them when they pulled up at the farmhouse. 'Come away in, this is a lovely surprise!'

'Mam, this is Kelton. I mentioned him on the phone,' said Carol.

He extended his hand. 'Happy to meet you, Mrs Cooper.' With his most charming smile, he presented her with a huge gift-wrapped box of chocolates.

'Och, you shouldn't have, thank you very much! That's very nice of you, Kelton,' she simpered. 'Welcome to Oldtown.' She led them into the kitchen.

Carol squirmed. How broad her mother's accent must sound to his ears. How plain the house must look!

Mr Cooper stepped forward. 'I'm Carol's father. How d'ye do?' he said gruffly.

Kelton grinned. 'Hi. Nice to meet you, sir.'

'We might as well sit down at the table. The two of you are probably hungry, aren't you? I'll just give the soup a wee pep-up, if you'll excuse me a minute,' fussed the mother. Carol followed her through to the kitchen, leaving the two men alone.

'Well, and what do you think of Scotland?' enquired Mr Cooper.

Kelton chuckled. 'It's great, but I'll tell you, I kinda wondered what I'd gotten myself into, the first few weeks in Aberdeen!'

The host eyed the guest sourly, hating the way he said 'Aberdeen' with emphasis on the first syllable. The arrogance of him, changing the pronunciation of a centuries-old name!

Carol sat a large tureen filled with thick vegetable soup on the table, and her mother came bustling through with four huge plates from Granny's dinner set, taken out of the cupboard and specially dusted off for the occasion.

'Try an oatcake, Kelton, I made them myself this morning.'

He took a bite. Carol watched as he slowly chewed on it, then rolled it round and round his mouth. A large spoonful of soup helped him swallow, but a fragment of the rough oatmeal had lodged in his throat.

'I hate to bother you, ma'am,' he croaked, 'but d'you think I could have a glass of water?'

'I'm sorry, Kelton. I should have remembered to give you something to drink with your meal!' Mrs Cooper jumped up from her seat to fetch a tumbler containing three inches of tepid tap water. 'There ye are now. That should do the trick,' she said kindly, patting his shoulder.

Carol cleared her throat. 'We've something to tell you. Kelton and I are getting married.'

Mr Cooper spluttered. 'You're *what*?'

'I said we're getting married.'

'Over my dead body!' growled the father. Turning to Kelton, he said, 'No offence to you, laddie, but the idea's ridiculous.'

'This is all very sudden, Carol,' said the mother, placatingly. 'What your Dad means is that you should maybe get to know each other a bit better first, eh?'

Mr Cooper glared at Carol. 'You're more needing to pay attention to your studies wi' your finals comin' up. You've a nerve to even bring *this person* here at all, after what you did to Alex just a few months ago!' he said. 'So we'll have no more mention of getting married.'

Kelton laid down his soup spoon. 'I'm sorry that's how you feel, sir, but this is for Carol to decide on her own.'

'I beg your pardon? I don't remember asking *your* opinion. Nobody talks to me like that in my own house!' bristled the father. 'With your "sir" this and your "ma'am" that, you may act as if you're God's gift to this earth ... but you're full of hot air! I've met your type before. Carol should marry one of her own kind when the time is right, and the same goes for you.'

Kelton would stomach no more of the old man's boorish behaviour. Quietly he stood up. 'Thank you for the meal, Mrs Cooper. It was a pleasure to meet you.' Looking at Carol, he said, 'I'll be outside in the car.'

'No, wait!' Carol cried, rising up from her chair, but already the door was closing behind him.

'What's all this about? You're not pregnant, are you?' asked her mother.

'Since you ask, yes I am! The baby's due in November.' Carol sat back down at the table, and folded her arms.

'You make me ashamed,' said Mr Cooper. 'You kept a decent laddie like Alex on the end of a string for years, then you lift your skirt to the first Yank you ever meet! I knew it would lead to trouble, moving into that flat!'

'Kelton's the best thing that ever happened to me. I don't care what you say.'

'You'll care ere you're done, mark my words. He's a rascal, that, had the nerve to sit at my table and eat my food, after what he's been up to with my daughter. Well, he'll never cross our threshold again, not as long as I live!'

Mrs Cooper protested, 'Don't say that. He seems nice enough.'

'Nice my arse! He'll be no part of *my* family! You and yours will always be welcome, Carol. This is your home, whatever happens, but that *clown* can go back where he came from.'

Ten minutes later, Carol joined Kelton in the car outside. Little was said as they drove back to the city, and for once neither one felt like singing along when *Happy Together* by The Turtles was playing on the radio.

*

Jill unwisely complained one day that they no longer spent time together.

'But I see you every day!' Carol sniffed.

'Well, I'm just saying I miss you. You're here, yet you're not. You're so distant, we never have a laugh about anything now.'

'That's rubbish.' Carol felt that Jill spoke out of jealousy. With that, and the rift with her parents, she felt strangely isolated. Much as she wanted to, she would not go home alone. Unless Kelton was accepted in the house, she would not visit. Only in June did she bring the standoff to an end.

Another parent might be ready to hug or plant a kiss on the cheek of a daughter he'd neither seen nor spoken to in six weeks, but Mr Cooper was made of sterner stuff. In his book, any display of emotion was a sign of weakness. Meeting her off the bus, he greeted her with a gruff, 'Well, quine, how are you doing?', though she could tell he was pleased to see her. As they drove, they listened to the weekly edition of *Farm Journal* on the radio.

Her mother emerged from the back door as they arrived, wiping floury hands on her apron, her arms so soft and plump they were worthy of a Rubens painting. Stepping inside, Carol realised how much she had missed the fragrant warmth of her mother's domain, the security of knowing things always stayed the same. Suddenly she loved everything that made *that* house her home, from the monkey-puzzle tree by the front door and the Toby jugs looking down from the kitchen shelves like old friends waiting to greet her, to the brass-faced grandfather clock in the hall, whose chimes rang out on the hour, day and night. The enormity of her decision hit her. Who could tell when – or if – she would return?

Not daring to follow that train of thought, Carol forced a smile. 'I've got news for you, Mam. Kelton and I are leaving for America next week. He's got the tickets. We fly through New York to Las Vegas to get married. Then it's on to St Louis for his job interview.' Even to her, the itinerary sounded unreal.

'Surely not before your graduation?' gasped Mrs Cooper, shocked.

'No problem, I'll graduate *in absentia*, and they'll send on my parchment.'

The mother bit her lip to hide her disappointment. For years, she had looked forward to watching proudly as her daughter stepped up to the podium in the Mitchell Hall, but now there would be no ceremony. Instead her little girl was pregnant, and calmly announcing plans for a wedding in Las Vegas. The family had seldom travelled. Her experience was restricted to their annual day trips that began at dawn, after the first milking. Dressed in their Sunday best, the three of them would pile into the family car, to drive eighty miles for breakfast at a country hotel along the way. Edinburgh was their destination. By mid-morning they would be strolling along the wide pavements of Princes Street, ready to do some shopping. Their lunch venue never changed, because the restaurant in Jenner's department store epitomised luxury to the Coopers. Later they would perhaps climb the Scott Monument or visit the Castle before driving north once more. Carol would curl up to sleep in the back seat, while her parents watched the road in companionable silence, exhausted by their taste of the high life. At Oldtown, the animals would be waiting patiently for their return, their udders swinging full and heavy as Mr Cooper led them back to their stalls at dusk. The routine of the farm was utterly relentless.

As she dished up lunch, Mrs Cooper noted the subtle fullness in Carol's face and slight thickening round her middle. It wasn't meant to turn out this way, she thought. She'd hoped to have her daughter close by in her old age, to watch her grandchildren grow up. Though the separation of recent weeks would be as nothing compared to what lay ahead, she had to admire Carol's courage in rejecting what was safe and comfortable, to leap into the unknown. Occasionally she wished she'd had the heart to do likewise, but she had long since accepted her own limitations and those of her spouse. Now she regretted not demanding that her husband climb down from his position on Kelton. Really, it was too bad of him to say the lad was not welcome in their home! Having decided on a course of action, Mr Cooper would not waver, regardless of the cost. The rigid inflexibility that seemed a strength in his youth turned out to be a weakness. He was not man enough to admit he was wrong.

In the afternoon, Carol went upstairs to take a few things from the wardrobe in her bedroom, then she hung them back up again, unable to face the finality of leaving a line of empty hangers. At five o'clock precisely, her father sounded the car horn, ready to drive her to the bus stop.

At the moment of parting, he patted his daughter on the back, and her mother gave her a brief, embarrassed peck on the cheek before Carol climbed aboard. From her window seat, she looked out at the two people who had loved her longer and better than anyone else on earth, Dad standing dour and stoic with one arm raised, while Mam's round figure grew smaller and smaller, till it was just a speck waving in the distance. Only then did she allow herself the luxury of tears, because the bittersweet reunion was also a last farewell to her old self.

Her life in the new world with Kelton was about to begin.

Chapter 8

'England and America are two countries separated by the same language.' – George Bernard Shaw

NEW YORK, LAS VEGAS, ST LOUIS. Never had Carol dreamed of seeing such glamorous places, yet already the names tripped easily off her tongue. Hard though it was to imagine she was going on anything other than a vacation, she knew this was for real. She was moving to live in America, and her apprehensions were easily brushed aside by Kelton. You bet he would soon have a job, he told her, and his Mom wouldn't mind if they stayed with her temporarily. They'd soon be able to afford a house of their own, the kind of money he would be earning, and everything would be fantastic. Carol hung on his every word, feeling only the odd pinprick of doubt.

Her pregnancy had caused little trouble during the first trimester, other than the inconvenience of morning sickness. The end of her fourth month brought backache. On the day of departure, her elation evaporated when they were three hours out of London. The flight she had so eagerly anticipated seemed interminable. Miserably she looked down at the grey cottony clouds that cleared to reveal the steely coldness of the vast ocean below. She realised the enormity of what she had done: she had abandoned all that was familiar for a virtual stranger, and a foreign land.

Kelton snored softly beside her.

Her misgivings vanished during the refuelling stop in New York. At immigration, Kelton did the talking, and before she knew it, a green card was inside her passport. Years afterwards, such ease of entry would seem inconceivable.

The flashing neon signs of Las Vegas danced and winked in the darkness as they circled McCarran Airport many hours later. A taxi dropped them at their hotel. Carol caught sight of herself in a mirror at reception in the Flamingo, her face doughy and pale in the garish light. Having crossed so many time zones, she had no idea how long it was since the start of their journey. Quiet and shivering, she stood in the chill air-conditioning of the hotel lobby, grubby and hungry, yet feeling almost sick, as though she'd overeaten. Gleaming crystal chandeliers, glistening marble floors, the ringing of phones and the jingling of slot machines all grated on her. Kelton's voice sounded far away when he spoke, but somehow they made it along an endless corridor to their room. After a quick shower she tumbled exhausted into the huge, glorious bed.

Next morning, Kelton propped himself up on one elbow and looked down at her. Gently he ran a finger around her mouth. She opened her eyes and smiled.

'How's it goin', babe?' he asked.

Carol gave a contented sigh. 'The second my head hit the pillow, I felt I'd died and gone to heaven. I didn't hear you come to bed. What's the time?'

He reached for his watch and turned on the radio. 'Coming up to 11:40 am.'

'I've slept for more than a round of the clock? I'm sorry, we'll have missed breakfast!' she said, throwing back the sheet.

He grabbed her, laughing. 'Take it easy! You're in the States now, they serve breakfast all day!'

'Is this a wonderful country or what?' she said lying back down again. To the strains of *All You Need Is Love* by The Beatles, she coiled her legs round his.

In half an hour, they removed the 'Do Not Disturb' sign from the door as they left their room.

*

Weird things amused her, like the menu in the diner, with its biscuits 'n' gravy, and pigs in blankets. Kelton ordered them each a short stack with bacon, sausage on the side, and two eggs over easy, all washed down with coffee.

The Strip was reminiscent of a fairground where glitz and glamour masked hollow desperation. Half an hour in the intense heat of the day was as much as she could stand, until Kelton led the way into an air-conditioned casino. As soon as he began feeding quarters into a slot machine, a scantily-clad waitress appeared.

'Something to drink, sir?'

He ordered two beers. 'Cheers, honey. Enjoy. These are on the house, even at the nickel slots.'

He clinked his frosted glass against hers. It was a different world, thought Carol with a shiver. Hot as an inferno outside. Cold as ice inside. Breakfast in the afternoon. Kelton slipped his last coin in the machine and pulled the lever. Three matching bars of cherries popped up, and money gushed like floodwater. This was the land of plenty!

They took a cab to the Clark Street Marriage License Bureau to complete the official paperwork: they'd get everything signed and sealed afterwards at one of the many wedding chapels sprinkled like confetti along the Strip. Next they shopped for Carol's dress, a cream silk sleeveless shift. As they rested on top of the bed with the window shades drawn, the room filled with the flickering light of the television. Kelton kept his eyes on the set. He was enjoying an episode of *Jeopardy*, and was scarcely aware of her presence. Ultimately he asked, 'Wanna get married tonight?'

Jet lag was taking its toll on her. Carol stretched and yawned. 'Could we leave it till tomorrow? We've still to buy rings.'

But the commercial break was over, and he was once more engrossed in the quiz. 'Sshh, here's the Daily Double!' he said.

Impatiently he howled at the screen, 'Come on, who is *Ben Franklin*?'

'So what do you think?' she asked.

The lead contestant had gambled big and lost. The host and the studio audience groaned and so did Kelton. 'Can you believe these guys?' After a few seconds, he turned round. 'What? Yeah, rings. Shops are open late, we'll pick them up on the way. It's no big deal. We're as well to get it over with.' He looked back at the screen.

Their wedding was of less interest to him than *Jeopardy*. But he was tired, she told herself, ruffling his black curls and kissing him before swinging her legs off the side of the bed.

'Give me half an hour to get ready, right?' she said, closing the bathroom door. A shower would revive her, help shake off this lethargy. She had to be upbeat. That was the American way.

Meanwhile Kelton lay back on the bed and stared up at the ceiling. This was it, the moment of truth. It would be a big adjustment, being married, always having to consider the needs of another person. But it would beat a stint in Vietnam.

*

They took the full wedding package. The chapel was as artificial as a stage set. During the ceremony, Carol carried a rented silk flower bouquet, while a stretched tape of organ music played wonkily in the background, and a paid witness stood by them. The vows were exchanged, and the minister droned, 'By the power vested in me, by the State of Nevada ...'

There was a pause. Thoughtfully he chewed on a piece of gum.

In the dramatic silence, Carol glanced sideways at Kelton, who stared straight ahead. She was suddenly filled with an insane desire to giggle at being married by a Roy Orbison look-alike, with tinted glasses hiding his eyes, and a black pompadour toupee that sat slightly askew.

The minister cleared his throat, and solemnly continued, 'I now name you husband and wife. You may kiss your bride.' He stepped to the side, lifted a burning cigarette from an ashtray and drew deeply on it.

With a nod, he signalled to the next couple waiting excitedly in the hallway.

*

Angie MacLeod met them when they arrived in St Louis. Carol's first impression of her mother-in-law was of a stylishly dressed beanpole with long black hair, a deep tan and red lipstick. Kelton had inherited his looks from her. The mother rushed forward, arms outstretched, and threw herself on Kelton, kissing him on both cheeks. 'My baby! You made it home at last. It's so good to see you! Have you lost a few pounds? I really think you're skinnier than before!' she cried, feasting her eyes on the son she adored.

Gently Kelton disengaged himself. 'Hey, Mom, this is Carol.'

Suddenly Carol found herself smothered in a perfumed embrace, then she was held at arm's length while Angie said, 'Why, look at you ... if you're not just cute as a button, and you must be *so* tired!' she sympathised, with a meaningful glance at Carol's stomach.

'Oh, I'm fine, thanks. It's lovely to meet you, Mrs MacLeod,' said Carol, but already the woman had turned away.

Kelton loaded the luggage on to a cart. Flirtatiously Angie linked her arm through her son's as the three of them walked through the terminal. Outside, Carol took her first breath of the hot, steam-bath air of a July day in the Midwest. Holding open the rear door of the car, Kelton made to get in beside her.

'Why not sit up front beside me, son? Your wife won't mind sharing you just a little bit. Will you, dear?' asked Angie, from the driver's seat.

'That's okay, Mom. We're fine here.' Kelton laid his hand over Carol's to bridge the vast expanse of cream leather between them. Angie raised one insolent eyebrow and jerked the Lincoln into drive.

50

From his description of his mother's place as a 'ranch', Carol imagined a white clapboard house with horse paddocks and white fencing, but the MacLeod home was a bungalow in two acres of manicured green lawns. With its white and gold décor the house was almost too perfect; it felt like a museum. Its cold pallor lacked soul. Only the kitchen, with its swing door and frilly curtains on the windows offered some refuge. It was airy and bright, with yellow checked wallpaper and a huge refrigerator, an oasis in a desert of wretchedness. It reminded Carol of *I Love Lucy*, one of her favourite childhood shows.

*

Angie lay stretched out on a lounger by the pool, where she spent most days working on her tan. 'Cora!' she called from behind her huge sunglasses. 'Bring us iced tea and sandwiches. The kids had an early start, they're hungry.'

'You have a beautiful home, Mrs MacLeod,' said Carol politely.

'Well, thank you, sweetie. Why don't you call me "Mom"? It would be better, save people thinking you're the hired help.'

Cora arrived bearing a tray. 'Will y'all need anythin' else, Miz MacLeod?'

Angie barely looked round. 'We're set. You can go now. See you tomorrow.' In a syrupy voice, she purred, 'Kelton, tell me more about this interview you have next week. I can't *wait* to hear all your news!'

*

At 4 pm each day, Angie showered, dressed and applied her make-up for the evening, then mixed a shakerful of martinis at the wet bar in the family room. Food was of little concern. Like Wallis Simpson, she believed you never could be too rich or too thin. By her second glass she was becoming almost pleasant. 'I hope you'll be comfortable enough.' Elegantly she nibbled on a pretzel. 'Kelton's bed wasn't really meant for two people.'

'It won't be a problem, I'm sure,' said Carol. She finished her drink and carefully placed her crystal glass on a coaster.

51

'Let me top that up for you.'

'No, thanks.' Carol couldn't remember when she'd last felt this ravenous. 'Could I start to prepare the meal?'

'Sweetie, you do what you wanna do ... just don't expect *me* to cook for you! All I can make is pbj's.' Angie drew deeply on her cigarette, sucking in her cheeks.

Carol looked blank and Kelton shrugged. 'Peanut butter and jelly sandwiches,' he whispered. 'Why don't we all go out for dinner, Mom?'

'You go if you like. I'm not hungry.'

Carol heaved a sigh of relief. At last the two of them would have some time alone! It had been a long day, and it was not yet six o'clock.

'She doesn't approve of me, does she?' Carol remarked.

'It's how she is, hon. She'll grow used to having you here. Do you fancy Italian food? I thought we could go eat at Cunetto's on the Hill.'

'Sounds good.'

Afterwards they drove to the riverfront and parked on the cobblestones of the levee, to stroll along the broad boulevard that separated the memorial grounds of the Gateway Arch from the banks of the Mississippi. The monument was both breathtaking and ridiculous, like a gigantic stainless steel hair band towering over downtown. Carol gazed around her. The Old Courthouse was dwarfed in the shadow of the Arch, and paddle boats bobbed on the river.

What the hell did it matter if her father or his mother disapproved of their marrying? She and Kelton were happy together, and she'd be damned if she'd let anything spoil that for her. *FTLOT*.

'What do you think of it so far?'

'It's terrific,' she replied.

*

Angie had already retired to bed when they got back. Her dirty
martini glass remained on the coffee table for Cora to clear up. A
ghostly emptiness filled the house with no smells, no colours and
no taste, its only sounds the on/off click of the air conditioning,
and the inane blare of the television. Suddenly Carol felt sorry
for her mother-in-law, who was surrounded by everything that
money could buy, and had so little of value.

Chapter 9

'The most terrible poverty is loneliness, and the feeling of being unloved.' – Mother Teresa

'DAD? HEY, HOW ARE YOU, it's Kelton!'

Andrew MacLeod smiled. 'Hey, son, you got back! How was Scotland?'

'Great. I'm on track to graduate next month, but I have even better news. I'm married, and you're gonna be a grand-daddy!'

'Son of a gun! Well, when do I meet my new daughter-in-law?'

'Is tonight any good for you and Cindy?'

'Any time's good to see you, son. Come about six, and we'll put on the grill. We've a lot of catching up to do.'

*

Upon hearing their plans, Angie's irritation was obvious. 'You're newly home and now you're running out on me,' she complained.

'Nobody's running out on you. Dad wants to meet Carol.'

'Oh, well. If you'd rather spend the second evening you're home with *him* ...'

She would never forgive her ex for leaving her. They stayed married until Kelton was fourteen. Suddenly for no apparent reason, according to Angie, he had asked for a divorce. It hurt her pride to be rejected by a man to whom she'd devoted sixteen years. She'd been faithful, kept a perfect home, had endured countless company parties, going out of her way to be witty and charming with one tedious boss after another, all to help Andrew get the next promotion. She'd given him her youth, and a fine son. Once he had shinned up the greasy pole, he turned round and kicked her out of his life.

He had the gall to ask for shared custody of the boy, but Angie's lawyer quashed that idea. Andrew could see him on weekends and some holidays. Angie tried hard, but it was impossible to put a wedge between them. Her only other weapon was to drain as much of her husband's resources as she could. For as long as she lived, she would make that bastard pay sweetly each month for what he'd done to her, and for trying to take Kelton away.

*

The happy, lived-in atmosphere of Andrew and Cindy's home, with its fashionable mustard shag carpeting, tweed sofas and avocado kitchen appliances, was a million miles from the icy grandeur of Angie's. Like Cindy herself, this home was welcoming and unpretentious: Carol felt relaxed. She was greeted not with a phony hug and air kiss, but with firm handshakes. Both Andrew and Cindy looked her in the eye when they spoke.

'This must be so stressful for you, Carol,' said Cindy gently, once they were all seated out on the deck. 'I just can *not* imagine how it must feel to leave your folks, your home and everything behind to come to a completely new country and get married! I think you're really brave. Isn't she, Andy?'

Carol blushed.

'Kelton tells me I'm to become a grandfather in a few months,' said Andrew. 'It's great you got together.' He raised his glass. 'Welcome to the family, Carol. I hope you and Kelton can be as happy as Cindy and I are. Here's to you!'

*

Angie worked her way through a second shaker of martinis in front of the television, her annoyance increasing with each hour that passed. Hearing a car pull into the driveway, she poured herself a refill and assumed her 'sober face'.

'Hi, Mom,' said Kelton, surprised to find her still waiting for them.

'Yeah, hi yourself. Where *the hell* have you been? I expected you back ages ago!'

He shrugged.

'You must have had lots to talk about. Had *ever* such a nice time with Dad and Cindy, did you?' said Angie in a mock-British accent.

Embarrassed, Carol looked at Kelton, then at his mother. 'I'm sorry if we kept you up,' she said.

Angie turned to her new daughter-in-law. '*Sorry*, are you?' she sneered. 'You should be sorry for getting yourself *knocked up*, that's what!'

'Mom, that's enough,' said Kelton. 'C'mon, you need to go to bed.'

'Excuse me?' said Angie, rising unsteadily to her feet. 'You think you can throw your weight about as if you owned the place, speaking to me like that in front of your *little whore*?' At the last two words, she poked him in the chest for emphasis.

He caught her by the wrist. 'You're way out of line. We're not taking any more of this crap.' He turned around to follow Carol to the bedroom, leaving his mother alone.

Accustomed to Angie's drunken tirades, Kelton had learned to disregard them. 'It's the drink that makes her behave that way,' he said, closing the door behind him. 'It upsets her when I see Dad. She doesn't mean half of what she says. Ignore her. She'll be fine by morning, won't remember a thing.'

'And what about *me*? I notice you didn't come to my defence.'

'Sweetheart, the situation's difficult for everyone. I need you to be strong.' He leaned forward to kiss her, but she stepped back.

'Has the air conditioning stopped working? This room's like an oven.'

'Mom likes it warm. She turns off the cooling at night.'

Carol took a shower, her third that day. She emerged from the bathroom to find Kelton spread-eagled across the bed, fast asleep. She lay down at the edge of the mattress, threw aside the top sheet, and turned off the lamp. Barely a week married, she'd been called a whore, but was expected to take it on the chin and be strong: she burned with indignation.

She watched the clock as the hours dragged by, while outside the crickets in the trees chirruped *Whee-Ooo-Whee-Ooo!* In the dark, stifling heat, she wondered what she'd got herself into.

*

Angie wrote a cheque for a shiny new Pontiac. 'That's my wedding gift to you both,' she announced grandly. 'I know you'd prefer something more sporty, kiddo, but I guess you're a family man now.'

Kelton graduated PhD, and was immediately hired by Devanacorp, a locally headquartered chemical company. Desperation for a place of their own pushed them to sign up for a cute house in a recently completed subdivision. They laid down a small deposit and signed up for a huge mortgage that left Carol aghast.

'Don't worry, these payments will look like chickenfeed in a couple of years. Before I'm done, I'll be sitting in Maxwell's chair, just you wait and see!'

She smiled at his aspirations to be head of the company: such self-assurance seemed naïve. In a long-overdue letter to her mother, she poured her heart out, describing their wedding in Las Vegas, their new home and Kelton's job.

'Want me to take this to the post office for you?' he asked, noticing the envelope on the hall table as he left for work.

'If you wouldn't mind.'

'No problem.' He slipped the letter into the side pocket of his briefcase.

By the seventh month of her pregnancy, Carol was desperately lonely. If only her mother were nearby! She had met two neighbours, women with children already in high school who showed little inclination to move beyond a wave and a cheery

'Hi!' Angie had declined repeated invitations to visit: her son knew where she was, if he wanted to see her. Andrew and Cindy were kind, but wrapped up in their own routines. Carol knew nobody and nobody knew her, nor wanted to, it seemed. All she had was Kelton.

If the solitude got too hard to bear, Carol drove around the suburbs. It was such a strange feeling, to live in a place where people smiled and seemed friendly on the surface, but rarely took things any further. The phone never rang, not even with sales calls, since their number was unlisted. Nor did she encounter a familiar face or hear a familiar voice. There were occasions when she envisaged calling it quits: she imagined boarding a plane out of St Louis to return home. Yet that was out of the question, however lonely she might become. She would be an object of pity and derision, her fatherless baby a constant reminder of folly and failure. She had chosen to come here, and would allow no one to think she regretted it. As Kelton said, she had to be strong.

Patiently she watched and waited for the mailman to bring a reply from Oldtown, but it seemed a forlorn hope. On one particularly down day, she stood in the checkout line at Schnucks grocery store, and her ears pricked up as a young woman talked to the toddler she held in her arms.

'I couldn't help hearing your accent,' said Carol, overcoming her natural shyness to approach the stranger who spoke with a comforting, lilting intonation like her own. 'Where are you from, originally?'

'Perth ... and my name's Marie. Have you time for a cup of coffee?'

'I've all the time in the world.'

*

Robert Andrew MacLeod made his entry to the world at Thanksgiving that year. He was a big baby, always hungry and filled with energy, with a head of dark curls like his father's. Kelton arrived at the hospital, jubilantly bearing an enormous basket of flowers for Carol and a pocket full of cigars for friends and co-workers. She wanted to cry, she was so happy. All that could increase her joy was contact with her own family.

Once she and the baby were home, Carol wrote a second letter to her Mam and Dad, enclosing a Christmas card and a photograph of the child. On the back, she wrote 'Your grandson, Robert, aged two weeks'. *That will bring a response*, she thought. Anxiously she watched for the mail, but the Christmas and New Year holidays came and went, with no communication from Oldtown.

FTLOT, she told herself. She had a wonderful husband and a beautiful baby, and that was all that really mattered. Still it hurt to think that her parents' hearts were hard as the ice that coated the trees after January's freezing rain.

Chapter 10

'I would rather be a little nobody, than to be an evil somebody.'
– Abraham Lincoln

K ELTON WAS DOING WELL at Devanacorp: his co-workers envied his success and hated his guts. Among themselves, they bitched about his ambition, his bumptious assertion that every problem had a solution. He irritated with his rash eagerness to excel, and his fearlessness in taking over projects that had defeated those older and wiser, but their resentment meant nothing to him. Everything he touched was a success: he was golden.

At his staff review, the boss declared, 'You sure hit the ground running!' – music to Kelton's ears. It was obvious from his swagger as he returned to his desk that something good had transpired during the interview, but he divulged nothing. The others would discover soon enough that he had got one up on them. He would leave the poor saps behind in a trail of dust. He came home with a bunch of roses for Carol.

'What's this for?' she asked as she placed the flowers in a vase.

'To celebrate my promotion to Senior Group Leader, that's all,' he grinned.

'You're kidding me! Already?'

'Already, and a decent salary increase to go with it.'

She threw her arms round his neck and kissed him. 'Hey, that's great. Congratulations! I'm really proud of you.'

He'd poured all his energy into the job in recent months. Leaving around 7 am, and not coming home till six each night, he threw himself wholeheartedly into what he did to get ahead.

It was natural that he'd feel a bit tired and crabby in the evenings, showing little interest in Carol or the baby. She envied him as he drove off in the Pontiac, dressed in nice clothes and ready to do a job for which he'd receive some tangible reward. Most of all she envied his daily opportunities to interact with other people.

Could it be only eight months since she'd first set foot in America, so eager for the wonderful new world opening up before her? It had all seemed so exciting at first, so much fun, apart from their spell at Angie's. Then after Robert's birth every day was the same, a marathon of solitary confinement where she tended the baby, cooked and cleaned the house. Conversations with Marie rescued her from utter depression. She felt exhausted the whole time, and grateful for the daily diaper service which was unknown in Scotland. When the infant cried during the night, he was her responsibility, because Kelton needed his sleep.

'It's ages since we ate a meal out. How about we ask Dad and Cindy to babysit this Saturday?' Kelton asked.

'Sounds nice.' Carol's joy was tinged with guilt. She was about to escape out to the real world, to be herself for a while, not Mommy.

*

This was almost how it used to be, she thought, like preparing to go out on a date. Could that have been just last year? It was more like a lifetime ago! Months had passed since she had bothered to set her hair in rollers: always twenty more important things required attention. It seemed hardly worth it, for a quick dash to the grocery store before the baby was due his next feed or change.

Tonight she was pulling out all the stops, doing her nails, hair and makeup. She wore the cream dress she'd got for the wedding in Las Vegas, only now she looked better. Though she had remained plump, Kelton said he loved her that way, found it a turn-on. Her eyes sparkled and her hair was shiny and bouncy, like in the television ads for the latest shampoo. There was a definite glow about her.

Kelton, too, had changed. Gone were the dark curls around his collar that Carol had so admired when she first cast eyes on him. Now he was a company man, and looked the part in his sharp suit, white shirt and red silk tie. His hair was short with longish sideburns, which were in vogue. Together they made a handsome couple.

The French restaurant had the hushed, rarefied atmosphere that comes with an outrageously overpriced menu – live piano music playing softly in the background, tuxedoed waiters hovering by candlelit tables, and tiny portions of exquisite food on enormous plates. As the night drew to an end, Kelton selected a cigar from the humidor and sat back, full of good food, good wine and good cheer. He leaned over the table and put his hand on Carol's. 'You seem miles away.'

'Sorry, I was thinking how sad it is that my mother never experienced anything as grand as this.'

'Well, I guess it all depends on the choices we make.' He was unwilling to let talk of his in-laws spoil things.

'I suppose so. Still, I'll never understand why she didn't reply to my letters.'

Biting down on his cigar with just a shade of impatience, Kelton laid his white linen napkin on the table and signalled to the waiter that he was ready for the bill. 'Honey, it's best to let it go. If they had any interest in us or their grandchild, they'd have got in touch. You've moved on to an entirely new life. You're American now.'

*

'Did you mail a Mother's Day card yet?' Marie asked Carol one morning as they trundled their carts round the grocery store.

Carol shook her head. 'I might not bother. I got no reply to either of my letters, and it's ages since I wrote.'

'Go on, don't be rotten,' said Marie. 'Give her another chance. Maybe the letters didn't get there.'

'Of course they did! Kelton mailed them at the post office.'

Marie smiled. 'Well, whatever ... but you only have one mother.'

Once Robert was down for his afternoon nap, Carol had time to think: how terrible to sulk and blame her folks for making no effort, when perhaps they were unable to trace her! Maybe at that very moment, her mother was wondering about the daughter who had gone off to America and apparently never looked back.

As on many occasions during the last few months, she looked at the phone and wished she could bring herself to break this silence that had gone on for too long. She tiptoed to the bedroom to check on the baby. He lay fast asleep.

Shakily she lifted the receiver to dial her parents' number. Suddenly an awful thought struck her: Southwestern Bell itemised all long distance calls on their monthly bill. Kelton would be annoyed if she called home, after the way her father had treated them. But she remained on the line. With a series of clicks the connection was made. She heard the ringing that jarred the cold silence of her parents' hallway, four thousand miles away. Much as Carol would have loved to hear her mother's voice, she couldn't risk upsetting Kelton. Abruptly she hung up.

Early next day, however, with Robert fed, bathed and dressed, she drove to the store to purchase the prettiest Mother's Day card on the rack. Again she enclosed a note with their contact details and a recent photograph of the baby. And this time she went herself to the post office, saying not a word to anyone.

*

Without delay, Kelton packed up his books and papers, ready to move into his new office. Those sad jerks who'd said he couldn't pull off the new formulation were laughing on the other sides of their faces, now that he'd got a promotion! This was just the start. He would show them! Before he was done, they'd all be bragging that they once worked with him, and were old buddies of his.

He whistled softly under his breath as he organised his new desk and cleared out his briefcase. Sifting through a wad of receipts and papers, he consigned some to the wastebasket and filed others. *Holy shit!* he said to himself when he checked the side pocket. Slowly he drew out two envelopes, both addressed to his in-laws: the same ones Carol had written months ago, which he'd promised to mail for her. *Tough luck*, he thought. Served the Coopers right anyhow. Carol was better off without them. She had him and the baby, didn't she? What the hell more could she need?

The second letter seemed bulkier than the first. Curious, he ripped it open and drew out the photograph with the inscription on the back. He smiled at the image of Robert lying there so small, yet so like himself, and stuck the print into the top edge of the corkboard on his new office wall. Then he strode purposefully through the outer area, past his secretary's desk, to a boxy piece of equipment next to the coffee maker. He pressed the green 'forward' switch and the device hummed and ground into action. Carefully Kelton fed the envelopes, the Christmas card and the handwritten pages into the vicious metal jaws of the shredder. Effortlessly its teeth sliced through everything, and Carol's correspondence to her parents spewed in meaningless strips into the trash can below.

Chapter 11

'There are two ways to be fooled. One is to believe what isn't true; the other is to believe what is true.
– Soren Kierkegaard

Things were not going well for the Coopers. Though used to being on their own, the knowledge that their daughter was half a world away in St Louis made it lonelier. Mrs Cooper's routine was the same as always, yet she lacked the energy for her daily chores. Her first thought each day was of Carol. All through the summer she was sure that the postman would bring a letter from America, but by the end of the harvest there was still no word.

A weariness sapped her energy, and she blamed her listlessness on her age. She devoured magazine articles where menopausal symptoms like hot flushes and irritability were coyly discussed. It wasn't for nothing that they called it 'the change of life', she grumbled, sitting down with yet another cup of tea. By November, when her grandchild's arrival was imminent, she attributed the searing pains in her breast to sympathy with Carol's condition. She'd be fine once they heard the baby had arrived safely.

As the agony grew unbearable, she resorted to stiff shots of whisky to help her through each day. Not until the spring of 1970 did she admit defeat by allowing her husband to summon the local doctor. Her weight had dropped, but she stoically drew reassurance from the absence of any lump: whatever her problem, it would not be cancer. After examining her, the GP announced that she would have to go to hospital for tests.

'What do you think it is?' she asked, her eyes wide with fear.

'It's difficult to give an opinion till they take X-rays and things. Don't worry, you'll be in good hands. With luck, you'll soon be back on your feet again.' Quickly he folded his stethoscope and snapped shut his black bag.

'Is she all right?' asked Mr Cooper, who stood waiting at the foot of the stairs.

'No, she's not. Pity you didn't call me sooner.'

Mr Cooper's usually ruddy complexion turned pale. 'Now, just a minute, you can't blame me. She's been having difficulties, but I didn't pursue it. Thought it was women's trouble, because of her age.'

'Yes, but I'm afraid there's more to it than that.' The doctor's tone was ominous.

*

Whatever was discovered during the exploratory surgery was not explained, making it easier to pretend that Mrs Cooper would eventually recover. Following a week's confinement in the sickly-sweet atmosphere of the hospital, she revelled in the pure clean air at home. She grew progressively weaker, and spent most of her waking hours upstairs in bed, with the window open a crack. The April sun streamed in and the thin nylon sheers fluttered in the cool freshness of the breeze as she fretted over the daughter who had abandoned them.

Little pink pills helped keep the pain at bay. She alternated between spells of delusion, almost happiness, where she dreamed Carol had come to visit with the baby. As the morphine wore off, so did her elation, and she wept to know she would never again see her daughter. Her sole comfort was that only her husband witnessed her decline: the ravages wrought by her spreading disease had transformed her into a whey-faced shadow of her former self. When she moved on to liquid medication, she recalled the whispered anecdotes of old. Prescription medicine laced with a favourite alcohol signalled impending death, an indulgence similar to the choice meal served to death row prisoners on their last night. The executioner's axe was poised to fall.

*

While she lay dozing away her last days upstairs, Mr Cooper boiled with silent rage. He was primarily angry at God, for striking his wife with this awful affliction; at Carol for running off to America; and at all those people who could go about their daily business, while his life was falling to pieces. He dreaded the dawn of each new day, and waking up to face the spectre of a woman once so rounded and bonnie, who now was shrinking before his eyes.

The hardest part was maintaining the charade that there would be some improvement. The illness was a punishment, he decided, though he'd been a faithful husband, kept a roof over their heads, and saw to it that their daughter was given a good education. He wasn't given to cursing, drank in moderation, and required only that his wife provide the comforts of a well-run home, attending to the woman's work of cooking, laundry and house-keeping. Was it too much to ask, that they should see old age together? She had endured terrible agonies of fear and pain, yet what of his torment? At least *she* was going a better place, leaving him alone in the world, barely able to boil an egg. He wished he could lie down and die beside her.

Things would have been simple if Carol had married Alex instead of dancing off with that Yank! As Mr Cooper saw it, that had been the beginning of the end for his wife, who had pined for their wretch of a daughter. Sadness must have weakened her resistance, he believed, making her an easy target for the cancer. Nothing could allay the bitterness he felt.

*

Mrs Cooper was propped up in bed, her claw-like fingers clutching the envelope that had come that day. She'd known Carol would write sooner or later! Time and again she had said so, while her husband grunted. She held the thing she most

67

wanted in all the world, and nothing could spoil the occasion for her. She slept a little, woke up to reread the Mother's Day card, and gazed in wonderment at the dark-eyed baby in the picture. Mr Cooper could not remember when his wife last looked so animated. In an unusual fit of magnanimity, he suggested they call St Louis.

His wife smiled sadly and shook her head. 'We will, once I'm a wee bit better,' she sighed. Then she lay back on her pillows, too exhausted to talk any more.

*

Carol's hands were full. Robert had begun teething in his sixth month, and though nothing had yet broken through, she could see a pearly gleam shining beneath his pink gums. His normal good nature was interrupted by sudden bouts of loud crying. An angry red dot would appear on each cheek, and his little chin was constantly wet with drool.

Spring in St Louis was one of the most beautiful seasons of the year. Carol was happy and settling well into her new life, while Kelton went from strength to strength at work. On weekends he toiled in the yard, transforming it into a beautifully landscaped area, complete with shade trees and a trellis for vines. One corner was a designated play area for Robert, with a swing set and sandpit. Neighbours' comments on his enthusiasm spurred him on to greater things. He instigated the formation of a homeowner's association for the subdivision, of which he became president. It was an opportunity to further his reputation as a man to be reckoned with.

One Sunday he announced he'd have to make a quick dash to the office. 'I need stuff for the meeting in New Orleans tomorrow,' he said. 'Damned secretary forgot to lay it out for me on Friday.'

'Can we come with you?' asked Carol. 'I'd like to see where you work.'

'Sure, if you want to.'

'You can show us where you spend your days,' she replied, slipping on her sandals. Many times she had driven by the Devanacorp campus, in awe of the immaculately maintained grounds, huge office blocks and labs.

As they entered the foyer of the main building, a security guard greeted Kelton by name, then the elevator whisked them up the three floors to his office so fast that her ears popped. Carol was impressed.

'I didn't expect it to be so fancy.'

He found the missing papers and stuffed them into his briefcase. 'Fancy, schmancy,' he said with a smile. 'You ain't seen nuthin' yet! This is just the beginning.'

He carried the baby to the outer office, and Robert chuckled with delight as they twirled in the secretary's chair. Carol turned to the corkboard near Kelton's desk, where drawings of new chemical formulations were pinned up alongside memoranda for upcoming meetings. In one corner was a photograph, an early one of Robert. She took it down, noticed the inscription on the back and took a deep breath. Puzzled, she replaced the picture. Either she was going crazy, or something strange was going on.

*

The most interesting part of his trip to New Orleans was Laura, the secretary who served coffee during his meetings. She reminded Kelton of Natalie Wood. Her demure smile was followed by a raising of her shapely brows when their eyes met, and he liked the swing of her hips in her pencil skirt. On his first night there, he attended a business dinner. Now it was Tuesday, and he had a free evening.

'Is there a decent restaurant nearby for a quiet meal?' he asked, lingering at her desk.

She stopped typing and smiled up at him. 'I guess it would depend if you'd like some company or not,' she replied with a twinkle in her eye.

He looked at his watch. 'So what do you suggest?'

'How about the Café de Paris, off Bourbon Street?'

'Wanna meet me at seven?'

'Sure.'

Kelton headed back to his hotel room to shower and change before calling Carol.

'Hey, how're things? You two doin' okay?'

'Yeah,' said Carol, 'we're fine. Robert's a bit crabby, but the gel's helping his gums. How's your trip going?'

'It's so-so,' replied Kelton. 'The guys down here, they don't get it, think they can keep doin' the same old stuff ... but I'll make converts of them yet.'

'No doubt you will,' laughed Carol. 'How is your hotel?'

'It's all right for a coupla nights. Nothing's as good as being home with you and the baby, hon. I'll see you about six tomorrow. Gotta go now. Love ya.'

He replaced the receiver, and switched on the television to watch the news, until it was time for his date.

*

The kitchen phone rang at eight the next morning. It was too early for Marie, nor would it be Kelton, since Carol had talked to him the previous evening. It would be a wrong number. She sat the baby in his high chair, and lifted the receiver.

'Hello?' she said uncertainly.

'Carol? Is that you?' shouted a loud, breathless voice.

She couldn't believe her ears. 'Dad! This is a surprise! Is something wrong?'

'I'm afraid so,' Mr Cooper replied heavily. 'Your mother's gone.'

'Gone where?'

'She's away. Died two days ago.' His tone was impatient, agitated. He'd been nervous of dialling such a string of numbers, and more so at the cost per minute.

The room begin to swirl around her, and Carol reached for a kitchen stool. 'What happened?'

'Cancer. She took ill at the start of the winter, got so bad she'd to go into the hospital, but there was nothing they could do. Typical doctors, useless when you really need them!' he raged. 'Opened her up, found it had spread too far and sent her home within a week. Then it was all downhill. Whole thing's been a bloody nightmare. If she'd been a beast, she'd have been put down. She was like a skeleton by the end.'

A sob rose in Carol's chest. 'Oh, I wish you'd told me Mam was ill.'

The father snorted. 'That's a good one. How could I tell you? For months, your mother pined for a letter from America. We had no address or contact number: not a cheep, until you got round to sending her that card.'

Crazed with grief and self-pity, he wanted to lash out at her. He had no idea of what the time would be in St Louis, nor did he care. He saw no cruelty in announcing the death so coldly, nor would he ask Carol anything about her new life or her baby. Certainly he would not mention that husband of hers. She had made her bed and she could lie on it.

'I wrote twice last year,' she protested. 'You didn't reply to my letters, not even at Christmas.' Her words went unnoticed.

Mr Cooper was watching the clock. He must have spent a fortune already! 'Aye, well, it's neither here nor there. The minister insisted I'd to let you know, so I've done my duty. The funeral's tomorrow.'

'Tomorrow?' Dazed, she could not believe what she was hearing.

The line had gone dead. As if sensing his mother's distress, Robert began to cry, and Carol lifted him, sobbing out loud as she walked him up and down the kitchen. The child's angry red cheeks brushed against her chalk-white face, and their tears mingled.

Chapter 12

'It has been said, "time heals all wounds". I do not agree.
The wounds remain. In time, the mind, protecting its sanity,
covers them with scar tissue and the pain lessens.
But it is never gone.' – Rose Kennedy

S HE HAD SCANT RECOLLECTION of the hours after the call, when she cried for the mother she'd not appreciated enough, and for the father who treated her so harshly.

Almost exactly a year had passed since she had last seen her parents, before leaving for America. The visit had gone well, though Mr Cooper had not said much; but then he never did. He'd been pleasant, and assured her she could always come home if things didn't work out. Now she was in shock at her dear Mam's death, and her Dad's hostility. Carol was stung by his claim that the Mother's Day card was her sole communication. Maybe he'd been drinking: it would be understandable, the stress he'd endured. She could scarcely imagine him coping on his own. He'd always been useless around the house. It hurt that he didn't ask how she and the baby were. He would not accept Kelton, but would it be so hard to ask about his own grandson? *If only I'd called home*, she thought for the hundredth time.

As she laid Robert down for a nap, a seed of doubt took root, the same one sown at the office three days previously. The photograph on the corkboard, with the inscription *'Your grandson, Robert, aged two weeks'*, might suddenly make horrible sense.

*

The clunk of the garage door closing meant he was home. Quickly she blew her nose and straightened up her hair.

'Hi,' she said, as Kelton entered the kitchen.

Immediately he could tell something was wrong. Her eyes were red and puffy, as though she'd cried for hours. 'Hey,' he said, taking her in his arms, 'what's up? Are you okay? You look a bit rough.'

Carol tried to speak, and sobbed. 'My Mam died two days ago.'

'Oh, God, I'm so sorry.' His brow furrowed with concern. Hell, he didn't need this, should have stayed in New Orleans! He hugged her tightly for a few seconds till a thought struck him. 'So, how did you ...? I mean, did your father ...?'

She could barely meet those dark eyes so caring, so sincere and perhaps so treacherous. 'Yes. My Dad called this morning.'

Kelton's face remained impassive. 'That hadn't been easy for him!'

'I'm sure it wasn't.'

That night, she fell into a restless sleep, unable to quell the chattering inside her head. Images of her mother haunted her. She dreamed of floundering alone in a stormy sea, fighting for air as an invisible force sucked her downwards into the blackness. Her struggle to survive grew increasingly desperate. When it became too much to bear, she woke up with a cry.

Kelton also lay awake into the wee hours. Somehow Mr Cooper had got hold of their number. The question was how?

*

He was so kind during the weeks that followed, that Carol felt guilty for suspecting him of any duplicity. One way or another, he and the baby would muddle along if she wanted to fly across to see her father, he said. The suggestion was impracticable, but she appreciated his consideration. It made her feel bad to have suspected him of deliberately withholding those letters she had given him to mail.

Carol found solace in cooking and baking. She laboured for hours on end, soothed by the rituals of mixing, kneading, whisking and beating, all learned from the mother who had given her so much. Comforting aromas from her childhood filled the house, and gradually her spirits improved. On their first anniversary, Kelton surprised her with tickets for a show at the Fox Theater, then dinner.

'There's something I've meant to ask you for ages,' she said as they ate.

He placed his wine glass on the table. 'Really? Well, fire away!'

She took a deep breath. It was now or never.

'You know the photograph of Robert in your office?' She paused, choosing her words carefully. 'Well ... maybe I'm wrong, but I could swear that was the one I'd sent to my folks with their Christmas card.'

Kelton gazed at her for what felt like an eternity, then his face broke into a smile.

'Why would you think that, hon?'

'Because on the back I'd written, "*Your grandson, Robert, aged two weeks*".'

'Yeah. Same as you put on the print for my Mom, and the one for Dad and Cindy.' Coolly he wiped his mouth with his napkin.

She was confused. Had she written anything on the others? She could not remember. That had to be the solution, of course it was. Fancy doubting him!

He saw her uncertainty. 'I'd better 'fess up. It's possible I gave Mom one with no inscription, and it's *her* one in the office.' He grimaced. 'My bad. Do you forgive me?'

'Oh, Kelton, I'm sorry. It's just with all that's happened, I can't seem to keep things straight anymore – thought I was losing my mind.'

He smiled his big toothy grin at her and raised his glass. 'You've been under a lot of stress recently. Here's to better days. Happy Anniversary.'

She sipped at her wine, and began to relax. Kelton always made it all right again. She was the luckiest woman alive, to be married to such a great guy!

*

'Why not come round to our place on Sunday, Mom, see Carol and the baby?'

'It's okay. I prefer having you to myself,' she replied as usual.

Angie refused to acknowledge the existence of her son's wife and child. It had been clear from the start that the two women would never be close friends, but Kelton had not expected the stand-off to last so long. Visiting her on his own had grown tedious.

'I can't make it next week.' He offered no excuse.

Her pride would not let her ask why. After all she'd done for him, she didn't deserve to be tossed aside! Like father, like son. 'Suit yourself. I'm happy to see you here any time.'

Kelton stood up. 'I'll drop by at the end of the month.'

She gave him a peck on the cheek, her lips a painted line of pique to see him leave once more.

*

Carol was apprehensive at his first mention of hosting a New Year's Eve party.

'You're the one who's Scottish round here,' he said. 'We should carry on the old customs! C'mon, it'll be fun.'

The date drew nearer and the growing guest list increased her anxiety. She cooked and baked till no more could be jammed into the fridge or the freezer. Everyone they knew was invited – neighbours, his family and people from the office. He would show them all how Hogmanay was meant to be.

'Fifteen pounds of shrimp?' Carol looked incredulously at Kelton's shopping list. 'Do we need that much?'

Kelton winked. 'You bet. Look at it as an investment. I have to create the right impression where it counts. It's all about networking.'

She said nothing. The decision had been made. Close to fifty guests showed up. Never had so many strangers milled around Carol's home, astounding in their familiarity as they rummaged through her kitchen in search of more ice or beer. She admired Kelton's ease as a host, laughing and joking his way round the room, taking extra care to schmooze with his bosses or anyone influential in the community. That night she learned his nickname. At work he'd become known as 'Big Mac'. In the years that followed, 'Big Mac's Hogmanay' became a tradition that filled the social calendar with return invitations.

A second son was born in June 1972 and they named him William James MacLeod. The loneliness and homesickness that plagued Carol during her first pregnancy had long since faded. An infant and a boisterous toddler left her little time to think of anything else. Kelton's career was moving along nicely. They were on their way up, he told her, and if he was happy, she was happy.

*

On a Sunday morning when yellowed maple leaves drifted lazily down onto the grass, he remarked, 'They're building single-family properties at Clayton Road.'

'Who'll be able to afford them? They're monstrous,' replied Carol.

'We should go and check them out.'

'Seriously?'

'Yeah. It bugs me, that truck they keep parked in the driveway next door.'

'Not enough to make you want to move, surely?'

'This was a great starter home, but now we can afford better. We should be in a decent catchment area, get the kids enrolled in the best schools.'

From the change in her expression, he knew she would resist no more. That year Big Mac's Hogmanay party took place in their brand new twelve-roomed house.

Fall 1974

It had been a rough week. First Robert then Will had caught a stomach bug. Following three sleepless nights in a row, Carol had returned to bed at five, glad to grab some shuteye before breakfast.

Kelton barged into the bedroom. 'Carol! You awake? Where's my best grey suit?'

'It's in the closet,' she murmured, snuggling beneath the comforter again while he raked the hangers to and fro along the metal rail.

'Is it back from the cleaner's?'

No response. She was asleep.

'Honey,' he called out in his most sarcastic tone, 'I hate to disturb you, but I need that suit now!' There was a dangerous ripple of annoyance in his voice.

Wearily Carol dragged herself out of bed. 'As if you couldn't wear another one ...'

'Yeah, right! In case you forgot, my meeting with Lenny Schwartz is today.'

'Look! What do you call this?' She pointed to the suit, hanging immediately in front of him, but received no apology or word of thanks.

He wrestled with the top button of a new white cotton shirt, selected his best silk tie, and slipped his feet into a pair of new black leather wingtips.

'See you at night,' he called as he strode out of the bedroom, slamming the door behind him. The noise woke Will.

As the car pulled out of the driveway, Carol watched from the bedroom window while her third baby kicked inside her.

*

'MacLeod! Good to see you. Take a seat.'

The two men shook hands firmly, and Kelton sat down opposite Lenny Schwartz.

'I won't beat about the bush,' said Schwartz. 'Your work on the TG5's has been outstanding. I wanted to know how you'd feel about moving on to manage the Alto project. That sucker needs turned around fast.'

This was the big break he'd been waiting for! He'd long looked forward to this day, and had toiled hard to make an ally of Lenny. Kelton maintained a deadpan expression. Managing the Alto project was a great chance to make his mark. 'I'd be excited to be given an opportunity like that, sir.' He had to strike a balance between ambition and humility.

'It won't be easy. Holman's had two years to hit the right formulation, but to be honest, he's getting nowhere. The guy's burned out. We can't afford passengers in this business, if you catch my drift,' said Schwarz, with a smile.

'Point taken. I appreciate your confidence in my abilities, sir.'

Kelton understood that if he succeeded with Alto, he would be a star. If he failed, he would be out on his ass, like Holman.

Schwartz stood up. 'Fine. I guess that's it, then. Glad to have you on the team.'

Back in his office, Kelton called home. 'Yeah, it's me,' he said, curtly.

'Hi,' replied Carol warily, since he'd left so angry that morning. 'You okay?'

'I guess so, since I've just been made manager of the Alto project.' She could hear the grin in his voice.

'Manager! Wow! Congratulations!'

'Find a babysitter for tonight. We have some serious celebrating to do. Talk to you later.' Kelton hung up.

The radio in the kitchen was playing softly in the background. The news left her so elated that Carol scooped up Will and Robert into her arms and danced around the kitchen, singing along with Gladys Knight and the Pips, *You're the Best Thing That Ever Happened to Me*.

However ratty Kelton might sometimes be, he more than compensated when things were good. That made it all worthwhile.

*

She reread the announcement of his promotion. At the end was a terse statement that Fred Holman was leaving the company to pursue other interests.

'Where's he moving to?' asked Carol, innocently.

Kelton laughed. 'Who the hell cares? "Pursue other interests" means you're out, baby, you're yesterday's man. That's what happens if you don't deliver.'

'And if *you* can't hit the right formulation either? Will you get the same treatment?' Heaven forbid that such a thing should ever happen: life would be impossible with him.

'Failure is not an option. Trust me, I can do this. You'll see me in Maxwell's chair before I'm done.' He knocked back the remains of his drink and looked at his watch. 'Where the hell is that babysitter? I'm hungry!'

Chapter 13

'JACK BERGMANN! I'LL BE DARNED. Must be six years since I saw you!'

'Hey, Brad, how're ya doin'?' said Jack, touching the other guy's shoulder.

'I'm doin' great, buddy. How 'bout you? You still as full of shit?'

Jack gave a good-ole-boy guffaw. 'This is my wife, Amy. Darling, meet Brad Taylor. We go way back.'

That was Jack's cue for reminiscing about the old days, and her heart sank.

Not again! she wanted to scream. *Who gives a damn what you did thirty years ago, before I was even born?*

Amy extended her hand to the short, bald guy at the club bar.

Brad looked at her appraisingly. 'Pleasure to meet you, ma'am.' To Jack he said, 'You ole dawg, this your wife? How come *you* got so lucky, huh?'

She tugged at Jack's arm. 'Got to go, sweetie. My lesson's in ten minutes. Nice to meet you, Brad.'

And don't fucking-well call me 'ma'am', she muttered to herself, as she threaded her way through the brunch crowd out into the hallway, towards the locker rooms.

These old guys were such phonies! Sure, Jack had been a savvy businessman in his day, and had amassed more money than she would ever need. But anyone who reckoned he was an old dog, whatever that implied, hadn't witnessed his pathetic attempts between the sheets. *She* knew why there were no children from his first marriage, despite the conventional wisdom that his first wife was infertile. That was the beauty of wealth, it could buy any illusion you wanted to create. Without money, Jack's failings would be exposed. He'd no longer be the envy of his geezer gang because no younger woman would give him a second look, let alone marry him.

Yes, she wanted to tell Brad, Jack was in fact full of shit.

Not that she could complain. When winter gripped the Midwest, they took off on their travels to warmer climates, and from the spring through fall, Amy enjoyed being at home in St Louis. Lunch dates, shopping and sessions at the beauty salon lent structure to each week, while hours on the tennis court kept her in shape.

Each summer the club employed a tennis coach: some student keen to earn a few extra dollars giving lessons to idle, rich women members with flabby arms and big dimpled thighs. Amy stood out from the crowd, with her lithe, tanned young body, blonde hair in a perky ponytail and the whitest frilly panties that only just peeped out from below a cheeky tennis skirt.

This year his name was Gary. From lunch after their game, it was a small step to intimacy. Amy saw it as a way of retaining her sanity. They harmed no one, these minor escapades off the court with a succession of immature, athletic, fun-loving guys who helped her forget Kelton, and lessened her contempt for Jack. If her husband was aware of these extracurricular activities, he made no mention of the fact. In her turn, Amy was discreet and respectful, careful to maintain the pretence her old man – *Daddy Cool* as she teasingly called him – was perfect in every way. Compromise bound the marriage together: they accommodated each other's needs and were happy in their fashion.

*

The Dom Perignon was chilled to exactly the right temperature, and Laura held up her drink. 'To your continued success!' she said, lifting the glass to her lips.

He ordered a selection of the finest dishes and wines while she lapped up the atmosphere of Brennan's, New Orleans' iconic French Quarter restaurant. She had taken special care with her appearance that night, and looked good; too bad they could not see or be seen from their side alcove, but Kelton liked privacy. She had learned that, if nothing else, in the four years since they'd met.

At the end of the meal, she leaned forward towards him. 'I always have the best fun with you, Kel. Bet that wife of yours doesn't know how lucky she is! This was a wonderful evening.'

He withdrew as the waiter approached. 'Glad you enjoyed it.'

They walked out onto Royal Street, her arm linked through his. 'Your place or mine?' she asked.

'I'm on the early flight tomorrow, I think I'll take a rain check.' Already he was tuning out, starting to plan his schedule for the next day. Best to quit while he was ahead, leave her on a high.

'I have a bottle of twenty-five-year-old Scotch at home you might like to try. We're almost there.'

That was sufficient to persuade him. 'Maybe just a half hour, then.'

Around one in the morning, Kelton got back to his hotel.

*

1975

Josie was a difficult child from the very start. Months of sleepless nights shattered Carol's illusions that a girl might be easier to raise than boys.

Kelton's energies had to be saved for the Alto project. His team of researchers lacked imagination and enthusiasm, but he was determined to whip them into shape. His calculated brusqueness fostered a jittery resentment of this new boss who was obsessed with results. Nothing less than total commitment was acceptable, he declared, and no freeloaders would be tolerated. The threat behind his words was clear. A newfound urgency to deliver results filled the lab.

As he passed his secretary's desk one morning, her external line rang.

'Good morning. Dr MacLeod's office. How can I help you?'

Kelton raised his hand, palm forward. He was not available. 'Thank you, I'll pass your message along,' the secretary said, scribbling on a pad.

Eventually he got round to reading the note:

Laura Donahue called from New Orleans.
Must speak with you ASAP.

Angrily he scrunched up the page, threw it into the trash can and instructed his secretary that on no account was she to accept any communications from Miss Donahue. Calling him had never been part of the deal. Unless Laura played by his rules, she would get the chop.

*

Carol bought one of the answering machines that had appeared on the market, because the phone that had remained so silent early in her marriage now rang night and day. She wondered how she could ever have felt lonely in St Louis. Marie was her closest friend, but she had many new acquaintances. A woman came in to help with the housework, leaving her free on weekdays for shopping and socialising. Saturday nights were for dinner parties, while the three children were left with a regular babysitter.

Then came the silent calls. Carol thought nothing of it, the first time the line went dead as she spoke. After several such instances, it became upsetting. One evening during dinner, Kelton answered, and abruptly said, 'I don't know how you got this number. Don't ever do this again.'

'Who was it?' asked Carol.

'A jerk trying to sell something.'

*

Carol's first job when she arrived home the following afternoon was to unload the grocery bags from her car. Having put Josie down for a nap, and settled Robert and Will in front of the television with cookies and juice, she began to prepare the meal.

As she laid the table she noticed the red light winking on the answering machine. She played the message, frowned and pressed rewind to listen once more. The pleading female voice on the tape reawakened her long-suppressed doubts. Old insecurities flooded back, and Carol felt a flush rise to her face. At the sound of Kelton's footsteps coming in from the garage, she hurriedly poured herself a glass of iced water. She had to keep her cool.

All he wanted was to have a drink and relax. It had been one helluva day, with wall-to-wall meetings from eight till five-thirty. Kelton felt he deserved a break.

'Hey,' he said, giving Carol a peck on the cheek.

'Okay, guys, Daddy's home! Dinner's almost ready,' she called to the kids.

Purposely she waited until he was seated, so that she could gauge his reaction. 'There's voice mail for you. Someone called Laura sounds very keen to have a word.'

Kelton laid down his fork. 'Laura? Laura from the office?' He felt his stomach lurch. 'I'll listen to it later.'

Carol rose from her seat, and pressed the replay button. 'You can hear it now.'

He jumped up, pushing his chair back so roughly it scraped the hardwood floor, but he wasn't fast enough. Already the voice was saying, 'Kel, it's Laura. I need to talk to you. Please call me.'

He shook his head in disbelief, wanted to pitch the damned answering machine straight out through the kitchen window. He clenched his fists in rage.

'So who's this Laura?' asked Carol.

'I told you, she works at the office.' He did not mention which office.

'And she addresses you as *Kel*? No one ever calls you that.'

He returned to the table. The best defence was attack. 'Geez, what is this, the *Spanish Inquisition*? You know what?' he continued, 'I've just about had it with everything today! This Laura woman, she's driving me nuts. It amazes me how she got hired! She has no concept of what's appropriate. You can see for yourself, she's completely lacking in common sense, bugging me at home! My regular secretary gets back from vacation next week – can't come soon enough!'

Thoughtfully Carol ate. If he was deceiving her, he really was good! Nobody in the middle of an affair could be that calm.

He shoved his food aside, his appetite gone. Desperate to change the subject, he turned to Robert. 'Hey, buddy, wanna go out and play ball in the yard before your bath?' (Though what he actually felt like was a large Jack Daniels on the rocks and an hour alone to stretch out on the sofa.)

'Not so fast!' said Carol. How am I ever gonna get them to clean their plates if *you* leave half your meal?'

Robert and Will giggled when Kelton made a goofy face and cowered as if to shield himself from a blow.

'*I'm sorry, Mommy,*' he squeaked.

'Not as sorry as you'll be if you don't finish what's in front of you.'

He lifted his fork. With so much adrenalin rushing through his system, every mouthful stuck in his craw, but eating was the price of proving his innocence. It had been a close shave but he got away with it.

Carol stacked the dishwasher and hummed to herself as she bathed the boys. How silly to imagine there was anything but a simple explanation for that stupid message! All was well with her world again.

He had barely sat down at his desk next morning when his phone buzzed.

'Your mother's on the line, Dr MacLeod,' said his secretary.

Kelton sighed. What the hell did she want this time? 'Hey, Mom,' he said. 'What's up?'

'I'm not feeling good. Can you come round?'

'What, *now*?'

Angie sounded scared. 'I'm sorry, baby, but I'm all shaky, and I've got that pain in my chest again. I think I'm dying.'

'Call 911 and I'll be over in ten minutes.' He grabbed his jacket. 'Family emergency. Cancel my meetings for this morning,' he called to Lisa as he dashed out of the office. The paramedics were already in the driveway. A gurney was being wheeled out from the front door. His mother's eyes were like gaping hollows in her gaunt face.

'I'll lock up, and follow you. You're gonna be okay, Mom.' He patted her hand.

Angie smiled weakly. With its siren blaring, the ambulance roared off towards St John's hospital.

*

'Is it her heart?' Kelton asked outside the examination room.

The doctor smiled. 'No. I'm glad to tell you her general health seems pretty good. More likely it was a panic attack, but we'll keep her in for observation for the next 24 hours, to make sure. I don't think there's anything to worry about.'

Hell, as if his life wasn't complicated enough without Angie starting to act up! Women, they brought nothing but headaches. It was just one darned thing after another!

Chapter 14

'An eye for an eye will only make the whole world blind.'
– Mahatma Gandhi

'WHAT THE *FUCK* DID YOU THINK you were doing, calling me at home?'

He was so angry, Laura scarcely recognised his voice.

'Kel? Thank God. I've tried to get in touch with you for a couple of weeks ...'

'Cut the crap,' he interrupted. 'You don't call me in St Louis, and certainly not at home. That was never part of the deal.'

'Nor was becoming pregnant, but sometimes shit happens.'

His face flushed in anger. Did she think he was stupid enough to fall for that old line? 'What's this to do with me?'

'Don't, please. Just come down to New Orleans so we can talk things over.' Receiving no response, she said, 'Are you still there?'

'Yes, I'm here. Look, I have stuff to deal with. I gotta make a few calls.' Time to plan was what he needed. 'I'll get back to you around five,' he said, hanging up.

*

His flight got in at seven the following evening. The taxi took him straight to Laura's apartment.

'Can I get you a drink?' she asked.

'Water.' Seldom had his eyes looked so black and menacing.

She placed the glass on the coffee table in front of him.

'Kel, I'm sorry I had to call you at home. I panicked, when your secretary refused to put me through to you at the office. I didn't mean to make trouble for you.'

'Like hell you didn't. So you believe you're pregnant?'

'I know I am. It was that night after Brennan's.'

'What makes you think it's mine?'

'Are you serious? Who else's would it be?' she asked, exasperated.

He shrugged. 'Listen, we see each other occasionally for dinner, when I'm here for meetings. What you do the rest of the time is your business.'

'Several nights a month for five years we've been together. You call that occasionally? I'll bet *your wife* wouldn't!'

'Don't bring her into this. I'm warning you: try to blackmail me, and you'll regret it.' He oozed hostility, pointing at her as he spoke. 'You're looking for a fall guy, but it ain't gonna be me, doll.'

She smirked. 'I have proof of the dates and times you were here.'

He gave a start. What could the conniving bitch have up her sleeve?

Laura paused, enjoying her moment of triumph. 'Don't you remember ringing Carol from my place? Like a dutiful husband, you checked all was well on the home front, to grab your bit of fun with a clear conscience. You even paid me for the calls, which was sweet. I would show you my phone bills, but they're in a safe deposit box with my other insurance policies.'

He sat with his head in his hands. 'So what do you want?' he said at last.

'It costs money to raise a child.'

'You don't want a baby! That's not your style.'

'Do I have any choice?'

'Of course. We're out of the dark ages now! You don't have to through with this shit if you're not totally committed. Get rid of it.'

She looked stunned. 'How can you say that?'

'Look at you: you're a smart, intelligent woman with a career. You want nice things. You have a future ahead of you. Are you gonna throw it all away because a tiny cluster of cells formed by accident? You're not thinking straight.'

Who was he to judge whether or not she was thinking straight? 'It would be on my conscience for ever. And maybe I'd *like* a baby.'

'Doesn't mean you need to mess up everybody's life in the process. Have a baby if you like, but don't involve me, okay? One of these days, a nice guy will come along, you'll get married and have a whole bunch of kids together.' He stared out of the window at the street below, a bored expression on his face.

'You don't give a damn how I feel, do you?' Laura cried. 'I was a good Catholic before I met you. My folks would go crazy if I even considered having an abortion.'

'Yeah, but you're a big girl now. It didn't matter what your folks would think when we were in the sack, did it?'

She winced.

Slow it down, he was saying to himself, try to sugar-coat his message. He could perhaps swing it yet. All he needed was time to make her see things his way.

'Look, it's a tough call: it's no walk in the park, being a single parent, and adoption's a hard way to go. Better to wipe the slate clean. Let me arrange everything. I'll meet you in New York, you'll travel first class. I'll see you through the procedure at a private clinic, then you'll spend a night or two at the Waldorf to recover. You come back and nobody's any the wiser.'

'And you'd be off the hook, right?'

Kelton shook his head. 'I'm just looking at the best solution for everyone. You can go ahead with this if it's what you really want ... or we can reach an amicable agreement and put this episode behind us. But if you take me to court, I'll fight you tooth and nail.'

He stood up. The conversation was over as far as he was concerned. 'Call and let me know what you decide.'

'Let me sleep on it.'

What he said was logical. She was powerless against him. After he had gone, she listened over and over to Linda Ronstadt's *You're No Good* and cried herself to sleep.

*

Trips to New Orleans would never be such fun again. Kelton saw to it that she was transferred to a different department. They no longer came in direct contact at the office.

It was not exactly a demotion, more a sidelining that left Laura little prospect of advancement. Her self-loathing grew to recall the solitary weekends and holidays she'd spent deluding herself that they had a future as a couple. How could she have imagined their relationship would harm no one? She had to face the truth. Big Mac, the company's rising star, was rotten to the core.

Shrouded in depression, she mourned the baby she'd aborted. Having let down herself and her family, she confessed her mortal sin to the priest, and sought repentance. It helped restore her self-assurance. Cowering in a corner was not the Donahue way. She would hold up her head and move on.

Don't get mad, get even. That became her mantra.

*

It was ten o'clock on a weeknight. Kelton had attended a particularly important business dinner, and returned to his usual hotel in New Orleans. Before turning in, he went for a quick nightcap in the lounge. The place was deserted, apart from a well-built man in his twenties. Slowly Kelton sipped his large single malt, consciously relaxing. Eventually he headed for the elevator, followed by the young guy from the bar.

Both stepped out on the fourth floor. No sooner had Kelton slipped his room key into the lock when a sudden, violent push sent him lurching forward, on to all fours. The door slammed shut behind him. Kelton tried to scramble to his feet, but received an upper cut to his jaw and went reeling backwards. With a sickening crack, his head struck the corner of the wooden luggage rack opposite the bed.

90

'*What the fuck?* Who are you, what d'ya want?' he whimpered. 'Here, take my wallet, my credit cards – whatever you like.'

'Keep your money, pal.' The assailant stood blocking the passageway.

With a groan Kelton raised a hand to his head, and felt the warm stickiness of oozing blood. 'Who are you?' he asked again.

'Let's say I'm a teacher, come to show you how it feels to be treated like a piece of shit. Now you know it was no fun for my sister, being messed around by a jerk looking for entertainment. Get it?'

As he tried to move, Kelton was dealt another sharp kick in the groin.

'Answer me. Do you understand?'

He could only nod as he lay curled in a foetal position, his head bleeding onto the carpet. Then finally he was alone.

*

He could conceal the bruises on his body after the incident, but there was no hiding the gash on his head.

'Oh, what's happened to you? Are you okay?' Carol immediately asked when he got home. 'You look ghastly.' She moved to put her arms round him, but Kelton backed away.

'Don't touch me. I got mugged last night.'

'No! Why didn't you let me know? That's awful! Did you report it?'

Closing his eyes, he shook his head. 'Just pour me a drink, would you?'

Hours later he recounted his version of the story. He'd been taken by surprise as he walked back to his hotel after dinner. Two punks had jumped him on a quiet street, beat him up pretty good. It had to be part of a gang initiation because they had no interest in robbing him. Wanton violence was their goal. The attack was totally random, he'd been in the wrong place at the wrong time, nothing more.

She listened, appalled. 'So why didn't you call the police?'

'And spend the rest of the night waiting to file a complaint about an assault with no witnesses? If they'd robbed me, of course I'd have reported it. I felt so bad, all I wanted was to get back to the hotel and into the shower. I guess I was in shock.'

'Darling, I'm so sorry.' Carol furrowed her brow. 'Why don't you take a really deep, relaxing soak? I'll run the water for you.' She ran upstairs and turned on the tap in the master bath. Carefully she laid out fresh towels and pyjamas, because at that minute, there was nothing she would not do to comfort him.

Chapter 15

'Prosperity suits some people, and they blossom best in a glow of sunshine; others need the shade, and are the sweeter for a touch of frost.' – Louisa May Alcott

1982

JACK LOOKED FIT, KEPT IN GOOD SHAPE, and had regular check-ups till one day on the golf course, the pain hit. Within an hour, he was in the emergency room of St John's Mercy Hospital where the junior resident buzzed the senior resident, who summoned the chief resident. Tests were ordered. Since the patient was comfortable, he was sent home. In two days, Jack went alone to hear the results.

'It doesn't look great,' reported the physician. 'Your ultrasound and CT scan both indicate a large abdominal aortic aneurysm.'

'You're way ahead of me here. I have no idea what that is!'

The medic explained, then sat silent, watchful.

'So, how do we treat this sucker?' The gravity of Jack's situation had not registered.

'We don't. It's because your aneurysm has gone undetected for a long time that you're experiencing discomfort. I'm afraid it's too advanced for us to operate on.'

Jack smiled feebly and felt he'd been whacked across the face with a spade. 'Hey, doc, you giving me a death sentence here?'

'By no means. Nothing's changed, except now you know the cause of the pain. You can carry on as normal, but once an aneurysm ruptures, that's it.'

Jack put on a brave face. Since so little else seemed within his control any more, he immediately arranged appointments with his broker and his estate attorney. He wanted to update the terms of his will and his revocable trust: at least his affairs would be in order.

When Amy got home from the hairdresser's, he was relaxing with a drink and watching the early news on television.

'Hi, honeybunch!' She kissed the top of his head. 'Doctor's visit go okay?'

'You want the good news or the bad news?'

She sat down in shock when he told her the diagnosis. 'We should get a second opinion. We'll go to the Mayo Clinic. There's bound to be something ...'

He put up his hand. 'Hang on, maybe I'm good for years yet. I'm still the same as I was yesterday, except they put a name to the condition. Come on, darling, I'm fine.'

Tears glinted in her eyes. 'We'll beat this, whatever it is.'

Jack put his arm around her. 'Enough already with the crying. We've all to die sooner or later. I'm not going to sit waiting for it to happen. I plan to enjoy every day I have on this earth.' He held out a clean tissue. 'Here, you go and fix your makeup, and I'll pour you a glass of wine. I made a 7 pm reservation at Dominic's. You won't get rid of me that easily!' he joked, though the discomfort in his stomach was telling him otherwise.

*

Kelton was at the top of his game again. His successes had propelled him into a director's position. A gleaming red BMW sat in his garage. Alongside was a new silver Chrysler minivan, a monster fit for all the kids and groceries Carol could ever need to carry. His promotion brought more money, responsibility, and extensive travel to Europe and South America. He was gone so much that Carol joked he was a guest who popped in to visit as he passed through St Louis. He laughed to hear her say that, though she was only half joking. No one could deny that he worked hard.

Too hard, his mother told anyone who would listen, justifying her successful son who lived close by but kept his distance. Angie lurched from one medical emergency to another. Whenever his secretary announced a call from his mother, Kelton groaned and reluctantly lifted the receiver.

But one day it was different. 'Dr MacLeod?' said Cora's voice. 'I hate to bother you, but you gotta come.'

Family could be such a pain in the butt! 'What is it this time?'

'Miz MacLeod won't wake up. I let myself in as usual with my key, and there was no sign of her. When I went through to her bedroom, she just lyin', never movin'. Can't git her to talk to me. I'm scared!'

'I'll be right with you,' said Kelton. 'It's probably nothing. Stay where you are.'

Angie had fooled him almost a decade ago, crying wolf over a panic attack, but he'd got wise to her tricks. No way would he call 911 again after that stunt! She'd most likely gone over the score with the martinis last night. Pity he wasn't out of town, then she'd get over it on her own, as usual.

Cora opened the front door as his car turned into the driveway.

'Mom?' Softly Kelton approached the bed where Angie lay. 'Mom?'

No response came. She was sound asleep, long grey hair spread over the pillow, her right arm with its gold bracelets resting on top of the sheet. Kelton bent over, reached out to place a gentle hand on hers, and almost jumped with shock, recoiling at the coldness of her skin. He dialled 911, though his mother was beyond help.

Cora began to cry, her anguished wails filling the silence. Kelton was glad of that show of emotion; all he felt was relief.

*

So much of his time and energy went on his job that he often had little to offer at home except bad temper, snide criticisms and dirty laundry. Weeks could pass when he and Carol hardly saw each other, let alone snuggle together in bed or have sex. Life with him was like living on the edge of a volcano: one minute everything was normal, till suddenly his anger spouted forth in a toxic stream of disapproval.

Perhaps work stress, or delayed reaction to his mother's death was the cause. Angie was gone, but was casting a cloud over them. What Kelton needed was a vacation, Carol decided. It would do them good to take a proper family trip for once.

'Let's go to Europe this summer,' she suggested.

'For the kids to meet the grandfather who doesn't know they exist? I don't think so.'

'They should get to see where their ancestors came from. Travel's an important part of their education.'

'There's a lot for them to see in the States.'

She persevered. 'And what about me? It's thirteen years since I left Scotland. Don't I deserve a trip home?'

He put his arm around her. 'Is that what you really want?'

'Yes. That's what I want, for us all to go as a family.'

'And we will, sometime, believe me.'

'As in *sometime never?*' she retorted, shaking him off. 'I wish you'd be honest, and say what you're thinking.'

'Goddammit, what more do you want from me? I already spend half my life hanging around airports or sitting on planes, and now you're annoyed that I don't want to cross the Atlantic yet again? Gimme a break, would you?'

No more was said on the subject. A trip to Great Britain would never be high on Kelton's list of priorities, nor would any big family vacation. Soon afterwards, he surprised her by purchasing a vacation home at Lake of the Ozarks, not that he had much time or inclination to actually use it. Like their huge in-ground pool in the back yard, it showed the world that he could buy anything his family could want – if it was *his* idea.

*

'Is that what you're wearing?' Kelton's tone was incredulous.

The boy's face took on a sulky expression. 'Yeah.'

'I don't think so. That T-shirt's fine for going out to throw a few baskets, buddy, but not for eating at the club. Okay?'

Carol dreaded these confrontations. If it wasn't the children's choice of clothes, Kelton found fault with mannerisms or phrases they had picked up at school. It would be so much simpler if they could go for brunch at Denny's!

'He's only a kid, let him be. It's no big deal,' she said.

Kelton whipped round to face her. 'I got us a membership that costs more than an apartment, and you want us to turn up at the club looking like the *Beverly Hillbillies*?'

'I'm thirteen, I can decide myself what to wear,' muttered Robert. 'Normal stuff's more comfortable.'

'You have a half-dozen Ralph Lauren Polo shirts in your closet. You telling me they aren't comfortable?'

'This is what I like.' The boy stood his ground, looking his father in the eye.

'Let me tell you something, buster. I've worked hard to get us to where we are. Appearances count. You want to come out as part of my family, you'll look the part or you can stay home.'

At the upstairs banister, Will was gleefully witnessing the scene. Putting one hand behind his back, Robert stuck up his middle finger to his younger brother, and glared defiantly at Kelton. Father and son stared each other out for almost a minute, until the boy turned around and went to change, lips moving as he mouthed every curse word he'd ever heard. Who gave a rat's ass about his old man's shitty club membership, anyway?

*

Amy spotted them as they entered the dining room. They would be hard to miss, the picture of young affluence, unlike the stale retiree crowd she was used to seeing. It had been fourteen years, but she'd recognise Kelton anywhere. Still good-looking, fuller in the face and with a touch of grey at the temples, he carried himself with the air of one who mattered. It amazed her that she had never run into him in St Louis, but it stood to reason: they moved in different circles. She watched the MacLeod family get seated at the far side of the room. The wife was pretty, like an older, heavier version of Princess Diana. The oldest boy was a replica of his Dad with the same head of long dark curls Kelton had back in the sixties. Likewise the little girl. Only the middle boy resembled his mother.

During the next hour, Amy enjoyed observing them. Her excitement mounted at the thought of Kelton's proximity.

'What are you looking at, darling?'

She hadn't realised she was staring, till Jack spoke. She gave a guilty start, and smiled. 'That couple, there's something familiar but I can't place them. Must have known them in high school.'

Every Sunday for ages afterwards, Amy primped and posed at the mirror before they went for Sunday brunch at the club, but to no avail. The sighting of Kelton and his family had been a one-off, but just thinking about him was a wonderful diversion. Air Supply's hit of that same year, *Even the Nights Are Better*, buzzed round in her head:

> *I, I was the lonely one*
> *Wondering what went wrong*
> *Why love had gone*
> *And left me lonely*
>
> *I, I was so confused*
> *Feeling like I'd just been used*
> *Then you came to me*
> *And my loneliness left me*
>
> *Even the nights are better*
> *Now that we're here together*
> *Even the nights are better*
> *Since I found you*

Then one day as she headed for the locker room, following a strenuous game of tennis, they unexpectedly ran into each other. Kelton literally stepped out into Amy's path.

'Whoa! Excuse me,' he said, coming to an abrupt halt.

'Kelton?' she said in genuine surprise. *Damn!* She'd wanted look her best, hair and makeup perfect for meeting him after so long. Instead she was slightly out of breath, hot and sweaty, her cheeks flushed and her long blonde hair slightly dishevelled.

Recognising her, he grinned. 'Hey, stranger! How are you?'

'Great. You?'

'Fine.' He could scarcely take his eyes off her, couldn't believe she still looked this good, maybe even better than he remembered! 'You play tennis here?' *Damn fool thing to say, when she has a racquet in her hand!*

'All the time,' she answered, cocking her head flirtatiously to one side. 'It's so funny, meeting you like this!' Her smile was dazzling.

Kelton looked at his watch. 'It's 4:15. Listen, I just got done with a round of golf. Will we have a coffee, a soda? Or how about a glass of wine?'

Amy smiled regretfully. 'Can't right now. Really, I'd love to catch up, but Jack's expecting me home at five.' She hesitated. 'I guess I could call and tell him I'm running a little late ... if you'll give me ten minutes to freshen up and grab my stuff?'

As she walked away, Kelton admired her snappy little skirt and her tanned legs. Club membership promised greater benefits than he'd bargained for!

*

Prosperity had swept the MacLeods into the trendy West County set, who shopped in the best department stores, ate only in select restaurants and paid for their children to attend exclusive private schools. In the early days Carol and Marie had shared similar aspirations. Together they'd laughed and cried, confided secrets and innermost thoughts, until divergent lifestyles cast a shadow over the friendship.

The weekend dinner parties Carol once found so smart had become boring, all idle chatter and one-upmanship, where superficiality reigned supreme. At home, she felt almost irrelevant, and queried whether anyone would notice if a live-in maid took her place. Depression often brought her to tears during moments alone. If she could call her mother, it would bring such comfort! Hearing that voice would let her feel loved again, and restore her lost sense of self.

On her birthday, Kelton presented her with an envelope. 'Special delivery for you,' he said, with a smile.

'What's this?'

'Something to cheer you up.' The gift voucher was for a complete makeover at the city's newest and most expensive beauty parlour.

'You think I need this, huh?' She forced a smile.

'Hell, don't jump on my neck. I thought you'd enjoy it.'

'Not exactly a subtle hint, is it?'

'Come on, babe, quit bein' so crabby. Break out of your shell, live a little. Get your hair blonded up – jazz yourself up a bit.'

He saw peroxide as a panacea for the futility of her existence! Despite thirteen years of marriage and three children, did he know her so little that he imagined bleaching her hair would magically bring contentment? She took the card and put it in her purse. 'Sorry. Thank you,' she said, trying to sound grateful since it was what he expected.

It was a lesson to her. Never had she told him what she wanted, nor given it much consideration. Her upbringing had encouraged submissiveness: blind obedience had turned her into the person her parents, and later Kelton, wanted her to be. Eager to please, she had allowed her real self to be submerged. The result was a life as pointless as that of the kids' caged hamster, that ran away its hours on a wheel, going nowhere.

Chapter 16

'Blessed is he who expects nothing, for he shall never be disappointed.' – Alexander Pope

KELTON AND AMY TOOK TO MEETING for an occasional drink at the club. Despite his glowing account of life with Carol and the children, his restlessness showed. Lingering over a glass of wine one afternoon, he took a quick glance around the bar, then began playfully stroking the back of her hand. 'Why don't we meet one evening for dinner?'

'And leave my poor old man at home on his own?'

'No big deal, for just a few hours. It's only a meal, for old times' sake.'

'Is that right? I suppose your next line is that your wife doesn't understand you?'

He laughed, and rubbed his leg against hers beneath the table. 'All I'm saying is that I want to be with you, should never have left you to go to Aberdeen.'

She had dreamed of hearing these words. Long ago, she would have melted into his arms, regardless of the consequences, but not any more. If there was to be anything between them, *she* would call the shots.

'Shoulda, woulda, coulda, huh? Sorry, it'll have to wait. Jack and I are off to Florida this week.' Carefully she moved away a little.

And he'd imagined he was making progress! 'How long will you be away?'

'Three months. I'll see you once we're home.' She picked up her purse.

At her car, Kelton said, 'I'll miss you.'

'Like hell you will. See ya!'

He stood watching her Mercedes convertible disappear round the sweeping curve of the driveway. He'd hoped they could pick up where they'd left off, but obviously Amy was no longer a pushover. She'd changed, but he liked the new self-assurance that maturity and money had brought her. It was no bad thing to meet some resistance. He'd always loved a challenge.

*

Her cool response to Kelton took every ounce of willpower she could summon up. He could still turn her on – and he knew it! Though Amy had not remained completely faithful to her husband, her little episodes after tennis had been purely physical. In her book, she'd remained emotionally true, whereas a fling with Kelton would amount to a betrayal. She had to remain loyal to Jack; it would be folly to do otherwise. After investing so many years in her marriage, she could not risk losing everything. Still, she had Kelton waiting in the wings, and nothing thrilled her more than being desired.

*

Waiting to check in for his flight at Lambert St Louis Airport, Kelton noticed a familiar face ahead of him in the line.

'Hey, Dave, how are you?' he called.

The guy looked round. 'Hey! You headed for Paris as well?'

Kelton nodded. At the counter, he requested a change of seat.

'Your reservation is for First, and your friend's in Business Class, right?' The ticket agent hesitated, wondering if she had understood correctly. Few passengers requested a downgrade. She consulted the seating plan. 'I can move you if you'd like.'

'Fine. Do it.' A new, cheaper ticket was charged to American Express and a refund processed for the original.

Devanacorp's travel policy was simple. Directors were entitled to travel in First; they charged air and hotel to their

103

credit cards, and subsequently submitted expense reports for reimbursement which went directly into their personal bank accounts. Kelton's Paris trip was exceptional in one sense only: he sat in a lower grade of cabin, with marginally less comfort and legroom. But when he came to submit *that* expense report, it seemed a waste to claim less than Devanacorp was willing to stump up for the journey. Why not charge the original fare? He'd be several hundred dollars in pocket, and no one would be short-changed. Why hadn't he thought of this before? Hell, he could be in profit to the tune of a thousand or two if trips to Asia or Latin America were involved. It was perfect, and so beautifully simple!

Amy was due back soon, and she had expensive tastes, with her Mercedes convertible and gold Rolex. The regular windfall he was now guaranteed would come in handy. He would have money to burn, hopefully enough to impress the pants off her. Unlike Carol or Laura, she wouldn't come cheap, but he wouldn't be spending from his own bank account. The scheme wouldn't cost him a penny, and was virtually untraceable. Airline tickets, hotel rooms, flowers, dinners, jewellery - all would be funded by the credits accrued on his business account. It would be like spending Monopoly money!

*

With no secretarial skills or work experience to speak of, Carol knew it would be an uphill struggle to find employment. Fruitlessly she searched the 'Situations vacant' section of the *Post-Dispatch*, till finally one day she noticed a tiny advertisement. Stuck at the foot of a column, it offered a part-time position with a local publisher. She screwed up the courage to submit an application, and almost fainted with shock when she was invited for interview.

'I may have found myself a job today,' she announced proudly to Kelton.

'You can *not* be serious.'

'I am.'

'I thought you'd want less to do, not more! You keep saying how tired you are.'

She resented his dismissive tone. 'Got to try this, or my brain will turn to mush. I'm picking up stuff to proofread tomorrow. It's a dry run to see if I'd be any good.'

'Whatever floats your boat, babe!' He smirked at the kids and rolled his eyes. 'It's not as if you need the money.'

She suspected he enjoyed seeing her miserable. While she grew fat and dependent on Valium, he went jetting all over the world, secure in the knowledge that she'd be at home waiting for him. She had nowhere and no one to run to.

The job was a small beginning, and might not pan out. But she *had* to do something, had to regain her individuality before Kelton had her scrunched completely under his heel.

*

In March of 1983, Amy and Jack had just returned from their winter vacation, both looking fit and tanned. Though he seldom complained, Jack's health was failing and he was frequently in pain. It came to an abrupt end one day as she arrived home to discover him lying barely conscious on the floor of the garage. Her 911 call brought an ambulance screaming up their street within five minutes, and he was whisked off to hospital, but it was too late.

After fourteen years of marriage, Amy was suddenly a beautiful, lonely widow.

*

In the weeks following the funeral, she hardly left the house, and avoided social contact. Sensing that her emotions were still raw, Kelton maintained a discreet distance. The longer the wait, the more attractive she seemed, and the more intense his longing for her. He called intermittently to check on her, and she thanked him for his consideration. He was determined not to mess up during that crucial period: this time around, he'd get it right!

Hurts So Good by John Cougar Mellencamp became his favourite song.

Amy, however, gave Kelton scarcely a second thought. Life with Jack had turned out much better than she'd expected. It had been a fair deal: she enjoyed the benefits of marrying an old man who was financially secure, while he gained the elevated status of having a young, pretty wife. Jack had been her protector, her safe haven, the Daddy Cool who always took care of her, no matter what a bad girl she'd been. His impotence assuaged her guilt at indulging in the occasional fling with a stranger. Overall, it had worked. She had not expected to miss him so much.

When she went to see the lawyer, it was in the firm expectation of inheriting her husband's estate. From day one, Jack had implied she would be a wealthy woman once he passed away. Since he had no offspring from his first marriage and no close relatives, Amy assumed that everything he owned would become hers, to do with as she pleased.

The first shock was learning how little actual cash would come her way. Reading the sum that would be transferred into her name, she protested, 'There must be some mistake. Jack's net worth was a lot more than this.'

The lawyer nodded primly. 'Yes, but your husband specified that you are to receive only one-third of those assets he accumulated since the date of your marriage fourteen years ago, as per your legal entitlement.'

She was scarcely listening. The officious dumb-ass sitting opposite had got it wrong! The number he'd shown her was a mockery, just enough to buy a scruffy house in a blue-collar area of town. This could not be happening to her: she might actually be forced to take a job!

'Look,' she said as calmly as she could, 'I don't understand any of this. Jack had a huge portfolio of stocks and bonds. Investing was one of his passions. He was the king of the rate chasers, *The Wall Street Journal* was his Bible! Yet you're telling me that this is all I'm entitled to? I don't think so!' Her face was red with indignation.

'Let me clarify, Mrs Bergmann. Whatever your husband owned prior to your marriage is irrelevant to the current situation. Yes, he was a shrewd investor, but the interest and dividends he earned went to maintaining the lifestyle you enjoyed together. He was fortunate in not having to dip into his capital to fund his retirement, as many people are forced to do. Sadly the situation is less advantageous for you, since little was actually *saved* in that period.'

She opened her mouth to speak, but he held up a hand. 'Let me continue. There is some better news.' He put on his half-glasses and sifted through the papers on his desk. Jack had placed the bulk of his wealth in a trust fund, he explained, from which Amy would receive a very generous monthly allowance for as long as she lived. She would have life rent of the homes in St Louis and Florida. At the discretion of the trustees, her income could be augmented by an occasional supplementary pay-out for necessary capital expenditures, such as a new car, medical treatment and home maintenance. At her demise, the trust would be liquidated and its proceeds donated to a range of Jack's favourite charities.

She started to breathe more easily. It wasn't as bad as she'd feared.

Her standard of living would remain unchanged. In the hours that followed, however, she could see only one reason for the arrangements Jack had made. He did not trust her. He'd found her unworthy of receiving his entire fortune.

Never had he demanded accountability, nor raised questions about where she went or how she spent her time. He'd known what she was up to, and had borne her deceit. Okay, she'd played him for a fool, but she'd been young – much too young to spend all her days imprisoned in his old world! He had passed sentence on her, one that would last for all her remaining years.

She resented the paltry amount he'd left her, was incensed at the prospect of begging the lawyer and other trustees for extra cash. How could Jack place her in such a demeaning position? The most disturbing condition had been added after the diagnosis of his aneurysm. A codicil stipulated that remarriage would automatically disqualify her as a beneficiary of the trust. For such an easy-going guy, Jack knew how to keep her reined in after his death, unless she was willing to forfeit her life of luxury. Like a waitress who'd served him her best years on a platter, she'd been stiffed on the tip.

One drink too many caused her rage to boil over. Grabbing a silver-framed picture from the coffee table, she hurled it into the brick fireplace with all her might. The glass shattered, but still Jack's face smiled up at her. He was having the last laugh.

Chapter 17

'You are only young once, but you can stay immature indefinitely.' – Ogden Nash

H E HAD ARRIVED HOME FROM WORK, eaten dinner and seemed surprisingly good-natured. Josie came up behind his recliner and began fiddling with his hair. 'Daddy,' she said, 'can I come up on your lap?'

Kelton sighed and made no reply. The boys knew better than to disturb him when he was reading. Even Josie usually kept her distance, but the girl had no fear. 'Daddy,' she said more loudly, 'I want up on your lap.'

'Come on then.'

Josie climbed up on his knee, and curled up, her face against his chest. This was one of her biggest tests yet. Often she and the boys had pleaded with Carol for a trip to Disney World in Florida. Invariably she told them to ask their father.

'Daddy,' she said quietly.

'What is it, Princess?'

'Can we go to Disney World?'

'Sure, sometime.'

'But when? Everyone in my class has been except me.'

Kelton smiled at her obvious lie. 'Is that right? Mom's taking you guys down to the lake for a couple of weeks. That'll be fun, won't it? Not everyone in your class gets to do that.'

'Yeah, but the lake's boring, not as much fun as seeing Mickey and Minnie. Oh, please, I would love you for ever and ever, if you would take us! Daddy?'

She looked appealingly up at him. Kelton's resistance ebbed at the sight of her big brown eyes in that face so like his own. He made a show of considering the idea. 'Maybe at Labor Day. *Just maybe*, mind!'

The girl threw her arms around his neck and planted kisses all over his face. 'Thank you, Daddy!' She clambered down off his knee, and ran upstairs to where her brothers were waiting.

'So?' asked Robert.

She held out her hand. 'Show me the money, then I'll tell you.'

The boys each fished around in their pockets for a crumpled dollar bill.

'Well? What did he say?'

'We're going in September, Labor Day,' answered Josie gleefully. 'Told you, I can make him do whatever I want.'

*

Carol's little pay checks brought a rare degree of satisfaction, proof that she was a person in her own right. A recent surgery, a tiny snip that eliminated the risk of another pregnancy, enhanced her feeling of wellbeing. For the first time ever, she went alone to their lakeside home with the children, since Kelton's work schedule was too full to take a vacation. No one said so, but it would be a lot more fun without him.

Rarely had he the house to himself. He figured he would enjoy the peace, with no kids to bother him, and no wife to nag at him. Instead the emptiness bugged him. Coming home at night was tiresome when no food was waiting on the table, and he was too lazy to defrost one of the meals Carol had prepared for him. Sometimes he grabbed a bite to eat at the club, otherwise he'd end up drinking in front of the television, gorging himself on Doritos or bread and cheese. By the start of his second week alone, the temptation to call Amy was irresistible.

Her months of solitude were over. Amy was back in the swing of things, playing with her tennis coach on and off the court. It was scarcely different from before, except no Jack was

110

waiting for her to get home, and his Cadillac was gone from the garage. No longer having to abide his geezer buddies was a bonus. Who the hell needed marriage, anyway? If Jack had imagined he could curtail her activities from beyond the grave, he was wrong. In fact if there was life after death, she hoped he was watching her. She would have however many men she liked, and squeeze every last penny out of that trust fund of his. It wasn't so bad, really, being on your own.

*

The phone rang as she was coming out of the shower.

'Amy? How's it goin'?' asked Kelton.

'Fine, I guess. You?'

'Good. Listen, I'm here alone for a few days. Carol and the brats are at the lake house. How about having that dinner we once spoke about?'

'Sure.' She kept her voice deliberately low key, though the prospect excited her.

'Would tonight work for you? I could pick you up around seven, if you like.'

'All right. See ya.' She hung up.

At forty, he felt like a teenager who had scored a date with the prom queen. He possessed the advantages of wealth and position that came with age, but the reckless passion of youth still burned in him. In the post-Laura years, he had been tempted into the odd one-night stand, and little else. With Carol, no spark remained: sex was boring, and she'd lost her figure. Marriage made everything too routine and predictable. No surprises remained.

Hell, what was life without novelty, a break now and then from the responsibilities that weighed on him? He missed the buzz of dating women whose secrets he had yet to uncover. Okay, Amy's body was not uncharted territory to him, but she'd changed. Her sassiness had him salivating at what the evening might hold.

*

It amused her to see him at his most charmingly solicitous, hardly able to keep his eyes off her. Amy wore a short little black dress, with a demure jewel neck that revealed no cleavage, as befitted a recent widow. When they'd last eaten a meal together, she'd been young and stupid. It was hard to believe that she'd have sacrificed anything to hang on to him, and had tolerated his boorish behaviour. She still smarted to remember his cruel indifference in McDonald's.

The thought of him might get her all hot and bothered, though sometimes she did not actually like him much. But he had taught her to look out for her own interests because no one else would. They were two of a kind.

*

'Can I bring you anything else? Coffee, a liqueur, perhaps?' asked the waiter.

Kelton looked at Amy, his eyebrows raised. She shook her head.

'Just the bill, thanks.'

As they left the restaurant, he let his arm brush hers, but she smiled and moved out of reach, teasing him, relishing the delicious tension between them. In the car, he inserted a tape of The Doors into the cassette player. On the highway, while they zipped along at a steady fifty miles per hour, she laid a desultory hand on his knee. Almost imperceptibly, it crept slowly higher on his thigh, then stopped. A minute later, her fingers spidered upwards towards his crotch.

He swung the BMW into the outside lane, easily overtaking everything in sight. *Geez!* His body responded involuntarily to her touch, and he pressed his foot harder on the accelerator. The speedometer hit ninety. Nothing had inflamed him so much in years. As they sped along, all he could think of was getting to her place. His blood pounded in time to her rhythmic caresses and the beat of *Light My Fire*. Man, this was living!

112

The blaring music drowned out the wailing siren of a vehicle following them. Noticing the flashing lights in his rear-view mirror, Kelton almost hoped it *was* a squad car in pursuit of him. *Yessss! Bring it on! Catch me if you can!* The Beamer could outrun any car on the road. But logic tamed his momentary, insane desire to put the pedal to the metal, to prove himself against a poor sap wearing a police badge, in a beat-up Chevy. He hit the brakes and swerved across the middle to the inside lane, sharply exiting on to Clayton Road. When he saw it had been an ambulance, not a police car, on his tail, he laughed out loud.

'You drive like a maniac,' was all Amy remarked as he pulled into her driveway.

'I live hard and play hard,' he replied, grinning.

After 2 am he finally got home.

*

True to his word, Kelton flew his family to Disney World in Florida for a sweaty, hot Labor Day weekend. Space Mountain, which was guaranteed to shake up even the most avid thrill-seekers, was top of Josie's list. The others were game, but Carol found a shady spot under a tree, and would not budge. 'Chicken!' scoffed Kelton. He and the kids were made of sterner stuff – they had MacLeod stomachs.

Feverish with anticipation, Josie grabbed her father and eagerly bagged the front seat. The two boys fastened their safety belts in the car behind. The lights were extinguished and the ride shunted forward. Exuberant screams rang out as they careered along, faster and faster, plunging at high speed into the darkness. To agonised shrieks of terror and delight, bodies were wildly thrown every which way as the cars jolted and twisted along the track. Downhill they rumbled until a deafening screech of brakes had them veering blindly to one side for a hair-raising few seconds, before yet another gut-wrenching drop into the black void.

113

On and on it went while Will sat paralysed with fear, gripping the safety bar. If he'd cried out, no one would hear. He closed his eyes, praying for the nightmare to end, gulping the warm air to stem his queasiness as the roller coaster relentlessly roared on. His skin became hot and clammy and he swallowed hard, his gorge rising. Suddenly he could hold it no more and with one heave of his stomach, a fountain of vomit spurted forth.

As soon as they emerged into the daylight, Carol knew something was wrong. Josie was running ahead of the others, crying, 'Mommy, guess what happened? Will barfed all over Daddy!' Behind her followed Kelton and the boys.

Carol caught the stricken look on her younger son's face.

'I'm sorry, Dad,' he was saying helplessly.

'Yeah, right,' replied Kelton sourly. 'You should have sat it out with your Mom. Why'd you come on, if you weren't feeling good, anyway?'

'I was okay at first. I didn't know I was going to throw up.'

'Whatever. Let's go back to the hotel, clear up this mess.'

'He couldn't help it, he's only a kid,' Carol said helplessly.

In the hotel room, Kelton was in no mood for excuses as he peeled off his stinking shirt. 'This weakness comes from your side,' he snarled at Carol.

'Give me a break,' she replied. 'Will gets sick, so it must be my fault? Can't be from you, because you're perfect, huh?'

She held open a plastic laundry bag for his clothes and went in search of a dumpster while he disappeared into the bathroom. When she returned, she switched on the television. Noticing that the wallet on the nightstand had not escaped poor Will's vomit, she reached into her bag for a wet baby wipe. He really had done a number on his Dad! As she carefully wiped the leather, a clear plastic insert slid out of the pocketbook.

Still she heard the sound of water gushing in the shower. Carol bent down to pick up Kelton's driver's license and credit cards, but a small foil package drew her eye, and she lifted it in disbelief. Not since before they were married had she seen him use a condom!

Precious seconds elapsed until she noticed that the noise of running water had stopped. The whoosh of the shower curtain rings along the metal rod brought her back to reality. Hurriedly she tried to jam the Trojan back into its tight little space, but suddenly she was all thumbs! She shoved it inside her bra and replaced the plastic insert in the wallet as Kelton emerged from the bathroom.

'Good shower?' she enquired.

'At least I'm clean.'

They'd get home to St Louis tomorrow, she thought, and then he was leaving for Belgium. Just as well. They'd had as much of each other as they could stand. How long could they go on this way?

*

'Carol!' he called. *'Carol!'* he shouted again, going out on to the landing.

'I hear you,' she replied, making her way up the stairs. 'What is it?'

'I had a stack of white shirts on the closet shelf, but there's only one here. What happened to them?'

'Maybe you wore them all, and they're still in the laundry room?' At one time, she would have apologised, would have scurried off for whatever he demanded.

She had changed, and Kelton did not like it. It was bad enough coming home to pack his own case, let alone finding his fresh clothes were not all immediately to hand! His requirements should be her top priority, not shoved aside while she indulged her fantasy of being a 'working mom'. He stood staring at her, his eyebrows raised in question.

'What?' she asked, though she knew full well what.

'Am I expected to fetch them?'

Carol shrugged. 'I'm not your slave!'

He grunted and shoved past her to go downstairs. 'I sometimes wonder why I bother to come home at all.'

'Yeah, that makes two of us.'

Chapter 18

'The first breath of adultery is the freest; after it, constraints aping marriage develop.' – John Updike

KELTON TILTED HIS SEAT to the fully reclined position as the plane lights were dimmed on the overnight flight. He spread the TWA blanket over his knees, glad the trip to Florida was behind him. Vacations were more hassle than they were worth, and the episode with Will had been the last straw. Like Thanksgiving gatherings, family expeditions were grossly overrated. *This* was more his style, the freedom to travel unencumbered: to spread out in comfort and be served a nice filet mignon with a few glasses of Cabernet. He relaxed and prepared his mind for the next day's business.

'Would you like another pillow, sir?' asked the stewardess.

'I'm fine, thanks.'

He looked to his left and Amy smiled at him.

'What are you laughing at?'

'I'm not laughing, just thinking what a cool guy you are,' she whispered.

Kelton grinned and put his mouth to her ear. 'And I'm with one fucking hot chick.'

She kissed him on the lips. 'Will you manage to sleep?'

'I'll grab a couple of hours. We land at eight, and my meeting's at ten-thirty. I need to read through these reports first, refresh my memory.'

That was the signal to leave him alone. A whole different universe was opening up for her, one that was exciting and dynamic. This was the life she should have had all along, married to Kelton or someone like him, the kind of guy who let nothing stand in the way of where he was going. Why, he was bringing her along on this trip, and insisted that her plane ticket was a perk of his job! That's what power could do! If his wife knew how to handle him, *she'd* be travelling the world with him. Then again, maybe it served Carol right, for letting herself go the way she had.

Amy cast a self-satisfied glance around the Business Class section. Kelton was like the other passengers she saw in the semi-twilight: suave, sophisticated men in well-cut suits, their attaché cases filled with vitally important documents. Such a change from Jack and the other has-beens whose existences revolved around the golf course and interminable stories of the good old days! Her marriage had been a rite of passage to an enviable lifestyle and winters in Florida, but now she had the best of both worlds.

She was where she belonged, among smart, well-heeled people of her own age. Still building their lives, they were not defined by glories past. She snuggled down into her seat, and tried to read till her eyes grew heavy. Then she drifted off to sleep, her head resting on Kelton's shoulder.

*

One hour before arriving at Brussels airport in Zaventem, Kelton emerged from the tiny plane bathroom freshly shaved and wearing a crisp new white shirt. A taxi dropped Amy off at the Royal Windsor Hotel in the centre of town, while Kelton went on to his meeting on the Avenue de Tervuren.

In the bedroom, she took a long hot shower, and fought the impulse to lie down. The starched white sheets and fluffy pillows looked so inviting, she would gladly have had just half an hour, though she knew if she once succumbed, she would fall into the night's sleep she had missed on the flight. She told herself not to be a wimp. If Kelton could get off that plane and go straight into meetings, surely she could at least venture out to do a little exploring.

Her previous travel experiences had been very different. Then she had been like a child, with Jack leading her each step of the way. Though his guiding hand had occasionally felt oppressive, he had kept her in a secure, comfortable orbit. Now she was entirely alone in an unfamiliar city, thrown back on her own resources. It made her afraid. But she had to learn to look after herself in those streets of strangers, whose language and culture were foreign to her. She would survive: she had to prove that to herself, and to Kelton.

That evening they dined on *moules frites* washed down with a bottle of Sancerre at Vincent's. Kelton's meetings had gone smoothly, and he was well pleased with himself. He was forging ahead in his career, had paid his dues to Carol by taking them all to Disney World, and he could look forward to wangling many more boondoggles like this with Amy. He had it made!

'So where did you go today?' he asked as they ate.

'I took a stroll down the Rue Neuve, looked in the store windows. Ate a waffle as I walked along the street, felt like a real Belgian,' said Amy jauntily. She didn't mention the courage it took for her to go out alone, nor her panic at getting lost in a warren of side streets, without any recognisable landmarks. Seeing the hotel doorman had been like arriving home, such was her relief to be back on familiar ground.

'Did you see the Grand' Place?'

'I did, kinda stumbled on it by accident, then I found the Manikin Pis. It's a bummer, no more two feet high.'

Kelton laughed. It was great to travel with an independent woman! After dark they strolled hand in hand along the narrow cobbled streets of the restaurant quarter, looking for all the world like a honeymoon couple.

'I think we should get married,' he said out of the blue.

She laughed. 'Aren't you forgetting you already have a wife?'

'Seriously,' Kelton asked, 'if I were free, would you marry me?'

'I never thought about it. Maybe. Maybe not.'

How things had changed! Who'd have dreamed he'd be eating out of her hand like this? She had revealed no details of her financial situation to him, nor did she intend to do so. It would take someone a lot more special than Kelton to make give up her income from Jack's trust.

Back at the hotel, almost before they had closed the bedroom door, he was tearing off her clothes. In an instant they were on the bed, all over each other, bodies writhing together as he reached for his wallet on the nightstand.

She fondled him and murmured, 'Come on, baby, I'm ready.'

In vain he fumbled for the Trojan. 'Coulda sworn I had one!'

'Shit! Well, forget it,' she said, trying to move away, but she was pinned under his weight. He would not stop. Her angry struggles increased his pleasure and he entered her despite her protests.

When it was over, she said, 'Don't *ever* do that again!'

He smoothed a strand of hair from her brow. 'I'm sorry. I couldn't help it.'

'Like hell you couldn't.'

She went for a shower. He was a bastard, but fun with it.

*

Their next adventure together was to London.

'This is a final boarding call for all passengers on flight TW 720. Please proceed immediately to gate 38.'

Amy looked at her watch. It wasn't like him to be late. Her stomach churned. What should she do? That bitch of a gate agent was staring at her. She had checked in her luggage, and had her boarding pass, but she absolutely could not get on the plane without him. It would be their fifth trip, and this had never happened previously. No way would she go up to the counter again to ask if there were any messages for her! She would stick it out and hope he showed up. Maybe his taxi had been in an accident. Or had he got sick at the last minute?

Suddenly in the distance she saw a tall figure in a Burberry trench coat that flapped open. Kelton came running along the concourse, in such a rush that he almost barged past her. Once they were settled in their seats, he sat quiet, catching his breath.

Amy placed her hand on his. 'I was afraid you weren't going to make it.'

'Yeah, I got held up with shit at the office, then I had to go home and pack. Fuckin' taxi was held up and I-270 was a mess.' Belligerently he leaned out into the aisle. 'Is there no beverage service before take-off on this flight?' he bellowed.

A stewardess appeared. 'I'm sorry, sir, the bar's closed. Please fasten your seatbelt.'

The plane moved slowly along the runway, and Amy pretended to read. He had slipped into taking her for granted. Nonetheless, she enjoyed these jaunts that cost her nothing: her fixed allowance had raised her awareness of how fast she went through money. So what, if Kelton was in a bad mood? Not her problem. As soon as the fun stopped, she could tell him to go to hell. Meantime, she would sit tight till the drinks arrived, and his mood sweetened. Some things never changed.

*

Dividing his time between Devanacorp and Amy meant Kelton was rarely at home. His wife and children had grown used to living virtually on their own. One night, an unusual call came for him.

'May I speak to Dr MacLeod, please?' a voice said when Carol answered.

'This is his wife. I can pass on a message to him.'

'Oh, okay. It's from TWA about his flight tomorrow afternoon. Departure's been rescheduled and his plane will leave an hour later. Just needed to let him and his companion know about the change.'

Companion? This was a new one! 'I'll tell him. By the way, who is he travelling with?' asked Carol smoothly.

The caller hesitated while she checked the names. 'Uh, give me a second. Yes, here it is. A. Bergmann is the other name on the ticket.'

'I'll pass along the information. Thanks.'

When Kelton got home, Carol told him of the departure time change. Casually she enquired, 'Who is A. Bergmann?'

He pretended not to have heard. 'What was that?'

'I said, who is *A. Bergmann*?'

'Why do you ask?'

She saw he was rattled. 'The person from TWA said that's who you're travelling with.'

'Oh, yeah, Amy. I've mentioned her before.'

She frowned. 'I don't think so. Isn't it unusual that you'd be ticketed together?'

'Don't ask me. Ask my travel agent.'

Earlier she would have accepted his story at face value, because she wanted to believe him. But not any more. Clearly he was lying.

*

Next day Carol sat reading a document, her reading glasses on the end of her nose. She hated wearing these things – such an admission of middle age! – and quickly removed them at the sound of a car door slamming outside in the driveway.

Kelton barged in. 'I'm late,' he said. Irritably he slapped down a manila folder on the table.

He headed upstairs for his suitcase and reappeared within five minutes to gulp down the sandwich she had prepared for him. He leafed through a stack of papers, then went to the hall closet for his coat.

She grabbed her chance. In a flash she had slid his folder down onto the seat of her chair, substituting it with the one she herself had been working on.

'Time I was outta here,' Kelton said, absentmindedly placing hers in his briefcase.

'You sure you have everything?'

He patted his breast pocket. 'Yup, wallet, passport, ticket. I'm all set.' He swept past her. 'I'm taking the car to the airport. Nearly missed my flight last week, waiting for the taxi. See ya!'

He was gone without a backward glance.

Carol waited for five minutes, then went out to her car, carrying Kelton's file. The traffic on highway I-270 had slowed to a crawl. She drummed her fingers on the steering wheel as the car inched its way along. If she made it before they boarded, she would see this Amy Bergmann, maybe put her mind at ease. If not, tough luck! Bluster would carry him through any meeting, with or without his notes.

In the terminal, she stopped to check the departure screens. His flight was now boarding, and damn it, the plane was leaving from gate 24, a long way from the entrance. Half walking, half running, she made her way along the concourse. She was within sight of the gate, and saw him by the agent's desk, standing beside a woman with long blonde hair. Carol watched her turn to him and touch his arm. He grinned, and said something as he looked into her eyes. She responded with a flirty smile and they turned to go through the jet way, his hand at the small of her back.

'Kelton!' Carol called out.

Hearing his name, he looked around. With a whisper, he gently thrust the blonde forward into the tunnel, towards the gaping maw of the plane door. Then in a smart about-turn, he strode towards Carol. 'What are you doing here? Something wrong?' he demanded gruffly.

'Your file. You lifted mine by mistake. These are the papers for your meeting.'

He took the folder, and fished hers from his briefcase. 'Wow! Glad you discovered that,' he said. 'Thanks for coming.'

A voice came over the loudspeaker. 'This is a final boarding call for flight TW 342. All passengers should proceed to the gate immediately.'

'Must go. See you in a few days,' he said, kissing her almost formally on the cheek. 'I'll call you.' He left her standing and disappeared through the glass door.

Slowly she made her way to the car park, unable to erase the image of Kelton and the blonde at the gate. The woman's face seemed familiar: was she a club member, or a parent at the children's school? If she was from the office, Carol might have been introduced to her at a company party ... yet surely even Kelton wouldn't be bold enough for a workplace affair. Or was he?

*

She called Marie. 'Hi, it's me.'

'How're you doin'?'

'I need a favour, and you're the only one I can ask.'

'What's up?'

'Will you make a call for me? Kelton's playing around.'

'Carol, come on, he wouldn't do that.' Marie sounded more sure than she felt. She could spot his type a mile away. He thought he was God's gift to every woman on earth. 'Maybe you're imagining things.'

'I don't think so.'

*

Next morning, Carol dialled and held out the receiver to Marie. 'Dr MacLeod's office,' answered a voice, 'how can I help you?'

'Hi, I'm trying to locate an A. Bergmann. Would she be in your department?'

'There's no one here of that name.'

'Oh!' said Marie, 'Well, thanks for your help, anyway.'

'That's it, the silver bullet.'

Now Carol knew he was playing her for a sucker. After almost twenty years she had to acknowledge that she was no match for him. He was a devil, more slippery than the soap in her bathwater.

Chapter 19

'There is no disappointment so numbing ... as someone no better than you achieving more.' – Joseph Heller

LISTENING ONE DAY TO Donna Summer's hit from 1983, *She Works Hard For The Money*, Laura Donahue decided to seek a life beyond New Orleans.

She got herself hired as an administrative assistant for a large corporate travel agent based in Chicago, and with evening classes she gained additional qualifications. Her subsequent promotion brought responsibility for several large clients in the Midwest.

By a strange irony, her docket included the travel arrangements for Devanacorp, her previous employer. Out of natural curiosity, she checked if Kelton was still with them. Though she had no desire ever to meet him again, he held a strange fascination for her. It became rare for a week to pass without her examining his itineraries. The remote surveillance gave her a kick. She tried not to think of it as voyeurism.

*

Kelton's willingness to accept credit for achievements not strictly his own, or to promise more than he knew he could deliver, had been instrumental in getting where he now was. He easily justified everything he'd done: when others didn't have the balls, he was the one who'd come forward and put his ass on the line. Whatever the situation demanded, he did it. Bluster was a necessary part of being successful in industry, and he always carried it off. He wasn't known as 'Big Mac' for nothing!

An invitation arrived by mail, addressed to Dr and Mrs K. MacLeod. A dinner was to take place at the home of Lenny

Schwartz, to celebrate Kelton's new appointment as Vice President for Licensing and Acquisition. While some in the company were surprised, Kelton saw the promotion as his due. It had taken years of tireless efforts to cultivate Dave Maxwell, the CEO, and his lieutenants – both on and off the golf course.

'Are you *ready*?' he called upstairs for the second time.

Carol struggled with the zip on her dress. 'Coming!' She stepped into her heels, and grabbed her purse.

'We're late as usual,' snarled Kelton as he reversed the car out of the driveway.

'Sorry to keep you waiting.'

Actually Carol was in no rush to get to Lenny's. He had been a friend and mentor to Kelton, but something about him got her back up. Lenny was the kind of phony who marked his fiftieth birthday by colouring his grey hair with Grecian 2000. Then he traded in his sedan for a convertible, and his wife of twenty-five years for an airhead in her mid twenties, named Tiffany.

Lenny greeted them at the door of his splendid new mansion. 'Hey, Mac! Come on in!' He kissed Carol on the cheek. 'Haven't seen you in a while, Carol. You look well.'

Kelton stepped into the foyer. 'Yes, she looks well, and you'll notice there's a *lot more* of her than before!' He guffawed while Lenny looked reproachfully at him.

The smile froze on Carol's face at the put-down. One of these days Kelton would pay for the hurts he'd inflicted on her.

*

Lenny's eyes followed Tiffany's every move. Whenever she was near, he couldn't resist touching her, playfully stroking her wrist or protectively putting an arm around her. He was besotted by her.

The girl was undeniably sexy, thought Kelton as he admired her firm little tush in the tight red leather skirt. It was a pity about that loud giggle of hers, but the occasion had to be daunting: any youngster would be nervous at hosting a dinner party for a bunch of company bigwigs. An almost palpable, obscene heat radiated between the newlyweds. This was as good as it got: like an ice sculpture whose fleeting beauty begins its meltdown from the moment of creation, their mutual attraction would vanish, yet it was strangely hypnotic to watch.

He envied Lenny's fresh start, admired him for throwing off the yoke of a stale, predictable existence in exchange for the excitement of youth rediscovered. Kelton contemplated doing likewise. For too long he'd endured a boring wife and ungrateful kids who treated him like an unwelcome interloper in his own house. He wanted to be carefree like Lenny, in a rush to leave the office at night, with a hot little piece of ass waiting at home for him! Amy would make life worthwhile again. She was older than Tiffany, but had twice the class. He could take her anywhere.

Lenny held up his glass to propose a toast. 'Here's to our newest VP. To you, Mac, and to your continued success!'

Kelton grinned at Carol, as if sharing his victory. For a split second their eyes met, before she looked away, unsmiling.

*

'Good meal, huh?' he remarked as they walked to the car.

Carol shrugged. 'It would have to be, the money he'd stumped up for the caterers. Why don't you give me the keys, and I'll drive?'

'No need, I'm fine.' He got into the driver's seat.

'Suit yourself.'

'What's wrong with you, anyway? You had on a face like a wet weekend.' He gunned the engine as they merged onto the highway, and the BMW streaked ahead of the other traffic.

'I didn't appreciate your crack about my weight. That was unnecessary.'

'It was only a joke, for goodness sake!'

'Right,' replied Carol sarcastically. 'You didn't mean to make me feel bad in front of everyone? Was I supposed to laugh, and be amused at your wit?'

'I don't know what to expect with you any more,' came the sour reply.

'I'd just like to feel you're on my side. I hate being stranded among the assholes you *think* are your friends. And it would be nice to enjoy an evening out without jokes at my expense, while you make a fool of yourself flirting with other men's wives.'

'*Excuse me*? What the hell's that supposed to mean?'

'You couldn't take your eyes off Tiffany the entire time. I was embarrassed for you.'

Kelton almost missed his exit, and cursed as he sharply cut off a car in the inside lane.

'So what if I enjoyed looking at her? She's an attractive woman! *You* were embarrassed for *me*? Let me tell you, dearest, I'm the one that should be embarrassed! Look at yourself: I've seen better-shaped sacks of potatoes.'

'Is that the best you can come up with? You're pathetic!' said Carol, jumping out of the car the minute he'd pulled into the garage.

Determined to get the last word, he followed her, through the kitchen and up the stairs to the bedroom. 'Pathetic? That's rich, coming from you! Here, swallow some Valium, calm yourself down a bit.' Roughly he seized her arm.

'Leave me alone!' she shouted angrily. 'You disgust me.'

'And how am I supposed to feel, huh? I give you everything money can buy, yet all you do is gripe. A lot of women would gladly trade places with you.'

She laughed mockingly. 'Like *Amy Bergmann,* for instance?'

'You're hysterical. You can't hold a rational conversation!'

'I saw you with her at the airport.'

'Amy isn't part of the equation. I knew her before I went to Scotland. If you hadn't been so ready to spread your legs, I wouldn't have been trapped into marrying you.'

Carol looked stunned. 'Well, there's the door. Feel free to go whenever you want, because even the children are happier when you're not here. Tell Amy I wish her all the luck in the world. She'll need it with a bastard like you!'

'*Shut the fuck up*!' he roared, menacingly raising one arm.

'Come on, asshole,' she goaded, 'let's see what a big guy you really are!'

Carol braced herself for the blow she was sure would come. But he thought better of striking her. With his mouth contorted in rage he turned away, and slammed out of the room.

*

Downstairs he poured himself a stiff whisky, and called Amy's number. She should be home at 11:45 on a Saturday night. Probably she'd be in bed, he reckoned when she didn't answer. To his annoyance, a recording began to play, and he slammed down the receiver. Hell! Was she out? Clenching his teeth, he pressed redial. Once more her taped voice asked him to leave his name and number at the tone. This time, he said, 'Amy, it's me. Pick up, would you? I must see you ...'

There was a sound in the hallway, and Josie appeared in her pyjamas. Kelton scowled. 'Why aren't you in bed?'

'You and Mommy were shouting. I couldn't sleep. Who are you calling, Daddy?'

He took a gulp of his drink. 'A friend. Just a friend.'

'I wish Mommy and you didn't fight so much.'

'Yeah, well *I wish* you would go back upstairs. Go on, git! Night-night, Princess.'

Kelton pressed the redial button. At the sound of Amy's recorded message, he swore under his breath. Where in hell's name was she, when he needed her?

*

Four miles away, Amy was blissfully asleep, the handset by her bedside switched off for the night. The first ring caused only the merest ripple of awareness. She turned over, wiped a trickle of saliva from her cheek and snuggled back into oblivion. In her dream, something tinkled again in the distance, until the insistent peal of the doorbell forced her to wake up. Her first reaction was fear. She looked at the clock radio, its glowing red numbers showing 12:40 am. Without switching on the bedside lamp, she padded across to the window and gingerly lifted one slat of the blind. She could make out the dark shape of a vehicle in her driveway, and wondered about calling the police. Then she heard Kelton's voice.

'Amy!' he bellowed. '*Come on, Amy, I know you're home!*'

Struggling into her robe, she went to the front door.

'What are you doing here?'

'I had nowhere else to go. I've left Carol.'

She led the way through to the kitchen. 'You sure can pick your moment,' she said, pouring herself a glass of water.

He sat down, shaking his head. 'I'm sorry, babe, I didn't plan it this way. We were out for dinner and the evening was a disaster. I can't stand it any longer. I'm going to file for divorce, cut the crap out of my life.'

'On what grounds?'

He shrugged. 'No fault, irreconcilable differences, whatever you want to call it. She'll go along with that. Split things fifty-fifty. Keep it simple.'

'You sure?'

'You betcha. She wants out as well. It's the one thing we agree on.'

'What about your children? You going for joint custody?'

'What do you think?' He laughed. 'I scarcely know the brats. Long as they get the stuff they want, they'll never notice I'm gone.'

Amy stood in front of him, a satisfied little smile on her face. 'So what can I offer you? A drink? Coffee?'

'There's just one thing I really need,' he replied, pulling her towards him and undoing the sash of her robe.

*

Carol took a long hot shower, and stood looking at herself naked in the full-length mirror. Kelton's remarks had stung. Sure, her breasts sagged a little, and her waist had thickened, but she'd had three babies! How dared he treat her like this? Already she knew the miserable answer: because he could. All these years ago, what she intended as a rebellion had been anything but. In going against her father's wishes to marry Kelton, she had simply given a different man permission to control her. She had rejected Alex, mistakenly regarding his respect for her as weakness. Now she saw how foolish she'd been.

She'd be better off on her own. Kelton could bugger off – and good riddance! Amy Bergmann was more than welcome to him.

Chapter 20

'And the danger is that in this move towards new horizons and far directions I may lose what I have now, and not find anything except loneliness.' – Sylvia Plath

HE LAY STRETCHED OUT on Amy's bed, and tried to recall the events of the previous night. Whatever he'd said to Carol – and it was difficult to remember exactly – she'd had it coming for a while. It wouldn't be pleasant or easy, to disentangle himself from his wife and children, but hell, if Lenny Schwartz could start over, so could he!

The old-fashioned solid cherry furniture in the bedroom surprised him. Probably it came from Jack Bergmann's first marriage, like most of the stuff in the house. Still, the place was roomy and comfortable. Amy had done all right for herself. What was taking her so long? Kelton got up, crossed to the door of the master bathroom, and tapped gently.

'You okay in there?'

No reply. Only when he tried the door did he realise that she was gone.

'Good morning!' she chirped, as he appeared in the kitchen.

Already showered and dressed, Amy looked like a twenty-something, though in fact she was closer to forty than she cared to admit. He smelled pancakes and bacon cooking on the stove. A jug of freshly squeezed orange juice sat on the counter beside a bowl of cut fruit and cereal packets.

'Hey, what's up? You expecting company?'

'Jack and I used to do this if we weren't having brunch at the club.'

Kelton downed a glass of juice and poured himself another.

'I have champagne, if you'd like a Mimosa.'

He grinned. 'You're really something, ain't ya?' This was the proper way to begin the day, with wine and a pretty face across the breakfast table!

'So, what's the plan?' she asked.

'I'll drop by the house, collect a few things. Shouldn't take long, no more than a couple of hours at the outside. Later on maybe we'll grab dinner and a movie ...'

'Actually ... that's not quite what I meant. Geez, Kelton, I don't know how to put it, but how long were you thinking of staying here?'

He laid down his forkful of bacon and noticed the real estate section of the Sunday paper that lay in front of her. *Fucking hell!* He hadn't expected this! He managed a tight little smile. 'I thought this would be it, babe: the start of you and me together.'

The nerve of him, turning up at her door out of the blue, ready to commandeer her house! He was still the same arrogant bastard he'd been all those years ago, imagining he had permission to take over her life, all because of a caper or two abroad!

Amy took a deep breath. 'I'd rather not be dragged into your divorce. You need a place of your own, to get your head straight.'

'You throwing me out?'

'Don't be stupid. But if you don't play by the book, that fifty-fifty split could be nothing more than a pipe dream. You wanna risk that?'

Hell, he'd assumed she'd have no objection to his moving in with her! Though it highlighted some inconvenient truths, he respected her clear-sightedness.

'D'you see anything decent up for rent?' he asked, pointing to the paper.

She circled advertisements, and he made a few calls. By week's end, he had moved into a studio apartment not unlike the one Amy had occupied as a teenager.

*

Carol jumped up at the sound of his car pulling into the garage. A flush rose to her face, and she went to the freezer to fill up her glass of iced water. Cool and collected, that's how she wanted to be. No matter what he said, she was determined not to lose her temper again.

'Hey, guys,' he said, as he entered the kitchen.

The boys gave him a nod.

'I came to pick up my stuff.'

'Be my guest.' Carol sipped at her drink.

He went to the basement for suitcases, then headed upstairs. It all felt unreal, as if he were preparing for just another trip, only he was embarking on a different kind of journey. He hauled underpants and socks from the dresser, collected his toiletries from the bathroom, and half a dozen pairs of shoes from the closet. The trunk of the BMW would never take the pile of dress suits, shirts and sweaters he'd laid on top of the bed. He almost tripped over Josie as he left the bedroom bearing his second mountain of stuff. She was seated at the top of the stairs.

'Hey, Princess, nearly didn't see you there.'

'Don't leave us, Daddy,' she wailed, throwing her arms around his legs.

He sighed. 'I'll still be close by, just not living here. Mommy and I need a break from each other for a while.' His arms shook with the weight of possessions he held. 'Come on, Josie, let me go, it's not for ever. Be a good girl.'

She looked up at him. 'Please stay with us.'

Let me the hell out of here, he was thinking, but the child clung to him.

'I've got to go, honeybunch. But you and me, we'll have fun real soon.'

'When?'

'I'll call you. Now knock it off, will ya?' He shook her off and squeezed his way past. Conversation in the kitchen stopped at

134

the sound of his footsteps. Laden, Kelton struggled with the door handle of the laundry room door, but no one rose to help him. Somehow he got everything tossed any old how into his car, and went roaring off down the street. What a bummer of a day!

*

'Yes, that's her, the woman I saw him with at the airport,' said Carol, flipping through a stack of photographs. The private investigator had done a thorough job. Before her on the table lay pictures of Kelton leaving the office at night, of him entering Amy's house with a key, and of the two of them together in various locations.

'He has a rental apartment, but stays with her on the weekends,' the guy said.

Carol studied a print of them in Amy's Mercedes. 'Has she kids, or a job?'

'No, she's a widow, childless, and pretty well set up.'

It was as well that Amy had independent means. Carol hoped that the chemistry between her and Kelton would last, because it was all he would bring to the relationship. Once she had enough evidence of his infidelity, she planned to take him for every last cent he had, and then some.

*

It was fun the first week or two, his bachelor existence of going to work and dating Amy. He had not banked on running out of fresh shirts and underpants, not right when he was due to leave on a trip! And he wouldn't be seen dead sitting in front of the coin-operated washer and dryer in the basement of his apartment block: he was above such drudgery. The following morning, his secretary found a plastic garbage bag filled with his dirty clothes by her desk.

'Take these to the cleaners for me, would you?' he said offhandedly, 'and go to Dillards for a half-dozen white cotton shirts, sixteen-inch collar, a six-pack of white Jockeys, and six pairs of black Gold Toe socks.'

135

She looked at him in surprise. 'What about these reports you wanted by noon today?'

'Forget the reports, this is more important.'

'But, Dr MacLeod, I really don't feel comfortable ...'

His gaze was stony. 'If you'd prefer to be back in the typing pool, I can easily arrange that.'

The secretary rose from her chair. 'No, no! I didn't want to fall behind schedule, that's all ... but it's no problem.'

'Fine,' came his curt reply.

*

'What are you doing at Thanksgiving?' he asked Amy early in October.

'The usual, I guess. I'll be in Florida. Jack and I always went in the winter.'

'Shit! You're running out on me, the first holiday we could be spending together?'

She pouted. 'Sweetheart, it's only for a month or two, and I love it. That sun feels so good while it's snowing in St Louis.'

He tried a different tack. 'You're not lonely, staying on your own?'

'Are you joking? I go to the club each day, swim, play tennis, whatever. It's fun, I've as many friends there as I have here. You must come down sometime.'

'I would if I was invited.' He'd thought she'd never ask!

'It can't be for Thanksgiving because my folks are driving down. They'll stay with me for a break, do their own thing. I haven't told them we're seeing each other again, and it would be awkward if you were there. You're not exactly a free agent, are you?'

Her quip irked him, but she was correct. He was anything but free. He'd imagined a glorious new phase when he could do as he pleased, but it hadn't turned out that way after leaving Carol. At night, he lay curled up on the cheap stained mattress that was too short for him, irritated by the music and cooking

136

smells that wafted through the thin walls of his unit. He'd landed in a cage, renting a shit hole they had the nerve to advertise as a studio apartment! Juan, the janitor who looked after the hallways, came in to tidy up for him once a week, which was another drain on his resources.

Most of all he resented maintaining the ridiculously large house Carol still lived in, with its recurring incidental costs like winterising the pool and the sprinkler systems. And that wasn't counting the kids' school fees! The faster he got divorced, the better.

Amy was running off to Florida, making him an outcast over the holidays: it really sucked, that the little bitch was so concerned with keeping her tan and pleasing her folks. She didn't give a shit for him! If he got a ring on her finger, she would just have to get used to St Louis winters again. Not that Thanksgiving had been that big a deal during his marriage, yet at least he'd had people around and the smell of a turkey in the oven. When Cindy called, asking him to join them for the day, he declined. What kind of loser did they think he was? He'd rather eat a frozen TV dinner on his own than that. He was a company VP, and needed no sympathy invitations!

He missed his mother as never before. If he were honest, he'd admit to scarcely giving Angie a second thought for a decade before she died, but now he wished he could go home. *She* would have understood the emptiness he felt, being left alone at Thanksgiving. Wherever he went, he would look lonely and ridiculous. Even the club would be closed. He vaguely considered taking a drive to East St Louis. It had been years since he'd crossed the Eads Bridge for a bit of action, not since the sixties. But his common sense prevailed: he wasn't that desperate. And so his Thanksgiving Day of 1986 was spent surfing endlessly through the television channels in the company of his new best friend, Jack Daniels.

*

Things had stalled with the divorce. Carol was being awkward, holding out for an unreasonably large settlement. It was all right for her, she had all the creature comforts anyone could desire! She wasn't cramped into two rooms, with a kitchen faucet that dripped and mould growing in the shower. He decided to try talking her round himself.

When he rang, no one answered, and he left a message.

'Carol, it's me. Give me a call back. I've got to speak to you.'

With no reply twenty four hours later, he called again to leave a message. After dark, he drove by the house, cruising slowly up and down the street like an animal stalking its prey. It was impossible to tell if anyone was at home or not. The lanterns on both sides of the entry were lit, like the table lamps in the front living room, but that meant nothing. They were all on timers.

A light came on in Josie's bedroom, and he saw the girl move around the room. Carol entered and closed the blinds. She was at home, then, and screening his calls! He got back to his apartment and rang her number.

'Carol, I know you're there. Quit playing games. We need to thrash this out.'

A further ten calls used up the entire micro-tape. Nothing more could be recorded. If she wouldn't speak to him, he'd make damned sure she could receive no other communications either.

Chapter 21

'THAT'S THE PHONE AGAIN, Mom!' Robert called.

Carol was about to step into the shower. 'Ignore it. In fact, turn off the ringer.'

She felt like a prisoner. For the last month, calls had come in at all hours of the day and night, and Kelton had taken to sitting outside in his car, which really creeped her out. Will had been first to notice the BMW, parked several houses away, when a friend had dropped him off after hockey practice. So strange, to see his father's face lit up in the sudden pale glare of headlights as he sat there alone in the darkness, watching.

Dad's sitting outside became the three words Carol most dreaded. She would dash through to the dining room window, usually just in time to catch the tail lights of Kelton's car as it disappeared from sight, but she knew he would be back. Then one night the doorbell rang while they were all watching television. Only one person would arrive unannounced at that hour! She went through to the hall without switching on the light, and looked through the spy hole.

'Let me in, Carol. We gotta talk.'

She stood quaking. The kids huddled around her while Kelton pounded on the door.

'Let me in, damn you!' he yelled.

'Contact me through my lawyer. I've nothing to say to you.'

He tried his key in the lock, but already Carol had hired a locksmith to change the barrels. He gave the door a vicious kick.

'I'm warning you, this is your last chance!' he shouted. 'Open up or you'll be sorry.'

She breathed in short, sharp bursts. 'Go away or I'll call the police.'

They listened to Kelton's footsteps retreat down the path. The car door slammed and his tires squealed as he backed out of the driveway.

*

Where he was in control, life seemed relatively normal. But outside the office, he felt Carol's stubbornness would drive him insane. Her refusal to talk to him face to face was running up thousands in lawyer's fees, while she hid behind her locked door. Noticing one day that his automatic garage door opener from home was still clipped onto the sun visor of his BMW, he had an idea.

The janitor was mopping the tiles at the entrance to the apartment building when Kelton strode in.

'Hey, Juan, how are you?'

'Good, Dr MacLeod.'

'Can I have a word with you?' Slinging an arm round the Mexican's shoulder, Kelton's tone was confidential.

With an incredulous smile, Juan responded, 'That's all?'

'You got it, buddy. Do we have a deal?'

'Sure thing, Dr MacLeod. I'll be at your place whenever you need me.'

'See you Saturday.'

Juan rushed to hold the door, anxious to help in any way he could. Dr MacLeod was a classy guy! For twenty dollars, he would lend him his old beat-up truck for half a day. But fifty, that was real money! Like in the Dire Straits song, it was *Money for Nothing*.

*

Carol, Josie and the boys remained oblivious to the Chevy pickup parked at the end of their street. The driver sat hunched in the cab as they drove by. Dressed in a workman's plaid jacket and baseball cap, Kelton started up the engine of the truck and kept a safe distance back, tailing Carol's minivan until it reached the mall parking lot.

Confident he was safe for at least an hour, he swung around to head for the house again. In less than ten minutes, he pressed his remote door opener and drove into the garage, waiting at the wheel as the overhead door slid shut.

The door through to the laundry room was locked. Pushing against it at the deadbolt, he smiled to feel it give a little: only the handle latch was on. He slid a credit card from his wallet between the door and the jamb, and bingo, he was in! Didn't even need the screwdriver he'd brought! Quietly he stepped into the kitchen and crept upstairs, feeling like a burglar in Carol's home. It gave him a rush, entering her world like this, and destroying her peace of mind, because really the place was *his*.

In the master bedroom, he almost laughed aloud with glee at what he was about to do. Pulling out his pocket knife, whose blade was sharp as a scalpel, Kelton went to the walk-in closet. With the precision of a surgeon in theatre, he systematically went along the rails of his wife's clothing. Dresses, pants, jeans, skirts, tops: random garments received a half-inch incision, every one of them a stab at Carol, the cause of all his woes. The frenzy of wanton destruction excited him almost as much as sex.

With that operation over, he carefully closed the knife, and made his way downstairs to the games room in the basement. On top of a low bookcase lived a brown and white hamster. Originally bought as a pet for the children till they lost interest, Carol had developed a fondness for the cute little bundle of fur. Seeing its cage door open, the tame little creature moved eagerly towards Kelton's hand, only to be roughly grabbed round the neck. In an instant the lifeless animal was back among the wood shavings at the bottom of its wire prison, its head and body partially covered.

Kelton wrapped his trophy and slipped it into the pocket of his jeans. He left as he had entered. As the garage door slid down he gunned the engine of the truck and sped off.

*

Back at the apartment, Juan was waiting.

'Don't forget, not a word about this. Anyone asks, I was here all morning while you cleaned the place up. Got it?' said Kelton, holding out the borrowed jacket and greasy baseball cap.

'You bet, Dr MacLeod. I say nothing.'

'Good. Here's your truck keys, and the fifty I owe you.'

To shake off the odour of Juan's clothes, Kelton grabbed a quick shower, and finished by splashing some aftershave on his face for the second time that morning. Then he loaded a suitcase into the trunk of the Beamer, and drove to the airport to catch his flight, singing along to Robert Palmer's *Addicted to Love* on the radio.

Two hours afterwards, he sat relaxing aboard the plane to Miami, well pleased with his morning's work. The filet mignon came rare, precisely the way he liked it, washed down with a fine Cabernet. Once lunch was cleared away, he settled down to enjoy the prospect of being with Amy again.

*

Carol discerned a difference in the atmosphere as soon as she got back home, though it was impossible to pinpoint exactly what had changed. Everything appeared the same as when they had left that morning. Yet upstairs in her bedroom, it was also there: the merest whiff of something she recognised. It was *his* smell, the Paco Rabanne aftershave that Kelton always wore. She searched the whole house for any visible sign that he'd been round, but nothing had been disturbed. Was she becoming paranoid? He would drive her nuts, if she wasn't careful. Before going to bed, she went to the basement.

'Come on, Hammy, supper time! Why are you hiding?' she cooed, reaching her hand into the hamster's cage. She felt for

142

him among his bedding: his soft fur was damp and sticky to the touch. Carefully she lifted him clear, and gasped.

Upstairs she wiped away the blood, wrapped the creature's body in a piece of kitchen roll and sealed it in a Ziploc bag. Unable to face recounting details of her gruesome discovery, she would say the pet had died of natural causes. After all, he'd been almost three years old, the expected lifespan for a hamster.

But for hours that night, Carol tossed and turned in the darkness. She could not wipe out the image of poor Hammy's blood-caked head that was missing an ear.

*

As usual, she planned to take the children out for Sunday brunch.

'What happened to your sweater, Mom?' asked Robert.

'What do you mean?'

'There's a little rip – looks like you've caught it, at the back.'

Puzzled, she went upstairs to change. The damage to her cashmere top was small. Selecting something different to wear, she carefully checked it over. It, too, was cut. An awful realisation came to her. This was Kelton's doing! He'd come by while they were out, had been in her closet, in the basement, and goodness knows where else! The kids were waiting for her, she'd best hurry. Frantically she slid the hangers along the rails, her dismay increasing at the extent of the destruction. Few items had escaped his ministrations.

It made her mad, but worse, it left her afraid in her own home.

*

The two policemen looked around the bedroom as she spoke.

'It was my husband,' Carol told them. 'He was here yesterday while we were at the mall.'

'You say you're in the middle of a divorce?'

'Yes. I should have called you before.'

'What's he actually been doing?'

'He harasses me constantly. Rings night and day, sits outside in his car, watching the house. One night last week he

143

battered at the door, but I was too afraid to let him in. The only way I'll talk to him is through my lawyer.'

The older cop sighed. 'Ma'am, we can't do much in this type of situation.'

'What do you mean? Everyone will tell you, he's made my life a misery for months.'

They remained sceptical. 'Has he voiced any specific threats against you?'

'He shouted I'd be sorry if I didn't let him in. Destroying my clothes is his way of trying to intimidate me.'

'You're having a rough time, ma'am, but look at the facts and the evidence: you claim your husband was here, but where are the witnesses who saw him enter and leave the premises? We can't be sure when the offence occurred.'

'Yesterday morning, I think.'

'Right. *You think.* But there's your cleaning lady and your kids. It's anybody's guess who's been in your closet.' The men edged away.

'Hang on!' Carol said, incredulously. 'It's an act of vandalism, so what action will you take?'

'We'll file a report of the incident.'

'I want my husband charged with malicious damage. He's one of the few people who wear Paco Rabanne, and I smelled it in the house yesterday. He *was* here!'

They smirked. 'Look, lady, we can't base a charge on something you *think* you smelled.'

'Will you at least question him?'

'Yeah, but it'll be his word against yours. You could apply to the court for a restraining order if he really bothers you.'

Carol opened the front door for them to leave. 'You don't think what he's doing is *really* bothering me?'

'Only a suggestion. You have a nice day, ma'am.'

Irritated, she watched from behind the blind as they got back into the squad car. They didn't believe her: virtually said she had no case against Kelton. Perhaps they even suspected her of the damage. They'd probably have laughed in her face if she'd mentioned Hammy.

'Did you check out these clothes? Everything had a designer label,' remarked one of the cops as they drove along Clayton Road.

'Rich bitch, and hysterical with it,' answered his partner, looking at his watch. 'Let's hit Dunkin' Donuts. I need some sugar and caffeine.'

Chapter 22

FROM THE MOMENT HE TOLD HER where they were going next, Amy couldn't get the tune out of her head. Already she visualised herself on the beach, in a white bikini, and she'd be exactly like *The Girl from Ipanema*.

Tall and tan and young and lovely
The girl from Ipanema goes walking
And when she passes, each one she passes goes 'Aaaah'
When she walks, she's like a samba
That swings so cool and sways so gentle
That when she passes, each one she passes goes 'Aaaah'

Kelton landed in Miami to find her waiting at the gate. She ran forward and threw her arms around his neck.

'Sweetheart, it's great to see you!' she said, kissing him.

'You too. Did you check if our flight's on time?'

'Exactly on schedule. I'm so wired!'

Maybe so, Kelton thought, but not as wired as he'd been just hours earlier! Each little slash of his knife had empowered him further. He smiled as he relived those minutes in Carol's house. What he had given, he could take away.

The plane touched down at Rio de Janeiro next morning. In the hotel, Amy stood drying her hair, humming to herself as she looked out of the bedroom window. Directly across the street lay the soft pale sand of Copacabana Beach, and its glistening blue waters. She could hardly wait to go sightseeing, it was so beautiful.

'Why don't we steal a half hour in bed first, before we go out?' Kelton asked, emerging from the bathroom with a towel round his waist.

'If you like.'

'You bet, I like,' he replied, coming to stand behind her at the window, his hands tenderly cupping her breasts. He hardened as he pressed himself against her, and steered her across to the bed, kissing her neck, nuzzling and nibbling gently at her skin. Then her bath robe was off. He entered her slowly at first, his rhythm quiet and steady, his conscious hesitancy heightening her anticipation of the next thrust. She arched up to meet him again and again, drawing him into her very core. He pushed deeper, more desperate to possess her than ever, easing off to come back stronger and rougher, till it seemed he would crush the life from her when their hot, tingling bodies climaxed in unison.

'You've reminded me what I've been missing in Florida,' Amy said, as they lay looking at each other.

'Glad to be of service, babe. I'm all yours, nobody else's.'

'No, you're not. You're still married.'

He grinned. 'Not for much longer. The divorce is pretty much a done deal. She'll cave on the last few sticking points.'

'Have you spoken to her?'

'No need,' was his confident reply. 'I know her. She tries to act tough, but I'd bet she's so fed up right now, she'll be willing to settle. That's why we're celebrating. Once I'm through with my meetings tomorrow, we'll drop by H. Stern's for you to pick out a ring.'

*

Carol lay in bed, weighing up her situation. Her privacy had been invaded, her property vandalised, and there was nothing she could do. Who knew what Kelton had in store next? It didn't bear thinking about. Perhaps she should accept the terms his lawyer proposed: though she would come out of the divorce with less, she'd get shot of him faster. But that was exactly the response he would expect from her. He would bank on her caving in, as always, to keep the peace. Well, not this time. She was done with being nice, manipulated by others: she would overcome her old fears and insecurities. The negotiation might drag on for years, but she would fight him. Somehow she would summon the strength to cope with whatever shit he might throw her way. If anyone should be afraid, he should!

*

The courtesy limousine pulled up outside the H. Stern building in Ipanema. Security guards dressed in business suits immediately appeared on either side of the vehicle. Amy and Kelton were escorted through vast plate glass doors to be met inside by a charming young receptionist, immaculate in a grey tailored dress and black high heels.

This wasn't just any old jewellery store, thought Amy, glancing around while she and Kelton sipped their welcome drinks.

'Is this your first visit?'

Amy smiled. 'Yes, it is.'

'In that case, might I suggest you take a tour of our facility, in order to appreciate the range of our merchandise?'

Amy opened her mouth to speak, but Kelton was faster.

Looking at his watch, he said, 'Thanks, but we know what we're after.' *Cut the crap, get this show on the road*, he thought.

'As you wish, sir,' replied the receptionist. 'One of our specialist consultants will be right with you.'

*

They were back in the limousine as it sped to the base of Corcovado. The massive statue of Christ the Redeemer towered above them, arms held out in blessing over the city.

'Would you like to take the elevator to the top?' asked the driver. 'The line's not too bad, probably half an hour's wait. Forty minutes max.'

148

Kelton declined. 'Nah ... we're done sightseeing. Take us to our hotel.'

All that interested Amy was the sparkle of her new diamond and emerald ring. 'You sure you can afford this?' she whispered, tilting her hand this way and that in the light.

Kelton grinned. 'Whatever you want, babe, I'll buy it for you.'

Though he'd been willing to cough up for a decent ring, maybe stretch to a few months' salary, he had not anticipated the sticker shock of signing the payment slip. But hell, like the guy above them with his arms outstretched, nothing was beyond his powers! The investment should pay off handsomely: sometimes you had to give a little to get a lot.

*

A call to his lawyer was Kelton's top priority when he got back to St Louis at the end of that week. 'What d'you mean, there's no progress?' he barked into the phone.

'Your wife's sitting tight, she won't accept the no-fault settlement. Says she'll drag you through every court in Missouri to get what she wants.'

In frustration, Kelton punched the wall. He would happily have socked Carol in the jaw if she'd been nearby. 'So what do you suggest now?'

'This situation is very common. It'll take time to thrash out the details.'

'Yeah, yeah. Don't bullshit me, I'm paying you to solve my problems. Just find a way to get me out of this.'

'That's precisely what I'm working on,' the lawyer began, but the line had gone dead.

His day at the office had stretched well into the evening. All Kelton wanted was to relax in front of the television with a large Scotch while waiting for a Domino's pizza to arrive for dinner. He went to answer his apartment door with money in his hand, but instead of the usual delivery guy, he was confronted by two uniformed policemen.

'Are you Kelton MacLeod?'

'Yes.'

'We'd like a word with you. Can we come in?'

For a moment, he was thrown. What could they possibly want to talk to him about? 'Sure. I thought you'd brought my pizza,' he grinned. 'Have a seat.'

The cops took it all in: the half-drunk tumbler of whisky, the fine wool suit jacket and silk tie slung carelessly over the back of a rickety kitchen chair, the Italian loafers kicked off beside the cheap tweed-covered sofa. This guy had taken a dive in his living standard.

'So, what's up?' asked Kelton.

The older one spoke. 'We're investigating an incident at the home of your wife. Somebody entered the house and slashed the clothes in her closet.'

'Wow! *Not* nice!'

'We need to ask where you were last Saturday morning.'

Wearing his most ingenuous smile, Kelton said, 'Last Saturday morning? I can tell you exactly where I was. Right here, packing for a business trip to Brazil.'

'You have any witnesses, anyone that can confirm that?'

'Yup. Juan, the building janitor. He comes in on a Saturday to tidy the place up for me.' Kelton made a point of looking each cop directly in the eye.

'Do you have a contact number for him?'

'Hell, I don't even know his second name! He's around the hallways most mornings.' He moved to get up. 'Let me pour you guys something to drink.'

'Appreciate the offer, but not while we're on duty,' one of the cops replied. They stood up. 'Thanks for your time, sir. We won't hold you up any longer – had to do a routine follow-up on your wife's complaint.'

'Sure,' said Kelton. 'You do a great job. Take care, now. Good night.'

Once they had left, Kelton swallowed the half glass of liquor in two gulps and poured himself another.

*

'I don't understand, Dr MacLeod. Why the cops want me? I did nothing!' Juan panicked when Kelton got hold of him.

'Cool it, will ya? I only said *maybe* they want to talk to you. If they show up, tell them you were with me at my apartment last Saturday morning. Okay?'

'But the cops come, talk to somebody like me, it's different. Maybe they start to ask other questions, ask about visa or social security card. Better I don't talk to cops.'

Kelton's patience was running out. 'Listen to me! If they come, you were with me in my apartment, right? That's all you need to say.'

Juan took a step backwards, his hands raised, palms forward. 'I did nothing wrong. I tell them that.'

'Listen, you stupid little fuck! This is not about you. You say I was here with you all morning, or you'll be on the bus back to Guadalajara next week.' Grabbing the janitor by the lapels of his jacket, Kelton pinned him against the wall. 'Got it?'

'Yeah, I got it. I'm sorry. Whatever you say, Dr MacLeod.'

The fifty bucks had seemed like easy money, but it had come at a price.

Chapter 23

'Nothing can stop the man with the right mental attitude from achieving his goal; nothing on earth can help the man with the wrong mental attitude.' – Thomas Jefferson

'YOU FREE FOR LUNCH TODAY?'

Kelton consulted his desk diary. 'Yup, free as a bird,' he said into the phone.

'Meet me at Bristol's at twelve,' said Lenny Schwartz.

Kelton got there on the nail. 'What's the big deal?' he asked, as he sat down.

'I don't want us to be seen together at the office,' said Lenny circumspectly. 'A little bird told me a big reshuffle is on the cards. The whisper is that Maxwell's on the outs and the board's set to appoint Carson as new CEO.'

'Wow!' breathed Kelton. 'Carson? He's not even fifty! Why the hell would they put him in Maxwell's chair? What does he know about running the business?'

'Enough, it seems. He has friends in high places. But the good news is that his promotion would open up a senior VP slot. Your name was mentioned.'

Senior VP! The words were sweet music to Kelton's ears. *Careful, gotta play this real cool,* he thought, frowning slightly to counter a smile. A little modesty was in order. 'You're shittin' me, right?'

Lenny held up one hand. 'As God is my witness, I'm just giving you a heads up, that's all.'

'I appreciate it, man.'

'Yeah, well don't forget it's still under wraps. You didn't hear about this from me.'

'Sure thing,' Kelton replied.

*

It became clear that Lenny had not been toying with him. In a call the following week, Kelton was summoned to Maxwell's office. Alone in the elevator up to the CEO's suite, he straightened his tie and worked his facial muscles. Pursed his lips tightly then stretched his mouth wide in a grotesque grin, before relaxing. Repeatedly he raised his eyebrows as high as they would go, then lowered them. If this was the big news he hoped for, no twitch of an eyelid nor hint of a smile would betray his reaction. He would show he regarded it as no more than his due.

It all felt unreal. Thick plush carpeting muffled his footsteps as the secretary ushered him into the hallowed silence of the chief's office. Carson stood up, while Maxwell remained seated behind his huge mahogany desk.

'Mac, good to see you!'

'How are you, sir?'

Maxwell cleared his throat. He did not tolerate small talk. 'Draw in a chair, MacLeod. Here's the situation. I retire at the end of this year, and my seat will go to Carson. I want the transition to be a smooth one. The future of Devanacorp lies with young Turks like Carson here, and yourself. Several greybeards are going to feel they've been passed over.'

Kelton nodded smugly, at being lumped along with Carson as a 'young Turk'.

'I like what you've done in this company so far. Carson agrees with me that your appointment to a Senior Vice President position would be entirely appropriate to our vision. How would you feel about that?' Maxwell leaned back and eyed Kelton over the top of his glasses.

This was it, the big one! 'I'd be honoured, sir,' he replied in mock humility. The promotion was effective the next month.

Later, he stopped at a liquor store to pick up a bottle. He stuck a tape in the cassette deck as the BMW belted along the highway, speakers blaring at full volume. It was another step closer to the top job he'd set his sights on. He swerved into Amy's subdivision, its tranquillity shattered by the beat of Kool & the Gang pounding out *Celebration.*

*

Following an energetic game of tennis, Amy had newly showered when she heard the commotion outside. From the window she saw Kelton's car pulling into the driveway. *Shit!* He knew she preferred him to call first, not to show up unannounced. She met him at the front door.

'Hi, honey,' she said brusquely. 'This is a surprise!'

Kelton grinned and presented her with a bottle of Bollinger champagne, already chilled. 'Thought you'd like a glass of this to celebrate.'

'What? Did the divorce go through?'

'Fat chance. In a way, this is more important. I've been made Senior VP.'

Her expression changed. 'Oh, sweetie, that's wonderful! I'm so proud of you!'

'The bad news is, nothing's signed and sealed yet. The good news is that money-wise, the sky's the limit. I'll get stock options up the wazoo.'

'You are amazing,' Amy breathed, pressing her body against him as she reached up to give him a long lingering kiss. Hell, with news like that, he was welcome to turn up at her place whenever he liked!

*

He found the studio apartment depressing. He had anticipated spending at most a few months there, but things hadn't worked out that way. It really pissed him off, being forced to bunk down in this pigsty. He could be so much more comfortable at Amy's! He'd imagined she might cut him some slack after the trip to Rio, but the five figures he'd coughed up for her emerald ring changed nothing.

154

Until he could produce divorce papers, they couldn't live together, she insisted. As for Carol, she had been hanging tough for almost a year now, refusing to settle. Well, not for much longer, he reckoned. Finally he was about to make a bit of headway.

'Are you quite sure this is what you want?' the lawyer asked at their next meeting, scanning the page of scribbled instructions. 'This jeopardises your future security.'

Any fool could stick to a conservative course! Taking risks had got Kelton where he was. 'Yeah, or I'll be protecting my future earnings, which are set to increase substantially. The longer I delay, the more dough she's gonna demand. Draft a document detailing the concessions I'm willing to make, and courier it across to her guy ASAP. Make it clear my offer stands for one week only.'

The lawyer took another look at the sheet. Perplexed, he took off his spectacles. 'This is an extremely unusual way of doing things. It's my fiduciary duty to ensure you realise the full consequences of your action. I don't want you coming back saying I failed to advise you correctly. It's a big risk, to leave yourself with such limited assets. Regarding your children, you say you're not interested in custody: but at the very least, visitation rights should be established.'

Who did this squirt of a lawyer think he was, anyway, second guessing him like this?

'Just do as I say, will you?' he interrupted. 'They're hardly children any more. What I'm offering my wife is a severance package. If she gets what she wants now, she can't bleed me dry forever more. She can have the lot – the house, the vacation home, and a good chunk of dough –a couple of million, by my calculation, but that's it, *finito*. No alimony, no college fees, no medical or pension benefits, nothing more. I want no strings, no connections. She turned the damned kids against me years ago, so I'm cutting them all loose.'

He was a maverick, and he'd show the world he could afford to kick Carol and the brats out of his life. No price was too high for his freedom. Visitation rights, custody? They could shove 'em! Once he and Amy were together, they'd have no room for anyone else.

The lawyer shrugged. 'As you wish.'

'Thank you.'

The two men shook hands.

*

There had to be a catch. It was hard to believe he would suddenly become so accommodating. For two days Carol had mulled over Kelton's offer and still she was uneasy, looking for the sting in the tail. Never had she dared hope to be completely rid of him. Now, as if to punish her, he was insisting on no future contact with her or his offspring.

'I accept,' she told her lawyer.

In a month, the formalities were taken care of. Carol marked the occasion by bundling the entire contents of her closet into plastic trash bags. Kelton's first gift to her had been a dress, which at the time had delighted her with its sophistication. Ironically, his knife had liberated her from the tyranny of wearing only designer labels. Feeling light and unburdened, as though she'd cast off a uniform, she watched the garbage collectors toss the bulging black bags into the crusher.

Chapter 24

'The real voyage of discovery consists not in seeking new landscapes, but in having new eyes.' – Marcel Proust

HE WAS ON TOP OF THE WORLD. Gleefully he submitted notice that he'd be leaving his apartment. The weekend couldn't come fast enough, when he'd move his last boxes out of that dump and into Amy's place.

'We should be able to get married in a month or two,' he said that night over dinner.

'There's no rush,' Amy replied. 'Let's live together first, take it one day at a time.'

'Whatever you like. I thought you'd prefer to set a date, that's all.'

How like a woman, to blow hot and cold on him, while he gave up almost everything he had, just for her!

Amy enjoyed having Kelton around now and then, but within a week, he had already thrown five dirty white shirts in the laundry basket. The guy had to be put straight on a few issues! She was not his handmaiden.

Being a gentleman, Jack had always used the guest facilities, granting her exclusive use of the master bathroom. Kelton lacked such consideration, neglecting even to splash some bleach in the toilet when necessary. Nor did he wipe his sink: she hated his spatters of toothpaste and the greasy scum left by his shaving foam. She broached the subject and he wasn't sure he liked her tone, though she softened the reprimand by smiling at his scowling reflection in the mirror.

*

With Carson as head of the company, Kelton's travel increased to cover his new areas of responsibility. Amy's plans for wintering in Florida were shelved, in favour of accompanying him on his foreign trips.

They were en route to the Far East. Several hours into the flight, she felt like talking, but he was engrossed in the movie. Once more she flipped through her Tokyo guide book, and nudged him. 'Can you believe we're actually heading for *Japan*?'

Kelton continued to munch on the warm salted almonds that accompanied the cocktails before their second meal. That was something he loved about long hauls, you could get drunk, sober up and get drunk again if you felt like it!

'Did you hear me?' she said.

'What d'ya say?' He made to remove his earphones.

'I said ...' Amy began, and stopped. His eyes had glazed over, and already he was looking back at the screen. He was so totally self-centred! 'Never mind.'

*

The sick feeling hit during the last part of the flight, and stayed with her right through the coach ride from Narita to the Imperial Hotel in the city centre. Queasily she looked down at the view from their twenty-ninth floor room. It was her own fault; she should not have eaten and drunk so much during the journey, but what else was there to do? How unfair it was, that Kelton never suffered, however much he consumed! She should have stuck to water, had one light meal and a sleeping pill; then she would have been refreshed, not nauseous and hung over.

'It's all yours, babe,' said Kelton, emerging from the bathroom, briskly patting his cheeks. 'A shit, a shower and a shave, and I'm like a new man.'

'I wish,' muttered Amy. Quietly she closed the bathroom door and sat on the toilet. She pinched the bridge of her nose until slowly the pressure behind her eyes eased.

*

A decent night's sleep left her feeling better, ready to go sightseeing while Kelton was in meetings. The city streets were busy yet clean and civilised. Only in the subway was courtesy temporarily suspended in the crush to board the trains. She loved the quiet gentility of the Ginza stores, where elevator girls treated her like visiting royalty. The smallest purchase was carefully wrapped in charming corner-fashion, and presented as though it had cost the earth. Middle-aged women in silk kimonos bowed interminable goodbyes to their friends, all backing away in steely determination to make the ultimate gesture of politeness. Downhill streets created a strange illusion: the bobbing heads of dark Japanese hair seemed to move like a river of black silk.

Tokyo was like no place she'd experienced: she felt safe, even when it seemed she was the sole Caucasian around. On her last day, however, in Harijuku, she suddenly became aware of someone right behind her on the sidewalk; it was a young man with cropped hair. As she increased her pace, so did he. Was he tailing her? Maybe she was imagining things. She speeded up, almost breaking into a trot, and he followed suit, weaving through the crowd to be almost level with her. Suddenly he caught up, and mouthed something in her direction. She looked away uneasily.

'You!' he was saying, 'You ...'

Amy darted to her left, and stood in an open shop doorway. She would scream if he drew any closer. She was damned if she'd give up her purse without a struggle!

Halting abruptly in front of her, the guy again attempted to speak. 'You ... you ...' he stammered breathlessly, with an embarrassed smile. 'You ... very ... beautiful.' Then he bowed and disappeared into the crowd.

Shaking with relief, she was flattered and amused at the same time. Fancy thinking he'd meant to harm her! It was a different world.

159

*

Her enthusiasm for all things Japanese was not shared by Kelton. Getting back to their hotel room that night, he threw down his briefcase and headed straight to the mini-bar, to pour himself a Suntory.

'Hi, sugar,' said Amy, who lay on top of the bed watching CNN on television, a glass of wine by her side.

'Hi.' Kelton tore off his tie, draped his jacket over a chair and kicked off his shoes. In one gulp he downed his whisky.

'So what kinda day was it?' she asked, though the answer was obvious.

'It sucked.'

'You didn't get the contract?'

'Sure, I did, but we'd to sweeten the deal more than I wanted to. They freak me out with all this bowing shit. Devious bastards act so polite and humble, till it comes to the bottom line and you discover they're screwing you over.' His tone was ominous.

Amy dreaded his dark moods. 'You got what you're here for, that's what matters. Where d'you want to eat tonight?'

He cracked open another drink. 'Anywhere they don't serve fuckin' rice or fish.'

'Poor baby,' she crooned, patting the bedcover. 'Come lie here, and I'll tell you what happened to me today.'

Kelton listened with half an ear as she recounted her little adventure in Harijuku.

'Guy must have been some kinda nut,' he remarked when she was done. 'How's about we go find a Wendy's or a McDonald's? I'd kill for a burger right now.'

His reaction disappointed her ... but it was typical. He belittled anything in which he played no part. For all he'd achieved in his career, he was still the same jerk he'd been twenty years earlier.

Chapter 25

'There's one way to find out if a man is honest – ask him. If he says "Yes", you know he is a crook.' – Groucho Marx

AS THE ESTABLISHED INDUSTRY LEADER in the sale of premium flight and hotel reservations, Laura's company beat out the competition. They offered the best for less. For years she had observed Kelton from afar, casually monitoring his movements through the Devanacorp account invoices that arrived on her desk. He sure did a lot of jetting around the world!

A disturbing trend had emerged in her department's revenues. Sales were slipping back, making her look bad and impacting her annual bonus. She analysed the spreadsheets for the root of the trouble. On looking more closely at Kelton's travel activity, she was puzzled to see that ten of the last twelve flights her office had booked for him were cancelled, though his hotel reservations stood. And he was not alone: the same had been happening to a lesser extent with others in the company.

Something stank somewhere!

The pattern was clear. Airline tickets were issued; within weeks, those reservations were cancelled, but no substitute purchased, at least not through her office. Here it was again! One first-class flight to Japan had been booked for Kelton, two months previously, then shortly afterwards the ticket was voided. Yet he apparently had stayed at the Imperial Hotel in Tokyo as planned. What was he playing at? She rechecked the most recent figures, and called Devanacorp in St Louis.

'It sounds weird. You're positive about this?' asked George Freeman in Accounting.

'It's in black and white, right in front of me,' Laura assured him. 'Have you new travel restrictions? From here, it looks as though several of your top executives have been grounded.'

'Give me a few days and I'll get back to you. There's probably a really simple explanation,' he said.

'Appreciate it. Thanks,' Laura replied.

*

One of Carson's first actions as CEO was to install new vice-presidents of Finance and Human Resources: not a popular move, nor was it intended to be. He was out to shake things up a bit, weed out the complacency that had crept in during Maxwell's tenure. The old guy simply had gotten too comfortable in the job, surrounded by yes-men who imagined the company could retain its competitive edge while sticking with the old ways of the previous decade.

Well, they had turned a corner. A new chapter was about to begin and Carson was preparing for the nineties. Already an edict had been issued that the costs of all departments were to be scrutinised and waste eliminated. No economy was too small to consider, down to paper clips and post-it notes. Any director unable to effect an immediate ten percent savings in his budget would be called to account, and heads would roll. Lean and mean, that was his motto.

At a brainstorming session with his veeps, the CEO particularly liked one of MacLeod's ideas for trimming waste. The proposal would force all employees below VP level to submit fresh applications for their jobs. It would bring home to them the reality of the new regime, and instil a healthy dose of insecurity to know the rug could be pulled from beneath their feet at any minute. Criticism of the procedure would be interpreted as a lack of commitment to the company, Kelton had added with a grin.

Now *there* was a suggestion that would scare the shit out of everybody, from the janitorial staff right up through the ranks!

The more he thought about it, the more Carson liked the idea. MacLeod was a man after his own heart, obviously. Might even be the one to groom as his successor – though that was still a long way off, God willing.

*

HR was totally swamped by a deluge of job re-applications. It meant nothing that everyone in the company had been interviewed and vetted before being hired. Whoever dreamed up this wheeze obviously had no concept of the damage to morale and disruption it would bring to the everyday operation of the company. Hundreds of reams of paper, cartridges of ink and man hours were squandered on a pointless exercise to reinvent the wheel, but to say so out loud would be career suicide. No one dared state that the Emperor had no clothes.

Uproar spread through every department. On Carson's orders, the bean counters were to have heavier workloads, and a reduction in headcount. All expense reports were to be gone over with a fine toothcomb, and strict new rules put in place to verify claims. There was to be no more waste or duplication of effort. For those who survived this purge, things would settle down eventually, as they always did. A new leader was obliged to inflict misery on his employees to please Wall Street.

George Freeman shifted a vast pile of papers to one side of his desk, and came upon a note in his own writing. *Damn!* He'd promised to look into that query from Laura Donahue, but it had gone clean out of his mind with the recent reorganisation. Weeks had passed since her call. He'd do it today, and score it off his list. Then he could return to the vexing question of the cuts he had to make.

*

'What do you mean, a *discrepancy*? I don't understand.'

On the other end of the line, George knew he'd better choose his words carefully. 'Nor do I, sir. I hoped you could set me straight with these numbers, because they don't make sense.'

'You're talking to the wrong person here. My secretary handles all my reservations and expense reports. She'll be more help to you than I am. Take it up with her.'

'Actually, Dr MacLeod, I already did, but she was unable to clarify things.'

It was like stumbling blindfold through a minefield! Everyone knew it was dangerous to get on the wrong side of Big Mac. That was the last thing George wanted.

'*Who* did you say you are again?' Kelton's tone was menacing.

'George Freeman. In Accounting.'

'Well, let me give you a piece of advice, Mr Freeman. You should find more productive ways to spend your time.'

George suspected he was on to something.

*

'Hey, Lenny!'

'Mac! Am I glad to see you!'

They sat in a quiet booth. Kelton ordered two beers.

'What's up?'

'Wanted to tip you off. Our finagling days are over.' Beads of sweat shone on Lenny's forehead.

'What the hell are you blathering about? You're not making any sense here.'

'An eager beaver from downstairs called me today. Asked all kinda shit about where I'd travelled in the last year, and where I bought my tickets. I don't have a good feeling about this. I couldn't get him off the line!'

'And you kept talking to him? For fuck's sake!' interrupted Kelton.

Was this the same Lenny Schwartz he had once looked up to?

'Don't tell me, I can guess: he was called Freeman.'

'Coulda been something like that. His questions really threw me.'

Kelton narrowed his eyes. 'You didn't give the game away, did you?'

'Nah,' laughed Lenny sheepishly. 'What kinda sissy do you take me for? Deny, deny, deny. Isn't that what they say you should do?' He took a long slug of his drink.

'Right.'

There was an uneasy silence. This could turn nasty. Kelton sure as hell wouldn't admit to anything, but who knew where Lenny's big mouth might land them? Abruptly he rose and grabbed his car keys from the table. 'I've gotta go.'

The more distance he put between himself and Schwartz, the better. If a ship was about to sink, he'd be as far away from it as possible.

*

'Can you spare that much time?' Carson asked.

Kelton's expression was ingenuous, his response less so. 'A month in Europe seems a lot, but I truly believe it's in the best long-term interests of the company. Of course, it would be easier to bring the individual country directors to headquarters here, and spell it out to them. But you know what'll happen ... they go back home, St Louis becomes a distant memory, and they're straight into their bad old ways again. This way, I'm the *only* one travelling and they'll be up to speed immediately. They're better at implementing new strategy when it's presented on their home turf. It's an investment that will pay dividends.'

The CEO nodded. 'You've obviously given this a lot of thought. I like your initiative. Go for it.'

Kelton stood up. 'I'll get onto it immediately, sir.'

*

'I can't come with you? But you told me it was a perk of your job, to take a companion on your travels!' In her indignation, Amy suspected he was jerking her around, as he'd done with Carol.

'All that stuff's on hold. Carson's out to make his mark. Everything's to be done exactly by the book and perks are suspended. I'm needed in Europe. End of story.' Kelton continued to throw things into his suitcase as he spoke.

165

'So at an hour's notice I'm left on my ass for four weeks?'

'Babe, I'm sorry, right? I have to go with the flow.'

'Yeah, yeah. Go. Don't mind me.' She pouted, yet maybe it was no bad thing. It would make a pleasant change to have her house to herself again, to be free to come and go as she pleased. She might in fact look for a bit of fun elsewhere, like in the old days. That would really spice things up!

A month in Europe for Kelton might just be what the doctor ordered.

*

Things at the office were becoming too hot to handle. Lenny Schwartz had George Freeman on the line twice more, and now a face-to-face meeting had been scheduled, to include a representative from HR! It sounded ominous. The very idea made Lenny's heart race. He should have walked away the minute Big Mac proposed the scheme, but it had sounded wonderfully simple. Hell, if others were doing it, why not? Who would it hurt, to generate a little tax-free windfall each time he sat in Business Class instead of First when travelling for the company? No one could have foreseen that the shit would hit the fan like this, nor that Big Mac would wangle a trip across the Atlantic, leaving everyone else knee-deep in it!

There was only one thing to do: he'd call Mac's secretary for his itinerary and contact numbers. He'd go nuts if he couldn't talk to somebody.

Back in his Madrid hotel room to freshen up before dinner, Kelton noticed that the answering machine was blinking. He listened to the message, muttered an oath, then pressed 7 to delete. During his shower, two further voice mails were left, the caller's tone growing ever more panicky. Once he had dressed, he reluctantly called St Louis.

'Mac? Thank God!' said Lenny. 'Listen, Freeman's turning the screws on me. We should have a discussion before I meet with him tomorrow, get our story straight.' The desperate neediness in his voice was transmitted loud and clear, despite the five thousand miles separating them.

That neediness made Kelton despise him all the more. 'Lenny,' he said coldly and deliberately, 'I don't know what you're on about. There *is* no story to get straight, so quit calling me. I've got nothing to say to you. You're on your own, buddy.' He slammed down the receiver. It was nine-thirty and the city below Kelton's window was coming to life. His thoughts were on the bottle of Rioja he'd have with dinner.

In St Louis, Lenny stared at his office phone in dismay.

*

The game was up. He felt like a rat caught in a trap. He couldn't be sure, but he suspected every word they said was being recorded, which increased his nervousness. Barclay, the HR representative, had mentioned that skimming travel expenses was a firing offence. Lenny blanched and for an awful moment feared he might throw up. Freeman sat taking notes.

Who would have dreamed their money-spinning scheme could be such a big deal? Lenny had everything to lose. If they fired him, he'd never be hired by another company at this age, let alone one that paid anything close to his current salary. His stock options and medical insurance would disappear down the tubes. With the alimony to his ex-wife, the mortgage and his car payments, he might even be forced to declare bankruptcy! He wouldn't see Tiffany's heels for dust. She'd be out of the door like a shot. It was all right for that bastard MacLeod. He'd worm his way out of any trouble, that one!

What he and Kelton had done harmed nobody. It was a victimless crime, yet it had put his ass on the line. One option remained: negotiation. Hell, his career had been built on striking deals! If he came clean, they might go easier on him. Hadn't he always been taught that honesty was the best policy?

He realised Barclay and Freeman were staring at him, waiting for an answer.

Lenny took a deep breath. 'Okay, I'll tell you everything – if I can hang on to my job.'

'That's not gonna happen,' said Barclay. 'The best you can hope for is an X-grading, though I can't promise, because I don't make the decisions. I'm just saying it's a possibility. Everything depends on your degree of cooperation.'

X-grading. Lenny hated the term. It was a career death knell, the end of the line. He'd have a job, but heaven knows what kind of loser position he'd be assigned to. His present salary would continue till retirement, without increases or bonuses. It was equivalent to being put in the stocks for the rest of his working life, publicly smacked upside the head for his wrongdoing, probably reporting to some upstart he himself had hired! He'd be an object of universal derision, the big shot who got greedy and was caught. He wished he could turn the clock back. Wished he'd never been foolish enough to jeopardise all he had for a few lousy bucks.

Barclay and Freeman sat looking across the table at him. With his silk handkerchief, Lenny dabbed at his brow, took a sip of water and began to spill his guts.

Chapter 26

'We don't know what we want, but we are ready to bite somebody to get it.' – Will Rogers

THE MAJOR LIFE EVENT they had come through left her trapped in a maze of self- recrimination and regret. Carol wrestled with the idea that perhaps she could have tried harder to make a success of her marriage, that somehow she was responsible for bringing out the worst in Kelton. Was it really *her* fault the three children were left without their Dad? It was difficult to gauge the effect of the divorce on the boys: Robert had left for college, happy to escape the restrictions of living at home, while Will was a junior in high school, more interested in his vegetable garden than anything else. But at thirteen, Josie had taken it hard. As instinct had guided her in tapping Kelton's meagre reserve of fatherly affection, the girl's never-ending stock of hurtful barbs now frustrated her mother.

Carol resolved one morning to give herself a holiday. For that one day she would concentrate on being happy: she would turn a deaf ear to Josie's comments, and would not permit herself to think of Kelton. *Don't go there!* she would command herself, banishing him from her consciousness. No more would she beat herself up about how things might have been.

Her job helped restore her self-confidence, but exercise became her passion. Early each morning she was at the gym with Marie. If she had the energy after work, Carol walked a brisk couple of miles which brought an exhilaration she had not felt in years. As the pounds dropped off, her compulsion to keep moving continued, because exhaustion brought the reward of sleep.

Walk, walk, step and walk. Carol marched through the blazing heat of the summer, blood pounding as she pushed herself forward. Her clothes could be sticking to her, the oily taste of sunscreen filling her mouth, and rivulets of perspiration trickling into her eyes that watered and stung behind her sunglasses, but she persevered. As the trees basked in the glory of their fall colours and the harsh winter freeze stripped them naked, Carol kept on walking. The cold dry air brought roses to her cheeks, her skin regained its healthy glow, and she felt content. Almost.

*

Kelton's taxi pulled into the driveway as Amy finished putting on fresh lipstick. She rushed out to meet him.

'Welcome home, sweetie!' she cried.

'Hi, babe. Let's go inside,' he replied, picking up his suitcase and giving her a perfunctory peck on the cheek.

He was in one of his moods. Okay, if that's how he wanted it ...

'I need to call my secretary before she leaves at five,' he said brusquely.

Amy followed him into the house. He made straight for the phone.

'Dr MacLeod's office, this is Lisa speaking. How can I help you?'

'Yeah, it's me. I just got home and wanted to touch base with you. How's my calendar looking for tomorrow?'

Amy studied him as he spoke. His brows were drawn, creating a deep furrow above his nose. Clearly he didn't like what he was hearing.

'He insists on meeting with you as soon as you get back.'

Kelton clenched his teeth as he listened. 'Well, you can tell him I'm busy tomorrow, and for the rest of the week. Say we can pencil in something up for the end of the month.'

'But, Dr MacLeod, he keeps ...'

'Do as I say, will you? I'll see you in the morning.' Kelton banged down the receiver and went straight to the bathroom.

In the kitchen, Amy poured two glasses of Chardonnay, and lifted the lid of the casserole on the stove, savouring the aroma of the coq au vin she had cooked specially for dinner that night. Precious time she'd spent shopping and preparing a nice meal, then the bastard struts into her house, with barely a civil word to her! Well, she would enjoy her evening, regardless. She took a long slug of her wine, quickly topping it up at the sound of his footsteps in the hall.

'Great to see you back,' said Amy with a bright smile, as they clinked glasses.

'Good to be back,' said Kelton, without enthusiasm, wishing he could have stayed in Europe. Anywhere would be better than St Louis.

*

It came as a shock next morning to see that Lenny Schwartz's office had been vacated, his bookcases emptied, and his desk cleared. The open door had been stripped of its nameplate. Worse was to come. When Kelton reached his own department, his secretary was typing at her desk. He caught the outline of a man's figure standing by the window inside his office.

'Mr Freeman's here, Dr MacLeod. I'm sorry, he won't take no for an answer, insisted he'd wait for you,' she said apologetically.

Angrily Kelton brushed by her. 'What do you think you're doing?'

Freeman turned to face him. 'I'm waiting to talk to you, same as I've been doing for the last month or more. So I decided we could arrange a meeting in person, rather than carry on playing cat and mouse.'

'I've been in Europe.'

'So I gather. And now you're back. So what works for you, morning or afternoon? Name it, and I'll be there.'

'I've a load of stuff to catch up on. My calendar's full for the next three weeks.'

'I don't think so. In fact, I notice you have an hour free today.' Freeman was leaning over the desk, his finger hovering over Kelton's day planner. 'Right *here*. Let's say four o'clock, and I'll bring Ray Barclay from HR. We'll see you then.'

So far so good, thought Freeman, walking out of the office.

The internal line buzzed. 'What is it now?'

'Todd Styles of Styles Associates is on the line.'

These guys never gave up! However rudely Kelton rebuffed them, headhunters called him regularly. 'Put him through. I'll soon get rid of him.'

But this time was different. Styles came quickly to the point. A small pharmaceutical concern needed someone with clout in the industry and a strong track record to come in as CEO. Someone like Kelton.

'What makes you think I'd be interested in moving to a tin-pot company?'

'I know you like a challenge,' replied Styles. 'With the right guy at the helm, this "tin-pot company" could be the next giant in cancer treatment.'

'Yeah, tell me about it. That's what they all say.'

'These guys are on to something big. They have FDA approval and statistics to back up their claims. You should think about it. Give me a call if you'd like more information, and we'll discuss a meeting.'

Amusing, thought Kelton. *And nice to be wanted.*

*

Barclay sat quiet as Freeman rang Laura Donahue's office, and turned on the speaker.

'Hi, Laura? George Freeman here. Listen, about the question of cancelled tickets. Could you double-check the reservations made for Dr Kelton MacLeod? I need precise dates and costs, as far back as you can go.'

'Sure, give me a couple of hours.'

'Just one more thing. If we're required to use this stuff in court, will you sign an affidavit that your office records are accurate?'

Laura whistled softly under her breath at the mention of an affidavit. Maybe Kelton's luck was finally running out. Somebody was gunning for him. 'No problem. I'll fax everything I can find by lunchtime.'

'Excellent. I appreciate your help.' George Freeman hung up. With any luck he'd gather enough evidence to nail the great Dr Kelton MacLeod.

*

'Come in, MacLeod! How was the trip?'

Kelton took a seat in the CEO's office. 'Excellent. Got a lot done, well worth the effort it took. I brought these new stats for you to look over. There's still room for improvement, but I think you'll agree, things are moving in the right direction.'

'Good stuff. That's what I like to hear.'

'But I'm puzzled, sir,' said Kelton. 'I noticed this morning that Lenny Schwartz's office is empty. Did something happen in my absence?'

Carson gave a humourless smile. 'You could say that. Lenny got caught playing games. The stupid fool denied it at first, then admitted he'd been skimming expenses.'

'Really?' Kelton's eyes were innocent. 'This is a surprise. You think you know somebody, but ...' Lost for words, he paused. 'So what's he doing now? Is he out?'

'As good as. He accepted an X-grading, but he'll get sick of that pretty quick.'

'Geez,' was all Kelton could say. It had turned out worse for Lenny than he'd ever dreamed it would. And he was next in the firing line.

*

At four sharp, Freeman and Barclay were shown into his office.

'Could I bring anyone coffee?' asked Lisa before leaving. The three men shook their heads.

'Thanks, that'll be all. Close the door behind you. So,' said Kelton, 'how can I help you?'

Barclay laid a small device on the desk in front of him. 'I must inform you that this interview will be recorded.'

'Fine by me.'

Freeman spoke as though reading from a prepared script. 'Several irregularities in your travel claims have come to our attention. We need you to clarify.'

Kelton leaned back in his leather chair. Raising his arms to rest his head in his clasped hands, he placed his feet on his desk with the soles of his shoes facing the two squirts opposite. 'I'll be happy to help after you tell me precisely where and when these irregularities occurred. In other words, I need *you* to clarify for me, including details of your sources. It's my right to face my accuser, isn't it?'

Freeman smiled pleasantly. 'Nobody is accusing you of anything. But there are inconsistencies, starting with a trip made to Paris more than five years ago.'

'Excuse me, did you say five years ago? *Years?* Is this some kinda joke? You really expect me to remember one particular flight I made in 1983? I travel so much, it's hard to keep track of where I was five months ago, never mind five years!'

'In that case, let me refresh your memory. Here's a list of flights you've booked since that date. Those with an asterisk against them are the problem. They were all booked by the same agency, all for travel in First class. You filed an expense report for each one, and you were reimbursed for the full cost of the ticket. Then the reservations were cancelled, sometimes at the last minute.'

'So you're saying I'm a liar? That I claimed for trips I didn't take?'

'Not at all. Just that you claimed for tickets you didn't use.'

Kelton glared at the pair of weasels who imagined they could corner him. 'You're way out of line, harassing me like this! An anonymous document with some random asterisks proves nothing. You accuse me of doing something wrong, you damned well better come up with concrete evidence to support it.' Reaching forward, he grabbed the tape recorder to switch it off, and threw it across the desk. It rattled noisily towards Barclay. 'And since we're off the record, I'll tell you something: you picked the wrong guy. I don't appreciate your attitude and you don't scare me. Now you can get the hell out of my office.'

*

'At last,' he sighed, slinging his briefcase down in the hallway.

'You look all in,' said Amy. 'Had a rough day?' She was treading warily, given the temper he'd been in last night.

'Yeah, I need a drink.'

'What's up, sugar? You not feeling good?' Once he'd sat down, she massaged his neck and shoulders.

'I'm tired, that's all. Jet-lagged, running on empty.'

'Where would you like to go for dinner? We could eat at the club.'

Kelton drained his glass and reached for the wine bottle. 'Hell, Amy, give me a break, would ya? Let's veg out tonight, eat something from a tray in front of the TV. Can't you grab a meal out of the freezer?'

'Like what, ice cream? That's all I got, unless you fancy calling out for pizza. Last night was your special welcome home meal. I'm sorry, mister, but you ain't with Suzie Homemaker anymore!' She smiled at her own joke.

He curled his lip in disdain. 'And don't I know it! You've no idea what it's like to live in the real world. Never had to work your butt off, day in day out, did you?'

She looked at him, surprised. Like a wild beast, he was calm one minute, but ready to spring without warning the next. She rinsed her crystal wine glass at the sink, and lifted her car keys.

'We need a time-out. See you later.' She had more sense than hang around to take the brunt of this black mood that had descended on him.

Left alone in the kitchen, he gnawed at a piece of stale cheese from the fridge. Half-way through the second bottle of Merlot, he got to thinking how it was during his marriage. In all their years together Carol could always rustle up something tasty at short notice! It was no big deal to produce a snack or a full meal for him at any time of the day or night. The freezer was invariably well stocked with home-made soups, entrees and baked goodies.

He polished off half a dozen crackers and a bag of popcorn with the remains of the Merlot, becoming increasingly maudlin and angry, regretting all he'd given up for a pampered pooch who did nothing but play tennis. True, she had a neat trick or two in the bedroom, but any hooker could give him that for twenty bucks! Amy was consumed by trivia. Her chief concern was the next hair or nail appointment. It stressed her out to make it to the club for tennis before lunch, then she expected to go out for dinner! She lived in cloud-cuckoo land, he thought, dozing off into a drunken stupor.

Getting home at ten-thirty, Amy found the two empty Merlot bottles on the coffee table, and Kelton stretched out on the sofa, fast asleep, wine glass still in his hand. He could lie there and rot, for all she cared. Even that was better than he deserved. She turned off the television, and went upstairs.

*

The following morning he woke with a splitting headache and a dry mouth. He crept upstairs to the bedroom, careful not to wake Amy as she slept. Quietly he selected clean underwear, socks and a shirt. He showered, shaved, flossed and brushed his teeth. If Amy was aware of him, she did not let on. As he left the house at six thirty, she seemed to be fast asleep.

The whole night through, she'd tossed and turned, mad at being taken for granted, and more mad at herself for being stupid enough to allow him to move in with her. All along, she'd suspected it wouldn't work out. She'd been blinded by the fun they'd shared together. There was no denying it, when he was good, he was really good. And when he was bad, he was horrible.

Chapter 27

'Diplomacy is the art of letting someone else have your way.'
– Sir David Frost

H E WAS READY FOR SOME SOLID FOOD again, after the previous day's upsets. No wonder he'd felt lousy when he woke up, with skipping lunch yesterday, and finding nothing in the fridge at night! Few things were as satisfying to Kelton as a breakfast of pancakes, bacon, eggs and sausage at Denny's, all washed down with several cups of strong black coffee. By 7:30 am, he was in his office.

Arriving at her desk, his secretary was surprised to discover his office door open. 'Morning, Dr MacLeod,' she called brightly.

'Hi, Lisa. Photocopy these documents for my presentation next week, would you?'

This one could make or break his career. It had to be a doozie! He had to show the Board positive results, and wow them with his profit forecasts. He knew what they liked to hear. Confident that his latest proposals would please, he'd leave Carson in no doubt as to his indispensability. It should further his campaign to be designated heir apparent to the CEO's chair. The thought made Kelton smile.

Next on his agenda was Amy. Amends had to be made for last night. What had he been thinking, to snarl at her the way he'd done? Being interrogated by Freeman and Barclay had rattled him more than he cared to admit. He called a florist to order the delivery of two dozen red roses. Then he called the airline, and booked two seats. Finally he made a hotel reservation, confident that he'd get back in her good books.

*

'This is such fun!' said Amy as a taxi whisked them from O'Hare to the Palmer House Hotel in the heart of Chicago.

Kelton grinned. She didn't sulk, that was one of her virtues. Once he'd apologised, she was always ready for their next adventure together. It seemed incredible that they'd never come here before. He'd always liked Chicago: liked the 'City of Big Shoulders'. He identified with its work-hard-and-play-hard spirit. There was an honesty about a town where they admitted that a little bit of graft got you where you wanted.

They had dinner and went to a show. Next day, they shopped the Magnificent Mile until his credit card was maxed out, but it made her happy. A twenty dollar bill slipped to the waiter had secured them a window table for a romantic dinner in the Signature Room that evening.

With the city lights twinkling in the darkness below them, Kelton leaned across the table, looking deep into her eyes, and laid his hand on hers. 'How would you feel about a Christmas wedding?'

Her smile froze. He had to go and ruin things, and she'd really been enjoying this jaunt! She frowned. 'Honey, it isn't the right time.'

The tic at the side of his mouth betrayed his irritation. 'You mean you'd rather wait till spring? That would work, but we should start planning, and formalise things. Or are we not on the same page?'

She bit her lower lip. Might as well get it over with in a public place, since it might turn nasty. 'I don't think I can marry you. Please don't be mad at me.' She preferred to live separately, but something in his eyes made her afraid to say so.

He sat back and folded his arms. 'Huh? Is this about the other night? I get stressed out, and you decide you can't hack it?'

She took a deep breath. 'I need space to look at where we're headed. I'm flying to Miami next week.'

He looked offended. 'Whatever.'

'You could come down for the holidays,' she said feebly, hoping to soften the blow.

He thought for a second or two, and abruptly snapped his fingers at a waiter hovering nearby. With the bill taken care of, they walked along Michigan Avenue to the hotel. Amy smiled graciously at the doorman who wished them goodnight. Kelton ignored him, staring stonily ahead as they entered the lobby. He had wasted enough effort for one night. She lay huddled and shivery at one side of the bed, he at the other, the atmosphere between them chillier than the October wind that whistled through the city streets.

*

Just when he was sure Freeman and Barclay had given up, the call came that they wanted to talk to him again. The meeting was to be in Barclay's office.

Freeman presented him with a file. 'These are the details you requested.'

Kelton flipped through the data, seemingly unconcerned. 'So?'

'We need you to explain why changes were made in your travel arrangements, but not in the amount the company paid for your tickets. The sums don't add up. We have to get to the bottom of it,' said Barclay. 'And by the way, I'm recording our interview.'

'Like I said before, I don't know what you're speaking about. I did nothing wrong.'

'Let me put it differently, said Barclay softly. 'The company will take a more lenient view of any ...' he paused, choosing his words carefully, 'any ... *misstep* from the past, if you concede that you perhaps failed to act strictly within the guidelines of our travel policies.'

'I don't believe you guys!' exclaimed Kelton. 'How many times must I say it? I did *nothing* wrong. So take your leniency and shove it! Any more of this and I'm calling my lawyer.' He got up to leave.

'Please sit down. It's not helpful to become angry. I don't think you understand the seriousness of the situation: your employment cannot continue at Devanacorp unless this matter is satisfactorily resolved.'

They were threatening to fire him! Had these jerks actually the power to give him a pink slip? This was how Lenny had got himself X-graded. He'd caved to the pressure. Like a ninny he'd admitted to the charges levelled against him and Carson had not saved his sorry ass. In fact, the CEO had probably instigated the entire witch hunt!

Kelton became aware that Freeman had spoken. 'Excuse me?' he said.

'I said, why don't you take a look at the file, and we'll review it again next week?'

Kelton nodded and rose. Without a word, he went straight back to his office, gathered up his briefcase and papers, and told Lisa he'd be out for the rest of the afternoon. Privacy was required for an important call he was about to make.

*

It was as well Amy was in Florida, he thought, as he dialled the headhunter's number. 'Hey, Todd?' Kelton said jovially. 'That start-up you mentioned a while back, are they still in the market for a CEO?'

Styles laughed. 'I was hoping you'd call! Sure, wanna talk some more about it?'

'Yeah, why not? You got me thinking. Might be worth a look.'

'How about lunch tomorrow? Are you free?'

'Let me check. Twelve-thirty would work for me.'

'Great. You like La Bonne Bouchée, on Olive?'

'Fine. See you then.'

Kelton sat on the sofa to look again at the Freeman file. Among the stack of invoices was a memo from the travel agent, citing every ticket he'd bought and cashed in over the years. The

181

sender's name jumped off the page at him: *Laura Donahue!* It had to be a coincidence. The Laura he'd known wouldn't have the guts to leave New Orleans. She wasn't the type to pick up and go elsewhere ... or was she? Had *she* dropped him in this mess?

The more Kelton drank, the more convinced he was that Laura was the cause of his present predicament. Women – the root of all his troubles! Laura had jeopardised his job, while Carol continued to wallow in luxury under the roof *he'd* put over her head.

At least he had Amy. One of these days, they'd be married, and everything would be back on an even keel. He hoped.

*

Todd Styles was already seated when Kelton got to the restaurant. They placed their orders, and then it was time to get down to business.

'So what's this company called?' asked Kelton.

'Braid Pharma. They're based in the north suburbs of Chicago, about thirty miles from downtown.'

Kelton sucked air. 'That's an expensive house market to move into.'

The headhunter shrugged. 'I'm sure a hiring bonus would be negotiable.'

That was a good start. 'So they have a reasonable amount of funding behind them? I'd be a damn fool to quit Devanacorp for an outfit that could go bust in a couple of years.'

'You should think seriously about this. They're well funded and have an attractive pipeline. Get in on the ground floor and you'll have it made.'

Kelton's mind was racing. Throughout his career, he'd been aiming for the chair that Carson now occupied. But who could tell how long that guy would hold on to the job? And nobody in the company knew where they stood, let alone what the future held. The more he thought about it, the more a move to Braid made sense.

'I guess there's no harm in sounding them out. See if we'd have a fit.'

Styles nodded. 'I think you'll agree it's well worth your while.'

'Hope so,' replied Kelton. 'I don't like wasting my time.'

'I'll set up a face-to-face as soon as possible.'

'Sounds good.'

They shook hands outside in the parking lot, and Kelton headed back to the office.

*

'Hey, Sexy, how's it goin' down there in Florida?'

Amy was surprised to hear his voice on the phone. It was unusual for them to talk two days in a row, especially with the way he'd been lately. 'Great. I won two games today, just got home. What's up?'

'Thought I might come visit for a weekend. Feels like forever since we were together. I'm missing you at night.'

'Well, baby, I've been kinda lonely too, all by myself.'

Even from a thousand miles away, she could turn him on. 'We've a lot of ground to make up!'

She giggled. 'Can't wait. Bring it to me, Big Guy!' This was the Kelton she liked. With luck, he'd still be this upbeat when he arrived.

*

The interview at Braid Pharma took place faster than he expected. From the start, Kelton felt at home. Not wanting to seem overly eager to leave Devanacorp, however, he feigned indifference to the generous salary and incentive package being promised. They had to believe their need for him was greater than his for them: that was how business worked. He rejected the initial proposal.

Two days afterwards, Kelton was informed that a revised hiring bonus was on the table. Furthermore, if Braid went public within three years, he would be given eighty thousand stock options. It was mind-boggling! He'd cracked it, manoeuvred them into making an offer he couldn't refuse.

Keeping his cool, Kelton said he'd get back to them in twenty-four hours, once he'd given it some more consideration. Nobody would ever say he was a pushover!

Chapter 28

'Humankind cannot bear very much reality.' – T.S. Eliot

AMY WAS STRANGELY NERVOUS. It felt like going out on a first date. In her excitement, she had gone shopping for a new outfit and shoes. Her hair was shiny and bouncy, her manicure matched her lipstick, and the Florida sun had tanned her skin to perfection. His plane had just landed. The flight crew appeared from the jetway, and then Kelton. She jumped and waved as he came towards her. He grinned, and swept her up in a bear hug that almost took her breath away.

'You look good enough to eat!'

'I've missed you so much,' she said into his ear, before he put her down.

They drove back to her place, with the convertible top down in the noonday sun. Kelton sang along to *She Drives Me Crazy* by Fine Young Cannibals on the radio. Within half an hour they pulled into the driveway. The garage door slid up, and she parked the car.

In the house they headed straight for the bedroom, Amy pausing only to take the phone off the hook and slat the window shades. The new designer dress that cost so much fell carelessly to the floor as he peeled off her underwear and feasted his eyes on her lithe body. Last of all, she kicked off her shoes. She lay down on the bed, and instantly he was on top of her, all over her, and nothing in the world mattered except for satisfying the animal instinct that had brought them to so many new beginnings.

*

'I've something to tell you,' he said.

'Surprise, surprise!' remarked Amy, sipping at her wine.

'What d'ya mean? You think you know me?'

She laughed. 'Come on, spit it out!'

'I've been offered a CEO position.' He could barely keep the grin off his face.

'Get out! Really? What about Carson?'

'Fuck Carson! And Devanacorp. I'm moving to Braid Pharma. They make chemotherapy drugs in Chicago.'

'*Chicago?* I'll never see you!'

'You'll see me all the time if we're married. What about it?'

She shook her head. 'I love being with you. Nobody else in the world can make me feel like you do. But marriage ... well, it's a big step.'

'We have a great future ahead of us, babe! Once this company takes off, I stand to make millions. Serious money. I'll retire early, we'll travel the world.'

She looked away.

He had hoped for a more enthusiastic reaction. Things were not quite going according to plan. He'd had it all worked out: the hiring bonus would cover the basic moving and set-up expenses, but Chicago properties were in a different league from those of St Louis. The home he envisaged buying would run into seven figures. The monthly mortgage payments would be easily met on his new salary, but he urgently required a hefty upfront injection of cash for the down-payment. That was where Amy came in. He needed her ... and her money.

Hesitantly she said, 'Don't you like the way things are? We have fun together, *and* we enjoy things on our own. If it ain't broke, don't fix it, as the saying goes ...'

He smiled patiently. 'Sweetheart,' he said, 'of course I do. But after a day at the office, it's like I'm *dying,* when I come back to an empty house. To earn the kind of salary they're offering I'll be under a ton of pressure. You get nothing for nothing. I want someone waiting at home for me, to knock the rough edges off the day, who'll help me recover for the next round ... to be on my side to share the ups and downs.'

Amy closed her eyes. There was the rub. The ups were all very well, but if Kelton was down, he made sure everyone around him was, too. What he needed was a human punch-bag! Years earlier, one look from his big earnest eyes could melt her resistance and she'd agree to anything. But not any more.

'I'm not moving to Chicago.'

He laughed. 'But you liked it, just a month ago.'

'To visit, not to live there. It's too cold.'

'Like hell it is!' She was starting to irritate him. 'Come on, cut me a bit of slack here. We'll go on a house-hunting trip, at least have a look at what's available.'

She shook her head. 'In your dreams.'

He pressed on regardless. 'Look, you sell the St Louis house and we'll get married. We'll buy somewhere real classy to live, splash out on a mansion on the North Shore. We could have a boat, if you like, go sailing on the weekends.'

'Got it all worked out, huh?'

'This is it, baby. You and me together. The world's our oyster if we pool our resources.' He drained his glass, and reached for the wine bottle.

'Yeah ... like I can up and sell the house in St Louis,' she said with a humourless smile. 'The way Jack set up his will, I don't *own* any real estate. I got life rent of this place and the house in St Louis, then they revert to his trust. Neither one is mine to sell.'

Kelton sat stock still. 'You're joking! Why would he tie things in knots like that?'

'He just did. If I marry you or anyone else, I lose out, big time.'

Kelton shrugged. 'There has to be a way round it. You can't let a fucking stiff dictate your every move! Hell, Amy, imagine the lifestyle we'll enjoy!'

'Not gonna happen, sweetie. I'd be nuts to give up all I've got, for something that might turn to shit.'

He couldn't believe his ears. 'Whadya mean, turn to shit? Come on, you're not seeing the big picture. Let the damned lawyer take the houses. Big deal!' Slyly he added, 'You weren't exactly left penniless, were you? With the cash Jack left, you can do what you like.'

'Right. And I do. I'm sorry, but I'm fine the way I am, thank you very much.' Did he reckon she was dumb enough to discuss the details of her finances with him?

'Sorry my ass! Was it good for your ego, to keep me hanging on the end of a string?'

'I've *kept* you, but not on the end of a string! You've been living rent-free, in my house, in case you'd forgotten. So don't act all offended that I won't rearrange my whole life for you!'

'I really thought we could make it, you and me. You were happy to choose a ring in Rio. Why didn't you come clean? You never said you didn't want to get married.'

'You were in no position to marry anybody! Your divorce wasn't even final! But you want this back? Well, take it.' Amy slipped the emerald ring off her finger, and sent it spinning across the glass-topped coffee table towards him.

'Keep the fucking ring,' muttered Kelton.

Already he was formulating plan B. Without a sizeable deposit for a home loan, he'd be forced to rent. It would be somewhere spectacular, overlooking Lake Michigan. He didn't need Amy or her money! She thought she held all the cards, but he would make her regret this day. She could keep the comfortable existence that Jack Bergmann had mapped out for her. Kelton turned on the television, with the volume up loud. He'd said all he was going to say. While he moved onwards and upwards, she could stagnate in her cosy little rut.

It had always been this way, and always would be, Amy was thinking. Out of the corner of her eye, she looked at the guy with whom she'd shared the best and the worst of times. Her marriage to Jack was one of convenience, yet they'd worked around their shortcomings to live in mutual kindness and affection. Like a fool, she'd misconstrued her husband's will as his revenge for her little infidelities. Only now did she appreciate Jack's foresight. He had safeguarded all he had from the greedy talons of some fortune hunter who might catch her in a moment of weakness. The strings he attached kept her grounded, tethered to reality when she might easily have been borne aloft in a cloud of hot air. Even in death, Jack was watching over her, protecting her.

Next morning, she was glad to drop Kelton off at the airport. He pecked her on the cheek and said, 'I guess this is it, then. Thanks for the ride. I'll mail your house keys to you.' He stepped out of the convertible.

'Okay,' said Amy, wishing he would just go.

He leaned over her car door for a final word, saying gently, 'You know, babe, there's one thing I've meant to tell you. A plastic surgeon could easily smooth these wrinkles round your mouth. Your age is starting to show.'

With that, he turned and walked off into the terminal.

*

Back in his St Louis office, Kelton was busily drafting his letter of resignation when his internal line rang.

'Who is it, Lisa?'

'Ray Barclay from Personnel. He's anxious to talk to you, says he was expecting you in his office fifteen minutes ago.'

'Put him on.'

There was a click. 'Hi. Did you forget our appointment?' said Barclay.

Kelton smiled. 'Actually, no. I had better things to do.'

'Look, why don't we quit playing games here? We need to straighten this out once and for all.'

'You speak for yourself. It's not my problem, buddy.'

'On the contrary,' said Barclay, 'it's very much your problem. You're doing yourself no good by not cooperating.'

Silence.

It took a second or two for Barclay to realise what had happened. 'I don't believe it!' he said. 'The prick hung up on me!'

'Nothing MacLeod does should surprise you,' Freeman replied.

*

It was a whole new ball game: being X-graded was worse than Lenny feared. From having his own splendid office, he'd sunk as low as he could go on the totem pole, relegated to a tiny cubicle, surrounded by purposeful twenty- and thirty-somethings. His parallel universe extended to the cafeteria, where suddenly he was invisible to those he'd formerly managed. Every minute was like an hour, each day a marathon of lonely futility, squandered on 'busy work' – shuffling useless papers and writing reports that nobody would ever read. Like a beached whale, he was ridiculously out of his element, unable to escape a predicament of his own making. The thought of his pay check kept him going: that and his faith that he'd find a way out of this mess.

His situation at home was no better. Tiffany was still with him, but only just. He wondered how much longer she would stay, now he was no longer the big shot she'd married. He had to get networking again. For the hundredth time he flipped through his Rolodex and Kelton's number appeared. Big Mac, he muttered, the biggest motherfucker that ever walked! One day they were both knee-deep in shit, and the next MacLeod came up smelling of roses. It had been announced that he was moving to become CEO of Braid Pharma. Some folks had all the luck! Lenny continued to sift through the cards, his desperation mounting. Reluctantly, he punched in Kelton's extension number.

'Mac?' he said. 'Hey, it's Lenny. Just had to call and wish you all the best in the Windy City!'

'Thanks, buddy. I appreciate it,' replied Kelton.

'Don't forget, now, I'm open to offers if there's ever a spot for me at Braid.'

'Sure.' The last thing Kelton would want around him in Chicago was a sucker like Lenny. But hell, he could afford to be nice for once.

Chapter 29

'Every parting gives a foretaste of death, every reunion a hint of the resurrection.' – Arthur Schopenhauer

St Louis, 1990

IT WAS 6:30 AM, AND JOSIE was chewing on a bagel for breakfast when the phone rang. 'Hang on, I'll get her for you,' she said nonchalantly to the caller. As usual, the ringer on her mother's extension would be switched off.

From the front hall, she yelled, 'Mom! Someone to talk to you.'

No reply. The girl sighed. She ran upstairs, and into the master bedroom where Carol was still in bed. 'Mom? Wake up, will ya? Phone for you!'

Carol felt that immediate jolt of panic that comes with being rudely wakened from a deep sleep. Her first thought was that Robert had been in an accident with his car. 'What's wrong? Who is it?'

'Dunno,' shrugged Josie. 'Didn't ask.'

Carol grabbed the handset on her nightstand. 'Hello?'

'Eh, yes ... hello, Carol,' said a male voice hesitantly. 'It's Alex here, Alex Murray.'

It was a shock to hear that familiar Scottish voice after so long. 'Hi,' she said. 'How are you, Alex?'

'I'm fine. Carol, I'm sorry, I've no idea what time it is for you in Missouri. I wanted to let you know your father's in a bad way. The doctors say he'll be lucky to see the week out. Maybe you should come and see him, if you can.'

She looked at the receiver, selfishly wishing she could hang up, and pretend nothing had changed since last night. Why should a single message from nowhere suddenly turn my world upside down? She cleared her throat. 'Is my Dad at home?'

'No, he's in the hospital, in Aberdeen. Ward 40, Foresterhill.'

How could she suddenly leave everything here, and go to Scotland? And with the treatment she'd received, why should she suddenly run to him at the drop of a hat? But as the idea occurred to her, she knew she would go. For years, pride had kept her from returning home for a visit. Now she had the perfect excuse.

*

'You're abandoning us? You can't be serious.'

Carol sat nursing a cup of coffee at the kitchen table. 'You've a freezer full of food. Marie isn't far away, if you have a problem, and Robert can come home at the weekend to check on you both. I'm only going for a week.'

Josie scowled. 'Just how am I supposed to get to band practice? Or go anywhere, like the mall?'

'Will can drive you,' said Carol.

'Unh, unh. I don't think so. You can't leave me at his mercy!'

Her brother smiled good-naturedly. 'Shut up, Jo.'

'Can we have a party? We'll clean up the mess before you're back.' Josie's eyes sparkled mischievously.

'Don't even think about it,' warned Carol.

'You go and do the needful, Mom. Don't worry about us.'

She thanked God she could depend on Will.

*

The layover at Gatwick airport felt like an eternity. The overnight leg from St Louis had left Carol full yet hungry, with dinner followed by breakfast a mere four hours later. In her raw, tired state, everything sounded far away and echoed inside her head. A children's ride-on car nearby repeated the same, inane, tinkling *Postman Pat* music over and over till she wanted to scream. Finally the display indicated that her flight north was boarding, and she made her way to the gate.

Homesickness hit as she fastened her seatbelt on the Aberdeen plane, and listened to the stewardess's safety instructions delivered in a Scottish accent. Filled with elation and trepidation, she left her second breakfast of the day uneaten. During the descent, the sight of Aberdeenshire's purple hills and its lush green fields bordered by dry-stone dykes brought a lump to her throat. After a brief glimpse of the city, the plane wheeled round, and touched down.

Orange-clad oil workers milled around the airport, waiting to be ferried by helicopter to rigs in the North Sea. So much had changed in the years since she left! She stood in line for her rental car, claimed her bag at the luggage carousel, and headed outside. A snell north wind immediately made her gather her jacket collar closer to her neck. This was the north-east she remembered!

She unlocked the boot and stowed her case, then got into the rental car. Took a few deep breaths. So far so good. She started the ignition, put the car into first gear and hoped she'd remember how to drive a stick shift. Keep left, she kept telling herself, must keep left! Already her face was damp with perspiration. Damned hot flushes! She pulled forward slowly, moved into second gear and out of the car park. At the first roundabout, she was too slow to change down, and the engine stalled. A brief panic followed, but she managed into first gear when a gap came in the traffic, and jerked forward into the flow. In minutes, she was sailing along with the stream of fast little cars on the main road, and it was as if she'd never been gone.

*

'He's in the third room on the right,' said the nurse at the desk.

Carol walked along a grey corridor with glaring lights, her shoes squeaking on the shiny vinyl floor. The stinky-sweet smell of illness permeated the air. She looked inside the room the nurse had indicated, but the patient in the bed was not her father. At the next door along she peeked in. Again, wrong room.

'Can I help you?'

'I'm looking for Mr Cooper.'

The orderly smiled. 'You've come too far, that's him back there.'

'Oh.' Was that living corpse really her Dad? Surely not!

Carol turned around, confused. Returning to the third door along she entered the ward, where a patient was propped up amidst a pile of pillows. Eyes closed, toothless mouth wide open, his nose pointed like a bird's beak towards the ceiling. Intravenous tubes sprouted from his arms, and alarming lights blinked off and on. From a monitor came irritating, high-pitched beeps. He lay motionless, his hair thin and white, his wrinkled skin grey-yellow against the starched white linens. *But Dad always had rosy, weather-beaten cheeks!* she thought.

Afraid to approach the sleeping stranger, she stood several feet away from the bed and tried to discern some recognisable feature. There had to be a mistake. These ears were way too big! They might share a name, but he was no relative of hers, or so she thought until she noticed the hands that lay limp on the counterpane. Illness and old age could not disguise them: the square, practical hands that long ago had guided her over the hurdles of childhood. There was no mistake. This was what remained of Mr Cooper.

The Dad she'd known had died along with her mother. That delusion had helped overcome the hurt of his silence, and allowed her to look objectively at this being who was her father, and yet was not. Keeping open the possibility of reconciliation, she had faithfully sent him a Christmas card each year. It remained unacknowledged, yet she had felt compelled to maintain the precious link.

Now she stood wondering about the twilight between life and death. Had the old man's brain ceased to function, or was he aware he was at the edge of the precipice? A discreet cough behind her made Carol jump.

'Hi, I'm Dr Brown. Sorry, I didn't mean to startle you. I understand you're Mr Cooper's daughter?'

'Yes. I hardly recognised him.' It sounded almost like an apology, yet why should she make excuses to this total stranger? 'We haven't seen each other for a while,' she added.

'To be honest, he's probably not aware that you're here, but it's nice that you came.' The doctor moved towards the door. 'You'll want a few more minutes alone with him.'

Actually, no. For twenty years, he's had nothing to say to me, she thought. Carol drew a chair nearer to the bed, carefully avoiding the catheter bag that dangled precariously at the side. Gingerly she placed her hand on one of the patient's, but he showed no reaction. 'Dad, can you hear me? It's Carol. Dad?'

Mr Cooper remained motionless. She stared at him, and stood back. As she did so, she noticed a miniscule movement, a fluttering so slight that she wondered if she had imagined it. Gently, she touched him once more. For no more than five seconds, the familiar, blunt old fingers closed feebly around hers then grew limp again – enough to leave her with a sense of closure as precious as any words.

He died that night.

Chapter 30

'For there we loved, and where we love is home,
Home that our feet may leave, but not our hearts.'
– Oliver Wendell Holmes

THE SUN WAS SHINING as she drove along the dirt road to the house. When she pulled up outside the back door, a car was already parked there. Alex stepped out, and a woman emerged from the passenger side.

'Hello, stranger,' said Alex, shaking her hand. He looked older and smaller than she expected. His hair had grown thin on top, his face ruddy and fuller than before.

Carol smiled. 'Alex, it's great to see you! I don't know how I can ever thank you for getting in touch.' Just in time she stopped herself from giving him a hug. This was Scotland, not America.

'Meet my wife, Kirsty.'

The woman by his side nodded. 'I'm sorry about your Dad.'

'Thank you. I'm glad I got to see him again, at least.'

'Here's the house key. Do you want us to come in with you?' said Alex.

It had been impossible to envisage returning here. The things that had made it a home were all her mother's doing. Now it filled her with dread to cross its muddy threshold. 'I'll be fine on my own, but thanks all the same.'

She waved as they left, bracing herself to push the big iron key into the box lock. The hinges creaked as the door swung inwards and she was hit by a dank, smoky smell. The air of the kitchen was colder than outside. She drew back the curtains, and raised the sash windows. Daylight streamed in, revealing the accumulated dust and grime of twenty years. She stood by her mother's stove, where countless meals had simmered and stewed, and hundreds of scones and cakes had been baked. Its enamel surface that once sparkled was now chipped and coated with sticky layers of rancid grease. Crumbs littered the kitchen table. A smeared knife lay by an open two-pound tin of Lyle's Golden Syrup, while a stained cup held the dregs of her father's last tea.

Bereft of home comforts after the death of his wife, Mr Cooper had lived like an unwelcome squatter under his own roof. When he could no longer manage the land, he rented it to Alex, continuing to potter around outside during the day, whatever the weather. Only at sunset could he allow himself to kick off the work boots that still lay by the hearth. In the hallway, his dirty dungarees were draped over the banister.

Climbing the stairs, Carol wondered if she'd grown taller. Or had the house always been so small and dingy, the sloping roof upstairs always so low and oppressive? Her room was as she'd left it two decades earlier, with the same pink candlewick cover on her narrow single bed, and her moth-eaten Teddy Bear perched on the pillow. Hundreds of desiccated insect corpses littered the window sill. Glancing into her parents' room, she turned away with a shudder.

She went down to the parlour. It had been forbidden territory during her early childhood, off-limits except on special occasions. In her mother's day, the room was seldom used, kept clean and polished ready for entertaining important, infrequent visitors like the minister. Now the sheen was off the furniture, and the wallpaper had darkened with age. Neglect had blackened the amber-handled brass kettle in the hearth and the brass candle-sticks on the mantelpiece. The same deep-pile rug lay on the floor between the two armchairs and the same pictures hung on the walls, but one patch of wallpaper seemed lighter than the rest. The butterfly box had been removed. In its place was a gilt frame.

A hot wave of shame washed over her. Right before her, lovingly mounted and displayed, was her degree certificate from Aberdeen University, her parents' consolation prize for years of scrimping and saving. Denying them the small pleasure of seeing her graduate, she had eagerly run off with Kelton, carelessly sweeping everything else aside! What had appeared as an effort to control her was merely their natural desire to keep her safe. But there was no rewriting history: the old Carol would have succumbed to the temptation of punishing herself for past actions. Now she would deal with the present and move on.

Hesitantly she touched the top of the walnut writing desk that had been her father's private domain, feeling like a trespasser as she turned the key and quietly dropped down the top. He'd been no housekeeper, but he kept his correspondence in order. Neat bundles of letters and receipts filled every pigeon hole, and a rubber band held together a pile of Christmas cards, the very ones she herself had sent over the years from St Louis. From another slot, she pulled a bulky brown typewritten envelope with a recent postmark. The top left corner bore the stamp of a law firm. Inside was a copy of Mr Cooper's last will and testament. Carol was named sole beneficiary of the farm, the house and contents, and all his assets, unless she predeceased him: then his estate was to be divided equally among her descendants. The sight of his familiar, scratchy signature at the foot of the document reduced her to tears.

She wished she could tell her parents she was sorry if she'd hurt them. Wished she could understand her father's rage and explain her side of things, but that was like crying for the moon. He was never one for words.

A mountain of stuff remained to be sorted, but it could wait. Tomorrow she had a funeral to arrange.

*

Following a simple service in the local church, Mr Cooper was laid to rest beside his wife in the tiny churchyard. The solemnity of the burial gave way to joviality at the wake, where mourners were invited to take a dram or two of whisky, and were served tea and sandwiches: mushy little triangles of cheap white bread with mean slivers of cooked ham and a dab of mustard inside. Anything more would be viewed as extravagance. By local standards, Carol had given her parent a good send-off.

'Will you be selling off the farm?' enquired several neighbours, politely curious.

She shook her head. 'Not for a while, at least.' There was no rush. Alex was happy to continue working the land.

It had been a heart-wrenching, exhausting week. Carol planned to spend her last evening alone in her hotel room, but was persuaded to eat dinner that night with Alex and Kirsty. She showered and changed. On her way, she purchased a bottle of malt whisky for her hosts.

Kirsty showed her in. 'Come away, you never need to stand knocking at *our* door.'

'Sit yourself down, Carol,' said Alex, drawing out a chair by the huge pine table in the middle of the big, airy farmhouse kitchen. It was an ultra-modern showpiece, a far cry from the step back into the sixties she'd expected. Partitions had been knocked down, windows added, and an impressive line of high-end German appliances stood along one wall. 'Wow, you've done a beautiful job here!'

'It wasn't my doing.' Alex pointed at Kirsty. 'The boss here planned it.'

His wife smiled. 'Aye, I'm the boss when you're out, that's all! Tell the lassies we're just about ready, will you, Alex?'

'Can I help you?' volunteered Carol.

'You could bring out some wine glasses from that cupboard over there, if you like.'

Gently pushing a six-year-old ahead of him, Alex came back into the kitchen. 'Carol, this is Catherine.' The child smiled shyly, to expose a gap where a baby tooth was missing. 'And here are Barbara and Fiona.' The two older girls moved forward to shake hands. They had a look of their mother about them. The youngest had inherited her daddy's pale blue eyes.

The food was plentiful and the atmosphere was happy. Carol wondered whether life would have been easier if she had stayed in Scotland, but she doubted it. Her restlessness had to be satisfied: that was why she had jilted Alex. Twenty years as his wife would have turned her into her mother, and driven them both crazy. He was a decent man, and deserved better.

Bickering and tension had marred many family meals during Carol's marriage. Deceit, lies and unhappiness had lurked constantly beneath the surface, yet she was grateful to Kelton. He had taken her to America, where she escaped the fate originally mapped out for her.

And leaving had taught her to appreciate the good things about home.

Chapter 31

'Of all the noises known to man, opera is the most expensive.'
– Molière

SATURDAY MORNING WAS ONE of the best times of the week for Laura, when she could eat a leisurely breakfast, and linger over the *Chicago Tribune* with a second cup of coffee. Quickly skimming the Business News section, her least favourite, she noticed a small item announcing the appointment of a new CEO at Braid Pharma, along with a picture of Kelton. Fifteen years had elapsed since she last cast eyes on him. She looked more closely: he'd gained weight, with a heaviness at his jaw line, wrinkles around his eyes and a sprinkle of grey in his hair but still she'd have recognised that face anywhere. It was a pity he had left Devanacorp, since she'd no longer be able to track his travels. Then again, the newspaper had become a whole lot more interesting!

*

The move north had been easier than expected. Kelton liked the idea of starting from scratch in a new company where he could call the shots. His introductory speech was inspirational. The auditorium at Braid Pharma was full, and the audience hung on his every word. Earnestly their charismatic new leader exhorted them to be the best they could be, because each of them carried a heavy responsibility. Their efforts might change the lives of millions. At stake was not only the future of Braid, but the future of mankind.

His expression became grave, almost threatening. Anyone lacking the commitment to give one hundred percent of their energies to Braid should feel free to leave right now, he said with a glower. He had no room for passengers in his organisation. Nobody should expect the job to be easy, because nothing worth achieving ever was, but the rewards would be great. The crowd sat quiet, no one daring to move. When the silence grew almost unbearable, Kelton signalled to an aide at the side of the stage.

'I'm sure you all are familiar with what you're about to hear,' he said, 'but today I want you to *really listen*. Think about the words, and make them your mantra. Apply them to all your efforts, not just today, or next week, but every day of your working lives, because here at Braid, we truly *are* in a race with destiny.'

He stepped aside, and the lights were lowered. The opening strains of Whitney Houston's *One Moment in Time* began to play and a screen was lowered. An image of the Braid headquarters flashed up, followed by shots of employees, from white-coated scientists developing new products in the laboratory, to sales presentations and scenes from a hospital where a concerned doctor stood by a patient undergoing chemotherapy treatment. The music crescendoed, then faded. The crowd was mesmerised and silence reigned in the auditorium. The lights came up and Kelton appeared back on the platform.

'For me, that song says it all,' he said soberly. 'Each one of us here is on a mission.' He paused and punched the air with his fist, and shouted, 'So let's go for it! Make today and every day *your* moment in time. Thank you all for attending.' To thunderous applause, he strutted off with a self-satisfied grin.

*

Whatever his personal failings, he achieved results in the marketplace. Within six months, the sales figures at Braid had risen significantly. On the social scene, too, Kelton was causing quite a ripple. He willingly accepted the many invitations he received to charity galas and benefits. His photograph regularly adorned the pages of glossy local magazines, always in the company of prominent North Shore socialites.

Often pictured amongst his smiling admirers was twice-divorced Judy Perlman. To be brutally honest, Kelton would not normally have given her a second glance. Her looks were a turn-off, as was her neighing laugh ... but she was heir to a string of grocery stores. An invitation to the Perlman summer residence was not to be sneezed at! Pulling up outside her spread on the shores of Lake Geneva, Wisconsin, he gave a low whistle. This was the kind of property only old money could buy, made cottages at the Lake of the Ozarks look silly. It was almost a castle, with its stone walls, turrets, slate roof and huge garden that sloped down to the water.

'Kelton, darling, you made it at last! It's wonderful to have you here. Come inside, my friends are absolutely *dying* to meet you.'

It occurred to him that he should have brought a gift. But what do you give the girl who has everything? He would find some other way to make it up to her.

'It's good to see you again,' he replied, kissing Judy's cheek. 'Nice house!'

She laughed and said, 'It's fun. My grandfather built it, way back when. Do come in.'

The inside was like a museum: the massive wood-panelled entrance hall had a mosaic floor. At its centre sat an antique mahogany table with a large flower arrangement, its perfume blending with the smell of furniture polish.

The afternoon passed pleasantly. They sailed on the lake, and at 5 pm everyone retired to freshen up for dinner. Kelton stood singing to himself as he showered, oblivious to the figure that had crept into his bathroom. Judy dropped her robe to the floor, opened the glass door of the shower cubicle, and joined him in the thick cloud of steam. He gave a momentary start then laughed and grabbed her round the waist, drawing her close. Piercing jets of hot water rained down as she leaned against the tiled wall, leg raised to rub her foot on the back of his thigh. With her hands clamped tightly on his buttocks, their bodies began to move together. When it was over she left as abruptly as she'd appeared.

Never had Kelton been so taken by surprise by any woman. Those long nails of hers had actually drawn blood, but he loved it. As he took his seat opposite her at the table an hour later, he had to grant that looks could be deceiving. She was what he'd been looking for all his life. Judy was his kind of girl!

*

Disillusionment came sooner than anticipated. The creativity of Judy's cook failed to match the grand surroundings. Dinner was a simple entree of pot roast and vegetables, followed by a dessert of apple pie à la mode.

Over coffee and liqueurs, the hostess produced a clipboard and pen. 'Now, my dears, I'm afraid it's that time of year once more,' she said, suddenly businesslike.

A guy next to Kelton groaned aloud. 'Hell, Judy, don't spoil the party!'

She flashed a brief, coquettish smile at him before her expression changed. 'The last twelve months incurred quite a number of unforeseen expenditures. Major plumbing work and a few structural improvements were necessary, so we must all dig deep.' Expectantly she looked at her guests.

'Ted, why don't you set the ball rolling?' said Judy.

Ted sucked air for a couple of seconds. 'Put me down for fifteen.'

The number was entered on Judy's chart. 'Mia, how about you? I see you did nine last year. Could you manage a *teeny bit more* this time?'

Mia smiled ruefully. 'Can't do it. I'm already heavily committed to four other projects. Nine's my limit.'

Judy barely concealed her irritation. 'If you say so,' she snapped, then suddenly she was all sweetness. 'Les, darling, I know you won't let me down.

'For you, angel, I would give the world. Go on, put me down for eighteen grand.' Leaning over the back of his chair, Judy planted a kiss on his cheek and whispered in his ear. With a giggle, she returned on tiptoe to her place while Les guffawed and called after her, 'I'm shocked! You're a *naughty girl*, Judy Perlman – you deserve a spanking!'

'Promises, promises ...' she replied archly before turning her attention to Kelton. 'Darling. That leaves only you. You're new to Chicago, and I'd hate you to feel I was taking advantage, but could you perhaps do five? Just for me?'

All eyes were on him. He looked bewildered. 'Gee, Judy, I must be missing something here. I'm still trying to figure out what you've all been talking about.'

She looked accusingly at the others. 'Gracious, how inexcusably rude of us all! I assumed you knew. It's for the Opera. I lead the annual fundraising. You do *like* opera, don't you?'

Kelton nodded. 'Yeah ... I like any music. Jazz, pop, classical – it's all good.'

'I knew you would, the minute I cast eyes on you,' gushed Judy. 'So what do you reckon? Would you like to come in at five?'

He was trapped, invited for the donation he'd be forced to contribute. That was the sting in the tail, but he couldn't give them all the impression that he was a cheapskate! 'Sure, in fact call it six.' One way or another, he'd devise a way of charging it to Braid.

The amount was noted. 'Thank you all so much for your support. Let's see, your donations tonight total forty-eight thousand, a respectable start to this year's campaign.' Judy stood up. 'Now let's retire to the drawing room, and we'll round off our soirée with some Mozart.'

Kelton gave a tight little smile as Judy linked her arm in his. 'Darling, are you familiar with *Don Giovanni*?'

'I don't believe so.'

'Oh, dear, and it's my absolute, all-time favourite! The music and the libretto are divine! Its message is as fresh today as when it was first performed in 1787!'

His heart sank. Who the hell wanted to hear stuff written two hundred years ago? He didn't belong with Judy and her artsy-fartsy friends.

'*Don Giovanni* has universal appeal. Men admire him, and women identify with poor Elvira, then everyone enjoys seeing the bad guy get his comeuppance,' she prattled on.

A day that began so promisingly had turned to shit. As strains of the overture to *Don Giovanni* filled the drawing room, the company sat bright-eyed, enthralled by the music, and Kelton thought of Amy. A bottle of Jack Daniels saved the evening from being an unmitigated disaster.

Chapter 32

'Nothing is so painful to the human mind as a great and sudden change.' – Mary Shelley

WHILE KELTON LEARNED TO NAVIGATE his way through Chicago high society, Carol and the three children went on a journey of a different sort. That summer they took a trip to Scotland. On a drizzly July evening, they arrived at Oldtown.

'We're here, guys,' announced Carol.

'Is *this* it?' asked Josie.

'I warned you, it's nothing special and it needs a lot of TLC.'

Robert and Will unloaded the luggage, while Carol led the way inside, glad she'd had a chance to do some basic scrubbing during her last visit. Josie looked disapprovingly around her and shivered, hugging her arms to herself.

'It's cold in here,' she said. 'Where do we turn on the heat?'

'There.' Carol pointed to the empty fireplace. 'Roll up a few papers from that stack, and use it to light the kindling from the basket. I'll put on the kettle.'

'Nobody told us we'd be camping, for goodness sake,' muttered Josie under her breath. She pushed past the others sulkily. From the front hall she peeked into the parlour, then made her way upstairs. 'This is like a bad dream. We're checking into that hotel in the village, right?' she said, returning to the kitchen.

'You wish!' replied Carol. 'This is it for the next three weeks, so you might as well settle down.'

'Excuse me? How can four people share one bathroom and two bedrooms? I don't *think so!*'

'Cool it, Jo,' warned Robert. 'This is neat.'

'Who wants to summer in a cold, godforsaken dump, when we could be playing tennis or swimming? This place sucks.'

Carol set down a pot of tea and unpacked the food they'd picked up at the store. Without warning, she grabbed Josie by the arm. 'Knock it off, will you? It's twenty hours since we left home. You're not the only one who's tired!'

Exactly as her father would have done, the girl scowled and ate in silence.

*

Things cheered up next day. Robert had risen early, lit the fire and already had a pan of bacon sizzling on the stove when Carol got down to the kitchen.

'Did you see the sun rise over the hill, Mom?' he asked, pointing out of the window. 'It's all so green, everywhere you look! I don't know how you could bear to leave it.'

'That was long ago. But I'm glad somebody likes it, at least. Your sister would be on the next plane home if she could.'

The back door opened and Will walked in.

'What have you been up to?' demanded Carol.

'Can't lie sleeping the day away with so much to see! I've been speaking to Alex Murray. Interesting guy. He was filling me in on the crops he's planted. I'm going out to the fields with him later.'

'Anybody would think you'd been brought up here, and *I* was the stranger!'

'Hardly! We're invited over to their house tonight. His wife's going to call you.'

How weird, Carol reflected, that she had not previously noticed how much her younger son resembled her Dad! Though they had never met, Will unconsciously adopted the same stance as his grandfather: tall and straight, with strong arms, and toes that pointed slightly outwards. And at Oldtown, he seemed completely at home, which seemed even weirder. They all laughed when he appeared wearing a tweed cap that was hanging in the hallway: it was Mr Cooper's best one, kept for Sundays and funerals. But what began in jest became a habit.

*

Robert had the same good looks as Kelton, and Fiona Murray blushed each time he addressed her. She was flustered by those dark eyes of his, though her smiles proved she enjoyed his attention.

'Nice folks, huh?' said Carol to no one in particular as they drove the two miles home.

'Robert sure reckons so,' piped up Josie. 'He's asked Fiona out.'

'Why don't you zip it, Jo?' he hissed. 'It's none of your business.'

'You haven't, have you?' His mother was astounded. History might be about to repeat itself.

*

Carol received a mixed reaction to her plan of redecorating the farmhouse. Never had any of them undertaken such a task.

'What's the point, if you're selling anyway? We're supposed to be on vacation!' whined Josie.

'A change is as good as a rest. The place needs freshening up, and it'll be fun for us to work on a project together.'

'Mom,' said Will one day as he and Carol painted the parlour walls, 'how would you feel if I didn't come back to St Louis for a while?'

'What about college? Your classes begin in five weeks.'

'It can wait, can't it? I'd like to take a year out, learn from Alex how to run the farm. I might never have another chance like this.'

The proposal had blindsided her, but Carol put on a brave face. 'You should think well about it. It gets pretty lonely and raw here in the winter.'

'I *have*. I've thought about nothing else since we got here.'

210

In vain she hoped that he would drop the idea of staying on alone, but his mind was made up. Of all her children, Will was the one she loved best, and now they'd be an ocean apart.

While Will had fallen in love with Scotland, Robert's affections found another outlet. Most nights after dinner, he spruced himself up to meet Fiona. Carol snoozed lightly till she heard the familiar creak on the stairs that meant he was home safely. It was nonsense, she knew, to worry about a twenty-one-year-old: during the college term, she had no inkling of the hours he kept. It seemed different with him under her roof.

On their very last night at Oldtown, Carol lay half asleep. In the distance the latch clicked on the back door and she waited for the sound of Robert's footsteps. She opened one eye to look at her watch. One o'clock. She dozed some more, then woke with a start. It was 2:30 am.

Without disturbing Josie, she went tiptoeing out of the bedroom and down the stairs. Light shone around the edges of the parlour door. Quietly she turned the handle – and gasped. In the room preserved for decades as a shrine of respectability, two figures lay naked on her mother's deep pile rug at the fireplace. One quick glimpse of them brought a hot flush rising in Carol's chest. Perspiration beaded on her neck, her face, and her scalp as she soundlessly retreated.

Irrational shock at her son's behaviour mixed with her guilt at violating his privacy. Yet if anyone's privacy had been violated, it was hers! She felt like a dirty Peeping Tom in her own house, almost wished she'd never brought her family there. And the Murray girl had seemed so shy at first! At the open bedroom window, Carol stood taking in the cool night air and dabbed at her face and neck with a tissue. *Breathe and relax,* she told herself, *just breathe and relax.* She would erase the image of Robert and Fiona *in flagrante*. Hell, it was almost funny in a way! By 4 am, she had unwound sufficiently to nod off.

*

It was extraordinarily painful for Carol to leave Will behind. As she drove off with Josie and Robert for the airport, her last glimpse of him in the rear-view mirror was uncannily reminiscent of her father as a young man. Holding the tweed cap aloft, Will stood waving at the road end till the car was out of sight.

The long flight from Gatwick to St Louis allowed her time to digest recent events. In a sense the vacation had been a journey into the past: they'd been taken back to basics, to live in a context alien to any they'd previously experienced together. Though not entirely painless, the process let them get to know each other better. More important, their self-knowledge had increased. Certainly Will appeared to have discovered his niche, and Carol told herself that she should be happy for him. There was no hanging on to children; self-sufficiency was the result of good parenting.

When the plane circled Lambert St Louis airport in preparation for landing, she caught a view of the Arch, shimmering in the summer heat. It had been wonderful to see Aberdeenshire again, but she had no desire to be there permanently. Her future lay in America. This was her home now.

Chapter 33

*'A clever, ugly man every now and then is successful with the
ladies, but a handsome fool is irresistible.'*
– William Makepeace Thackeray

TRANQUILLITY REIGNED IN AMY'S St Louis home. The
months after Kelton's departure had been an adjustment
to life completely on her own, yet in an odd way she
missed him. In the dentist's waiting room one day, she sat idly
flipping through the pages of a magazine, and noticed the
headline:

Annual Charity Auction:
Meet Chicago's Most Eligible Bachelors!

Right before her eyes was a picture of Kelton in a tuxedo,
surrounded by other captains of industry. Each held up a
champagne flute to toast the bevy of rich, glamorous women who
stood with their cheque-books at the ready. A date with the man
of their choice was the prize for the highest bidder among them.

'Mrs Bergmann?' said a voice. 'How are you today?'

Amy jumped, hastily replaced the magazine on the rack, and
followed the hygienist through to the treatment room.

*

Business was booming at Braid Pharma. Any doubts about its new
leadership were quashed as the discovery effort for new, safer,
more effective chemotherapy drugs progressed by leaps and
bounds. Sales figures for existing drugs rocketed. *The Wall Street
Journal* hailed Dr Kelton MacLeod as having the Midas touch.

For all that, something was missing. The CEO position he
had coveted was a double-edged sword. Judy Perlman had left

him wary of society women and he was no longer at liberty to pick up any female that took his fancy. On the few occasions he had ventured out, he was conscious of being observed and already he had received unwelcome attention in the gossip columns. Isolation was a penalty of high office.

Lonely and half-drunk one Saturday evening, Kelton dialled a St Louis number.

'Hey, Sexy,' he said when Amy answered. 'How're you doing?'

Hearing his voice only days after seeing his picture at the dentist's came as a surprise.

'I'm okay,' she replied guardedly. 'You?'

'Yup, everything's going great here.'

'So, how does it feel to be one of Chicago's most eligible bachelors?'

He laughed aloud. It was comforting to hear that familiar voice, to be free to act naturally without worrying about the impression he was making!

'That load of crap? It's a publicity stunt, but it's fun, and I guess it's for a good cause. How come you heard about that, anyway?'

She chuckled. 'That would be telling.'

'Anyway, I wanted to say hi, and ask how things are in St Louis.'

'St Louis is the same as ever. Hot and humid, the dog days of summer. You know how it goes.' *If things are so damned great in Chicago, why is he calling on a Saturday night?*

'Oh yeah, I remember.' Then, as if the thought had just occurred to him, he said, 'Hey, why don't you come up next weekend? We could take a boat trip out on the lake, get the wind in your hair.'

She paused. 'I'd have to check my calendar. Listen, sugar, I've got to go, I'm behind schedule as it is. Let's talk again real soon, right?'

'Fine, I'll give you my number ...'

He got no further before the line went dead. Amy plumped her sofa cushions, kicked off her sandals and put her feet up. Reaching for the remote, she turned on the television in time for the opening credits of that week's episode of L.A. Law.

*

He called next day, and she sounded genuinely enthusiastic about the visit. 'Give me your office and your home numbers, in case I need them,' said Amy.

He reeled them off, and she repeated them back, to make sure.

'I'll book your flights, and TWA will FedEx the tickets directly to you.'

'Sounds super! I can't wait to see your new apartment.'

'You'll like it, babe. The view over the lake is stupendous!'

Big deal, she thought.

'I'll meet you at O'Hare, unless I'm kept late at the office, in which case a limo driver will be waiting for you at the gate, to bring you to Braid.'

'Aces! See you Friday.'

'It's been too long since we had fun together.' He hung up and smiled. The thought of having her around put a certain spring in his step.

*

Kelton had come up with a new wheeze. It would require someone he could trust implicitly, who could hold down a position of responsibility, and who was hungry enough to risk everything for the huge rewards it might bring.

At the first ring, Lenny Schwartz lifted his phone.

A woman's voice said, 'Dr MacLeod of Braid Pharma is on the line for you. Please hold.'

Lenny sat up straighter in his chair, and took a mouthful of lukewarm coffee from the mug on his desk.

'Hey, Lenny,' said Kelton. 'How're ya doin', man?'

215

'Mac! I'm good. And from what I hear, you got things moving fast at Braid!'

'Yeah, we're on a roll. Listen, would you be interested in a visit? I might have something here to offer you.'

'Really?' replied Lenny calmly. 'What's cookin'?'

'Why don't you come up to Chicago – say on the nineteenth? We'll talk. You can have a look around, get a feel for what we're doing here.'

'Sounds great. Yeah, I'm looking at my calendar and the nineteenth would be okay.' *As would just about any other day!*

'We'll catch up then,' said Kelton. 'Say hi to Tiffany for me.'

'Will do, Mac. Thanks for the call.'

Lenny put down the receiver, made a fist, and laughed to himself. He deserved a break, a chance to escape from this job where he'd no real work to do, and all day to do it. Whatever MacLeod offered, it would be better than spending the rest of his career as an X-grader.

*

Friday: the day Amy was due to fly up to Chicago.

Kelton rose early, whistling to himself as he dressed. At the office he was irritated to discover that a 4 pm meeting had been scheduled, making it impossible for him to be at the airport for Amy's arrival. Well, maybe it was for the best. The limo driver could drop her off at Braid Pharma. His corner office suite would impress her no end!

A bottle of champagne was chilling in the personal fridge by his desk, a nice touch to celebrate their reunion. Would they perhaps play around a little on his sofa by the window? The idea brought a smile to his lips as he buzzed his secretary. Instantly she appeared in his office doorway.

'Susan, call my regular limo driver, would you? Tell him to pick up two dozen red roses on his way to the airport. And check that he spells "Bergmann" correctly on the card.'

Amy was to be given the star treatment.

Three hundred and fifty miles south of Chicago, she was on the tennis court, determinedly working out before the temperature reached the nineties. At 11 am, she emerged from the club locker room, freshly showered, and headed for the beauty shop to have her hair and nails done. After lunch with her sister, she drove home and put her feet up.

*

The arrivals screen at O'Hare showed the plane was on time. Hank made his way early to the barrier, to bag a prominent position right where he'd be easily spotted by anyone coming off the St Louis flight. It was some mighty big shot he'd been sent to meet, he reckoned, from the fuss made about these damned flowers! At least the MacLeod guy was a good tipper. For a few dollars, Hank could forgive a lot.

What he could not forgive was waiting till every last passenger had left the plane, when there was not a single Bergmann among them. For a full hour he'd stood waiting, like a chump. The airline representative refused to divulge information about the passenger list. From a public phone box, he dialled MacLeod's office number, only to hear a recorded message that Braid's headquarters were now closed. Hank slammed down the receiver. Almost half a day he'd squandered on this trip, and nothing to show for it! MacLeod would pay sweetly for this.

*

Like a caged tiger, Kelton paced to and fro in his office. The traffic was always bad during Friday rush-hour, but this was ridiculous! If Amy had boarded, then take-off was delayed, she'd have had no way of contacting him. On his secretary's desk he found a customer service number for the airline: he was startled to learn her flight had been on time. Next he rummaged around for Hank's card.

'Executive Limo, Hank here.'

'Hank? This is Dr MacLeod. What the hell's going on? You were supposed to pick up Ms Bergmann off the St Louis plane!'

217

'Yeah, and she was a no-show! I waited forever. I tried calling your office, got kicked onto the answering service. Same thing happened with your home number. So why don't *you* tell *me* what's goin' on?'

Damn! He'd forgotten that the switchboard did not transfer incoming calls outside business hours. 'Hold it. Are you certain you were in the right terminal?'

'Don't insult me. I know my job.' Hank's hackles were rising.

'Whatever. Bill me for your costs – I'll take care of things. You won't be left short.'

'Sure thing, Dr MacLeod. Enjoy the weekend!'

Something had happened to Amy on her way to Lambert airport: that had to be the explanation. Kelton dialled her home number. When her answering machine kicked in, he said, 'Are you okay, babe? Call me at the apartment as soon as you can. I'm going nuts, worrying about you.'

He gathered up his briefcase and headed to the underground parking. On the way home, he picked up a burger at a McDonald's drive-thru, then wolfed it down in his spotless, empty kitchen. A tiny, flashing red light caught his eye. Hell, why hadn't he checked his home voice mail earlier? He pressed the play button.

'Hi,' said Amy's voice, 'it's me. Since we last saw each other, I've thought about your parting shot. You said I looked older, and I'm also wiser. It took a while, but I finally got over you, Kelton! So have a good life. Love ya!'

The colour drained from his face. She had called at lunchtime! She'd been playing him along, had never intended coming. He'd been well and truly dissed! Pursing lips in rage, he yanked the answering machine loose from its connections and hurled it with all his strength across the kitchen. It grazed an unopened wine bottle, which also crashed to the floor.

An angry soup of sixty-dollar Burgundy with green glass smithereens spread slowly across the pristine white tiles.

Chapter 34

'A journey of a thousand miles begins with a single step.'
– Confucius

IT HAD BEEN A ROCKY FEW MONTHS for Lenny and Tiffany. A lot had changed since the wedding. He lay gazing at her as she slept, her dark roots showing against the long blonde tresses that straggled across the pillow.

It felt like years since she'd played the glamorous trophy wife, living proof that he was still viable, capable of attracting a girl less than half his age. Tiffany had sparkled during their early, dizzying whirl of dinner parties and company-paid travel. That was life in the fast lane. Then the awful day dawned when he ceased to be important. Suddenly they were friendless, and had to endure whole weekends alone together. A table for two at their favourite restaurant bored her. Where previously she'd hung on his every word, believing she'd hooked a winner, now she treated him with contempt. He was a loser. A nobody. Maybe today's trip would change all that.

Grabbing the alarm clock before it buzzed at five, Lenny rose and ate a quick breakfast. Back upstairs he tiptoed silently into the bathroom. He cleaned his teeth twice, flossed and rinsed with peroxide. Carefully he applied a dab of hair colour to his sideburns and eyebrows, which had to be left for exactly five minutes: long enough to trim and file his fingernails. He stepped into the shower. Quietly he dressed, selecting with care a brand new shirt and a designer silk tie. He had to look good for this interview! With his suit jacket over his arm, and holding his dress loafers in his other hand, he leaned over the bed to place a kiss on his wife's cheek.

'See you about seven tonight, sugar,' he whispered. 'Have a nice day.'

Tiffany barely opened one eye to grunt a response. She snuggled down under the comforter, and was snoring by the time Lenny was downstairs.

His plane took off at 8:15 am. By ten he was in a taxi on Chicago's I-294, adrenalin pumping. Unless he could secure a big new job, *become* somebody again, his marriage would be over, he'd be finished. His entire future hinged on this meeting with Big Mac.

*

For fifteen minutes, he was left to admire the artwork in the CEO's outer suite until he was shown into Kelton's inner sanctum.

'Lenny! How are you?' They shook hands.

'Great. It's good to see you again, Mac. Pretty impressive joint you got here!'

'Nah,' said Kelton modestly. 'But it will be by the time I'm done, I hope. It's still early days. Let me show you round, and we'll talk business over lunch.'

*

'We're on track to go public in just over six months,' Kelton said as he ate. 'That doesn't leave much of a margin for you to get up to speed.'

Lenny took a deep breath. 'Not a problem. If we agree a deal, I could be ready to start in four weeks.'

'What about Tiffany? Would she be up for living in Chicago?'

'Sure,' Lenny replied without hesitation. But under Kelton's steady gaze, he averted his eyes.

MacLeod knew him too well!

Fidgeting with his napkin, Lenny smiled sheepishly. 'To be candid, it's anybody's guess how Tiffany's going to take it. A change might bring back a bit of the old excitement. But she might tell me to go to hell, she wants to stay put. Either way, I'm glad to come on board if you want me.'

Kelton looked thoughtful. This was not what he wanted to hear. Lenny could be an asset to Braid, but without Tiffany he could become a liability, too distracted to perform well at work if he became embroiled in a separation or divorce.

'Here's what I suggest. You go home tonight, tell her you've had a job offer. Everything goes on hold till the two of you make a trip up to Chicago. You'll stay at the Palmer House or The Drake – your choice. All expenses paid. Show her the sights, see a couple of shows and look at a few homes. Do whatever is necessary. If she doesn't bite, that's okay. No hard feelings.

'Thanks, Mac. I want you to know I appreciate this.'

Kelton interrupted, 'Don't thank me. I'll be upfront with you: someone carrying a load of baggage can't give one hundred percent to the job. There's no deal if this move would bust up your marriage. It would be bad for you *and* for me.'

Lenny gulped. Somehow he'd have to talk Tiffany round.

'Call my private number in a day or two. Keep me posted.' Kelton stood up. The interview was over.

'Sure thing, Mac.'

They parted outside the restaurant.

With an hour to kill at O'Hare, Lenny browsed the stores, stopping at a glass display case of gold jewellery to buy a trinket. It would require a lot more than that to sweeten Tiffany up, but it would be a start. Now his ass was really on the line.

*

Carol felt she'd lost both her boys during the summer. She had been forced to acknowledge that her elder son was a grown man after discovering him and Fiona in the parlour at Oldtown. Robert had returned to his studies, at the University of Missouri, Columbia, and Will's eagerness for a year alone on the farm was proof of his self-sufficiency. Only Josie remained with her.

One Thursday, she popped into the agency to drop off the manuscript she'd been working on. As she left, the owner, Mike, came out of his office.

'Carol!' he called, gruffly, 'I'd like to see you for a minute.'

'Sure.' She took a seat at his desk.

'I'm in a bit of a dilemma.'

Was she about to be canned? 'Have I done something wrong?'

'No, no, far from it. We're losing one of our best full-timers, and I wondered if you could fill the gap till we find a replacement. Ideally, I'd like if you could manage four days a week in the office … just to tide us over.'

Carol hesitated. Four days was a lot. How would she fit in her exercise routine, in addition to taking care of her house and family? Though with only herself and Josie at home, she had no reason to refuse. 'All right, I'll do it for a month or two.'

For the first time ever, she saw Mike smile. 'Thank you. You've no idea what a weight you've taken off my mind.'

'You must be nuts!' said Josie that night.

'Why?'

'Mom! Why would you sit in a stuffy office when there's loads of fun stuff you could do? It's not as if you need the money.'

'It's not about money.'

'What about the gym, going out for lunch, shopping and seeing movies?'

'There's more to life than that,' said Carol with a smile. A high-school junior would never understand her yearning for some intellectual challenge, nor the importance of building a framework for the solitary years that might lie ahead.

But sticking to the office schedule was vastly different from handling stuff at home. Seven hours at a desk each day curtailed her liberty; she learned to savour the sweetness of weekends. Once Josie got her driver's license and her own set of wheels, Carol would be off the hook for the school run, and would join the payroll as a full-timer.

*

'Happy Thanksgiving, honey!'

'Hi, Mom! Happy Thanksgiving!' replied Will. 'How're you guys doing?'

'We're all fine. We've been thinking about you. Is everything okay?'

'Yeah, but it feels funny not to be at home today. No turkey or pumpkin pie here in Scotland, just the same old, same old ...'

Carol heard a tinge of disappointment in his voice. 'So, what are your plans for the weekend?'

'We're going into Aberdeen, see a movie, grab a bite to eat.'

'*We*? Who's *we*?'

Will laughed. 'I knew you'd ask. Me and Fiona.'

'Fiona Murray?' said Carol in surprise. 'Well, say hi to her for me. I'll pass you over to Josie and Robert. Take care, now. Love you.'

Later she grabbed the chance of talking to Robert alone. 'Is Will actually *dating* Fiona, d'you think?' She tried to sound casual.

Robert looked surprised. 'I dunno. Could be.'

'But, well, I thought she ... didn't you say you were going to stay in touch with her?'

She should keep quiet, but how could she forget what she'd seen?

'Mom, come on, we were together for three weeks. Sure, I liked Fiona, but if Will wants to see her, I'm cool with that. No worries.'

'Oh. Right.' Like her parents before her, she found the relationships of her offspring incomprehensible.

*

Tiffany and Lenny spent a spectacular few days in Chicago, all at Braid's expense. She squeezed his arm as they sauntered round Bloomingdales on the Magnificent Mile.

'There's another one, see? That woman's carrying the Louis Vuitton bag I told you about.'

Discreetly he looked at where she pointed. 'And?'

Tiffany smiled, and gave a flirtatious little shrug. 'Well, if you needed help deciding what to get me for Christmas ...'

He bit the bullet. 'Why wait? Tell me you're willing to move here, and we'll buy it today, to celebrate.'

She turned around, took his face in both hands, and planted a kiss right on his lips. 'Of course I am. Did you ever doubt it?'

He smiled and thanked his lucky stars.

*

It all went like clockwork. By the spring, Kelton had knocked Braid into good enough shape to go public. He'd delivered, and now it was time to collect the options promised when he was hired. The more value he brought to the company, the richer he would become.

Lenny's remuneration package far surpassed what he'd earned previously, but even more astounding was the number of IPO stock options he'd been granted. Now six months into his position as Director of International Business at Braid, he felt a particular debt of gratitude to Kelton for rescuing him from a downward spiral. It was great to be tight with Big Mac, to be second in command of this firm that was really making its mark! And Tiffany was like a new woman; at the company party the previous week, she'd looked radiant. Her scarlet dress had drawn admiring glances from every guy in the room. Lenny was back on top of the world. Life was wonderful.

*

Carol put the final touches to her lipstick, and became aware of Josie standing in the doorway of her bedroom. 'How was school?'

'So-so.' Josie stood closer to her mother, and peered at her hair. 'Since when did you have blonde highlights?'

'Since today. I left work early. Do you like them?'

'Yeah, they look okay, I suppose.'

'They cover my grey streaks. You're on your own tonight. I'm going out for dinner.'

224

'Well, that's a first. Who with?'

'Mike Martin.'

'Eeuww! From the office? That's gross!'

'What do you mean, it's gross? He's a perfectly nice guy.'

'I mean, he's *old*! He must be at least fifty!'

'So?'

'Where does he get the nerve to ask anyone out?' *How ridiculous for Mom to be going out on a date!*

'I'll see you later, tell you all about it.'

'That would be too much information.'

*

At the restaurant, Mike stood waiting for her.

'Hi,' he said. 'You made it.'

She smiled. They were seated at their table, menus in hand, and began speaking at the same instant. They laughed. It amused her that his entire forehead seemed to lift, taking years off his face.

'I'm sorry,' she said. 'Go ahead.'

'No, *I'm* sorry. I'm not very good at this. Out of practice, I'm afraid. This is my first date since Anne died.' He stopped, embarrassed at revealing so much.

Carol smiled. 'I'm flattered. Just so you know, you're the first man I've gone out with since my divorce. We're in the same boat.'

The waiter appeared back at the table with his notepad. 'Did you decide yet?'

'We need a few more minutes, if you don't mind,' replied Mike.

Carol smiled to herself at his dour seriousness. That was the same face he wore at the office. Dour but kind. When he ordered, it was with a quiet, pleasant authority, so different from Kelton's peremptory posturing. They ate during laid-back conversation and calm, comfortable silences while they stole secret glances at one another.

The bill came and Carol reached for her purse. 'Let's go Dutch. I'll pay half.'

Mike shook his head. 'I'm the one who invited you out, remember. Please, I'll get it. I'm an old-fashioned guy.'

'Well, if you insist. Thank you.'

They walked outside together and he saw her to her minivan.

'It was a lovely evening, Mike. Thank you, I really enjoyed it.'

'Not as much as I did. Could we do it again sometime soon?'

'I'd love to.' She leaned forward, kissed him lightly on the cheek, and got into the driver's seat.

'See you Monday,' he said.

She nodded and waved.

He stood watching her tail lights disappear into the distance.

Chapter 35

'Life is rather like a tin of sardines – we're all of us looking for the key.' – Alan Bennett

BEADS OF PERSPIRATION appeared on Lenny's forehead. 'Hell, Mac, you're winding me up, right?'

'Wrong. I'm serious. That's the plan. That's what I want.'

'No. Hold on. Think about it … we can't ask a supplier to do that! It's unethical.'

Kelton laughed aloud. 'Excuse me? *What* did you say?' He sat with his head back, to look across his desk from beneath lowered eyelids.

Lenny was afraid. He shifted uncomfortably. 'You heard me. It's unethical.'

'*Unethical my ass*! Listen to me. The poor bastards who lap up our junk, they're on the outs anyway. We're their last hope. They're all fuckin' terminal, in such bad shape that they're better off going sooner than later!'

'If that's your opinion, why don't *you* do the dirty on them, and set this up yourself?'

Kelton thumped the table and glared. '*Because it's your job!* You're supposed to be my goddamned Director of International Business! Or don't you have the balls for it?'

'This isn't what I expected, when you hired me.' Lenny gulped.

'Nor did you expect the options I've put your way. But you didn't object then.'

There was no answer to that. 'You really reckon Xiang Yang Chemical will play along?'

Kelton shrugged. 'We're the client, they're our supplier. Where is the difficulty?' His expression softened. 'Come on, wise up, Lenny. It's simple math. We want double the volume, half the strength, that's all. You negotiate this deal, our profit and the stock price shoot up. You and me, we'll become *wealthy*, not just rich!'

'Maybe.'

'Don't bellyache. Think positively. You're in charge of International, and you can make this happen. You're my main man, buddy. I'm placing my faith in you.'

'Even if Xiang Yang goes along with it, it's risky. You get wind of a low reading, you're supposed to inform the FDA immediately, you know that.'

'So make sure Xiang Yang provides appropriate numbers. It's part of the deal.'

'I don't like it. It's like mugging a blind guy, pulling a fast one on folks who are on their last legs.'

'How? We're still producing CK58, just at half strength. Want me to tell you what difference it'll make to some ordinary sap drawing his last breaths?'

'Tell me.'

'He'll get two weeks less on this planet, that's all. You'd be doing him a favour! Whine all you like, Lenny, but it's a win-win situation. Nobody gets hurt if we can carry this off. Okay, the stock might tank if it ever comes to light, but by then we'll be the hell out of Braid.' Holding his hand horizontally, Kelton flicked his fingers up and down, like waves on the ocean. 'We'll be cruising the Caribbean on our private yachts.'

Lenny smiled. A fleeting image of turquoise waters and Tiffany sunbathing in a skimpy bikini flashed before his eyes. Hell, if he backed out now, he'd be kicking himself when Mac walked away with millions! He was in this far, with no alternative but to go along and hope for the best.

*

It wasn't meant to be like this! When Cinderella married Prince Charming, it wasn't to be dumped on her butt in a strange city with no one to talk to! The novelty of Chicago was wearing thin. Lenny's paperwork claimed most of his waking hours, then he'd go jetting off to China or India again, leaving Tiffany high and dry. She lay in front of the television, staring glassy-eyed at one daytime soap opera after another. Often it seemed scarcely worth getting showered and dressed. She was trapped, could end up passing the rest of her life as a nameless, faceless nobody and Lenny wouldn't even notice!

During his travels, her hobby was combing the stores at the mall for new clothes and shoes. Her closet was crammed with ranks of unworn things, but a girl needed *some* fun! It was all right for him. He'd no idea how it felt to live without friends, with only your hairdresser, your manicurist, and your favourite assistant at the Clarins beauty counter to give you a smile. Being greeted with *'Hi, Mrs Schwartz! How are you today?'* kidded her that she mattered.

She arrived home around five one afternoon, her hair and nails freshly done and her car trunk filled with packages. Outside the apartment Tiffany rummaged for her house keys: again and again she fumbled unseeingly through the junk at the bottom of her purse, without success. She must have dropped the keys in the car! Cursing under her breath, she dumped her bags in front of her door. They'd been heavy to lug up in the elevator, without trailing them back downstairs. She trudged back along the corridor. But as she'd feared, her search in the underground parking garage proved fruitless.

Upstairs, she looked around helplessly. The hallway was empty as usual. This *would* happen when Lenny was ten thousand miles away! A locksmith was what she needed, but for that she had to find a phone. Well, she was damned if she'd go begging for help at the door of some asshole neighbour she'd never met! Humble wasn't her style.

Of course, she could get into her car and drive, leave this shitty, lonely existence behind. She could beat a retreat to St Louis where she had friends and family. With Lenny so caught up in the new job, he scarcely paid attention to her anyway, whether he was home or not. But if she left him, then what? Then nothing. She'd be right back on her ass where she started, which was not a nice prospect.

She stood staring at the deadbolt. If she thought hard enough, a solution would come to her. In a wonderful, blinding flash of inspiration, she recalled Lenny's mention of a spare house key in his office desk. What an idiot she was, to forget! Relief washed over her as she gathered up her parcels and headed to the elevator. All she'd to do was go to his office, pick up the key and things would return to normal. Come to think of it, normal wasn't all that bad!

*

The evening security guard looked up in surprise from his *Sun Times* at the sound of Tiffany's heels on the marble floor of the foyer at Braid Pharma.

'Can I help you, ma'am?'

Hi, I need to get into my husband's office. I've locked myself out of my house, and there's a spare key in his desk.'

'What's your husband's name?'

'Schwartz, Lenny Schwartz. Director for International Business? He's abroad, on a company trip to China.'

With a shrug, he spoke quietly into his walkie-talkie, then said, 'I need some ID.'

'What are you running here, Fort Knox?' Impatiently Tiffany held out her driver's licence. A minimum-wage moron had no right to keep her hanging! A pen was thrust at her.

'Just doin' the job I'm paid for, ma'am. Please sign here. You need to wear this security pass.' *Who the hell does she think she is, this up-talking bimbo?* 'Walter here will take you to Mr Schwartz's office,' he said, as a second uniform appeared.

The building was deserted. In Lenny's office, Tiffany went straight to his desk, and tugged at the top drawer. Like all the others, it was locked.

'Can you open this for me?' she demanded.

Walter folded his arms. 'Unh, unh. No way. You wanna get me fired, lady?'

Shit! She was within inches of her key, would have found a way to break the lock on the damned drawer if this jerk hadn't stood sneering, watching her every move! Again she tugged as hard as she could, but it refused to budge. Snatching up a copy of the Yellow Pages, she sat herself down on Lenny's sofa to scan the list of locksmiths, when she heard a familiar voice in the outer office.

'Is there a problem?'

Walter jerked his thumb back in Tiffany's direction. 'Guy's wife lost her house key.'

Kelton barged past him. 'Tiffany? I didn't expect to see you here! I thought I was last to leave.' He smiled and kissed her on the cheek.

'Oh, Kelton! You've no idea how glad I am to see you! I locked myself out of the house and now I can't get into the drawer for Lenny's spare key.' She grimaced, showing off her line of even white teeth, then flicked her bangs off her eyebrows.

'This is ridiculous!' Kelton snapped at Walter, 'Go down to the lobby, and tell Dan to give you the blanks that are hanging at the top left corner of the board.'

'Right away, Dr MacLeod.'

Kelton shook his head. 'I'm sorry about this. These guys, you know, they're not the sharpest crayons in the box.'

'No, it's not your fault! I'm so grateful you came along and made everything better,' she simpered. 'It's difficult, sometimes, in a strange city ...'

Cheerily jangling a bunch of pass keys Walter reappeared, suddenly a model of efficiency and helpfulness. Within minutes,

Tiffany had her house key, and the desk drawer was securely locked again.

'How can I ever thank you?' she breathed as Kelton escorted her to her car.

'It was nothing. Happy to help. You know, I drive right by your block on my way home. D'you want me to stop and make sure that house key actually works?'

'Oh, that's so sweet!'

'It's my pleasure. You lead, I'll follow you.'

*

Tiffany unlocked her apartment door. 'Home and dry!'

'You're all set, then.' Kelton stepped back, and turned as if to leave.

'Wait! You should come in for a drink, or something.'

'Thanks, but you don't have to do that.'

'Really, it would be no trouble.'

He smiled and looked at his watch. 'In fact, I was just going to a little Italian place for a bite to eat. It's been a long day. Why don't you join me?'

Throwing her department store bags carelessly down on the polished hardwood floor, Tiffany struggled to contain her exhilaration. She bit prettily at her lower lip.

Kelton backed away. 'Hey, I'm sorry. I'd no business putting you on the spot like that, with Lenny away. I thought ... well, I guess I didn't think.' He gave a frowning smile and looked at her intently.

She caught his arm and giggled. 'Oh, no! I'd love to. It was a surprise, that's all!'

'You're sure Lenny wouldn't mind?'

'Absolutely,' she replied with certainty.

Lenny could go to hell.

Chapter 36

'With rebellion, awareness is born.' – Albert Camus

THE MUSIC TRANSFORMED the girl's room into a no-go zone, a fortress protected by a raucous barrage of sound. Now sixteen, Josie was a big fan of grunge rock, a passion heightened by her mother's distaste for the genre.

'Mike's car's in the driveway!' called Carol from the front hall. 'Let's go!' Receiving no reply, she went upstairs. 'Turn that thing down!' she bawled, opening the bedroom door.

Sitting cross-legged on top of her bed, Josie feigned surprise. She reached over to her stereo and muted the deafening racket. 'What's up?'

'You were supposed to be ready. Mike's waiting for us!'

'I changed my mind. You two go by yourselves. I want to finish my term paper.'

'Why didn't you say so earlier?' Carol said. 'Come on, doll, you'll enjoy the show. Mike got really good seats, then we're going for dinner.'

'He's your friend, Mom. Leave me out of it.'

'Come on, don't embarrass me like this.'

'I told you, I'm not going, okay?' Josie turned up the volume once more, and stared straight ahead. A CD by Pearl Jam blasted out *Why Go?*:

> *She scratches a letter into a wall made of stone,*
> *Maybe someday another child won't feel as alone as*
> *she does.*
> *It's been two years, and counting, since they put her in*
> *this place.*

Carol was torn between confronting the alien creature her daughter had become, and salvaging what was left of her birthday. She turned and closed the door. It would have to wait till tomorrow.

*

'We need to talk about what you did last night to Mike. It was very rude.'

'Huh? I chose to get on with my homework.'

'You accepted his invitation. When you say you'll do a thing, you should *do* it.'

Josie tried to brush her off. 'Didn't feel like it, okay?'

'That's not an answer.'

'*It's my answer*. Who do you think you are, anyway?'

'Excuse me?' said Carol. 'What do you mean by that?'

'Nothing.'

'I want to hear what's eating you. You're not leaving until you tell me.'

The girl stared sullenly at the wall. Suddenly she burst out, 'You're such a phony! If you'd shown half the concern for Dad's feelings that you do for Mike's, he might have stayed with us!'

Carol blanched. 'You never really knew your father.'

'Oh, didn't I?' retorted Josie, years of resentment rising inside her. 'Well, maybe I would if you'd treated him better. You kicked him out, and now I'm expected to accept Mike instead. But why should we all dance to your tune?'

'I can't believe you're saying this! I didn't kick your Dad out, as you put it. And nobody's trying to take his place!'

'Duh! Even if he wanted to, he could never come back, not with *your boyfriend* always hanging around.'

'Your Dad and I will never be together again. You must accept that.'

'And life goes on, huh? It doesn't matter to you that I still miss him every single day.'

'But the marriage was no good for either of us ...'

The girl interrupted, '*So what?* It maybe sucked, but you took him for better or worse, didn't you? You weren't supposed to turn him against his own kids! Have you any idea how it feels to be ignored by the person who spawned you?'

Carol took a deep breath. 'Actually, yes. I know how much that hurts, and I'm sorry you're being put through it too. But I *did not* turn him against you and the boys. Don't blame me for his actions. I'm not responsible for what he does.'

She would not defend herself further. Some things were best left unsaid.

'No, you're never to blame for anything, are you?' snorted Josie.

'Know what, I've had it up to here with you! Anything bad that happens, you take it out on me, and I'm sick of it!' Carol's voice rose. 'I've taken too much of your guff already! I only did what seemed right, and it hasn't always been easy. You will apologise to Mike.'

The girl sat motionless apart from the quivering of her mouth. Shakily she said, 'Okay. Tell him I'm sorry about last night.'

'Not good enough. Do it yourself. Now.'

For what seemed a long time, they stared, unblinking, at each other, till Josie dropped her eyes. With an exaggerated sigh, she reached for the phone.

Carol had made a breakthrough of sorts.

*

'This is the most fun I've had in ages!' said Tiffany.

Kelton smiled. 'So what do you think of it so far?'

She looked around the restaurant. 'Nice. I like it.'

'No, I meant how do you like living in Chicago? You starting to feel at home here?'

'Kind of.'

'Takes a while, huh? I've been there, done that, and it's not easy,' he said gently, gazing at her with eyes that felt her pain.

She was tempted to break down, to tell him how miserably lonely she often was, but she knew better. Sipping at her wine, Tiffany sized him up over the rim of her glass. Men like Lenny and Kelton were turned off by neediness. Why else had both ditched their wives and families? Fun was what they were after, and it was all she had to offer. She'd been naïve in believing Lenny was a catch. Buyer's remorse had set in. She put down her drink, and impulsively reached across the table to touch Kelton's arm.

'Do you believe in fate?'

'How do you mean?'

'Like tonight: perhaps it was meant to be. How weird is it that I got locked out just when my husband's on the other side of the world? I mean, what were the chances – let alone that you'd still be in the office, and come to my rescue like you did? It's uncanny.'

He interlaced his fingers with hers, examining her pearly pink, almond-shaped nails. 'You really have beautiful hands. Has old Lenny any idea how lucky he is to be married to a girl like you?'

'How many times did you use that line?' she laughed, unashamedly fluttering her eyelashes.

The steady gaze of Kelton's dark eyes was hypnotic, his compliments intoxicating. Already Tiffany looked forward to their first kiss, wondered how those lips, those teeth and that tongue would feel against hers.

Chapter 37

'Absence of evidence is not evidence of absence.' – Carl Sagan

'MISSION ACCOMPLISHED.' Lenny dumped a pile of papers on the desk.

'*All right!*' Kelton walked over to close his office door, then sat down again. 'You'd no problem making them understand exactly what we need?'

'Met some pushback at first,' smirked Lenny. 'Usual Chinese bullshit ... they acted offended, like I was trying to squeeze more out of them for the old price. Claimed the formulation of CK58 couldn't be changed without screwing up the numbers. When I offered the monthly "premium" you and I talked about, it mysteriously became doable. They've agreed to dilute it and adjust the data for the FDA.'

'Good job. When does production start?'

Lenny smiled triumphantly. 'It already has. As we speak, they should be churning out the first batch of our next shipment.'

'And the label?'

'No change. Vials will look exactly the same on the outside, bio-assays will reflect same results as before. Money makes all things possible at Xiang Yang.'

Kelton leaned back in his chair, one foot up on his desk. 'Okay, so we're ready to rumble, huh? From today, all communication with Xiang Yang takes place exclusively through you. Everything in writing is strictly for your eyes only, and you assume total control over all our dealings with them. CK58 is your baby.'

'No other bastard needs to know a thing about it.'

'It might mean you've to spend more time in China.'

'Whatever,' shrugged Lenny.

'Is that a drawback?'

'Nah. A while back, it might have been, but now I think Tiffany kinda likes it, with me gone.'

You bet she does, thought Kelton. *You've no idea how much!*
'Women, they're all the same,' he said nonchalantly. 'Can't live with 'em, can't live without 'em, huh?' He grinned and showed Lenny out of the office.

*

1992

Steve Paul was a leading light in the research community at Washington University in St Louis, the kind of guy who happily devoted whole weekends to working tirelessly in his quest for a better cancer therapy. Pharmaceutical companies might occasionally do some good by throwing millions at research projects, but mostly pissed him off. Masquerading as heroes of the day, the head honchos cared only about the bottom line: claimed to be changing the arc of history with their medical advances, when really they were feathering their own nests with huge salaries and obscene bonuses! A genuine quest for knowledge was not part of the equation. That was for lowly academics like himself, who toiled unappreciated beneath the radar. The certainty that his efforts would ultimately leave the world a better place was Steve's reward.

In recent months his entire focus had been on Braid's new chemotherapy treatment. Having witnessed its consequences on experimental mice in his lab, it bugged him to see the product hailed in the press as a new 'wonder drug'. Sure, a number of cancer victims gained slightly more 'quality time' on earth following their course of CK58. But what of those unable to tolerate its side effects? These patients meant nothing to Braid, were swept aside as irrelevant losers.

To Steve, they became an obsession. There *had* to be a protocol that would increase the percentage of subjects able to

238

benefit from the treatment! For weeks, he conducted trials, treating batch after batch of cancerous mice with CK58 while juggling around dosages and timing, feverishly noting the minutest variations in vital signs and side effects. It almost drove him crazy. Then miraculously, he got it right. By doubling the approved dose for two days, withholding it completely for three days and resuming it, a higher proportion of his test group showed an upward trend in general wellbeing. Yet another trial confirmed his results, and he was jubilant. His perseverance had paid off!

Or so he believed, until a third round of experiments made absolute nonsense of his previous successes. With that batch of cancerous mice, the new protocol elicited an unexpectedly weak response, in comparison to the control group injected with saline. Something had to be wrong! Steve wrestled with the problem. A careless mistake by a technician could have fouled up the experiment. He would run the damned thing again, and this time nobody else would be allowed near it! Painstakingly meticulous though he'd been along each step of the way, the poorer results were replicated precisely. The test mice displayed little or no response. He had unfairly misjudged his staff. The fault had to lie with his latest sample of CK58.

*

They had a window table in Spiaggia, looking out towards the lake. 'You still haven't told me what we're celebrating.'

'Braid earnings have exceeded analysts' expectations. You'll see an article about it in tomorrow's paper, but you might find it kinda boring.'

'Yeah?' Slipping off her shoe, Tiffany ran her foot up the inside of his trouser leg.

Kelton grinned. 'Bring a bottle of champagne while we look at the menu, would you?' he snapped at a passing waiter.

It was 10 pm before they left the restaurant. At his apartment, he poured drinks while Tiffany went to freshen up.

'Is it tomorrow your beloved gets back from Shanghai?' he asked as she reappeared.

'Yup,' she said, looking at her watch. 'He'll have had breakfast. Could be on his way to the airport as we speak.'

Kelton held up his tumbler in a drunken toast. 'Here's to Xiang Yang Chemical. And a very special thanks to Mr Leonard Schwartz, the best henchman a guy ever had. Me and Lenny, we're better than the Lone Ranger and Tonto!'

She screwed up her face in distaste. 'Lenny's an idiot.'

Seizing her arm, he pulled her down on the sofa beside him, and shoved his face so close to hers that they were less than an inch apart. 'Are you really so dumb? Don't you realise it's your old man who pulled off my little scheme for CK58?'

'Let me go! You're *hurting* me!'

He eased his grip on her to take a gulp of his drink, then topped up his glass. When she made to speak, he silenced her with a finger to her lips.

'I'm gonna tell you a modern-day parable, and you're gonna listen real good. Remember hearing at Sunday school, how water was turned into wine?'

'Huh? You'll have to tell me. I didn't go to no Sunday school,' she huffed, examining her nails.

'Well, old Lenny, he went one better. He turned the water into dollars! Without him, we wouldn't be partying ... and don't you forget it.'

Unimpressed, Tiffany raised a hand to brush her hair off her face, and suddenly felt a wet tongue in her ear. She hated when men got drunk and slobbered over her!

'Screw Lenny,' she muttered, pulling away.

'Prefer to screw you ...' slurred Kelton, his eyes heavy.

'Not tonight you won't!' Already he had passed out. Quietly she left him to sleep it off. What should have been a nice evening had gone completely down the tubes.

*

'Braid Pharma, how may I help you?' said the receptionist.

'Hi, could you transfer me to Dee Morley in the oncology lab?'

'Sure, no problem. One moment, please.'

After several minutes on hold, a voice said, 'This is Dee.'

Steve Paul described the most recent, unexpected test results yielded by CK58.

'Doesn't sound right. All I can recommend is that you scrap the stuff you have, and we'll send a fresh supply for you to redo the trials.'

'Hmmhh. And you've had no negative feedback from any other source? Half a dozen labs are testing this drug,' Steve persisted.

'No other complaints, you're on your own. Has to be a rogue result.'

From the woman's dismissive tone, Steve knew he was wasting his valuable time. It was pointless to press it further with her. Already his mind had changed gear. There was more than one way to skin a cat!

*

Laura Donahue's attention was caught by a headline on the front page of the *Chicago Tribune*'s business section:

Braid Pharma Reports Blockbuster Results

Braid was going from strength to strength. Earnings had doubled in the last quarter, and analysts had upped the stock rating to a 'strong buy'. A forty percent leap in the value of the company was forecast. Disappointingly, the article carried no picture of the CEO. It did, however, quote Kelton, who credited his second-in-command, Lenny Schwartz, with Braid Pharma's spectacular gains.

Was he this altruistic? It seemed unlikely to Laura that this leopard could change his spots.

*

Steve Paul's new batch of CK58 results were as poor as those from the two preceding tests. But from his cabinet, he had unearthed a small quantity left over from the previous year. Using that in a side experiment, he compared the data with those of his three recent trials. To no one's surprise, only the *earlier* sample matched Braid's claims. *Let them explain that away!*

Once more he called Dee.

'Gee, that's really weird. I think you should talk with Lenny Schwartz. Let me give you his extension number.'

*

'No way,' said Lenny adamantly. 'Our product is rock solid, same as it always was. Nothing has changed.'

'No adverse effects reported? No drop in patient survival rates?'

'Not to my knowledge. Look, I don't have to prove anything to you. Our sales figures speak for themselves. Braid couldn't claim the number one spot for chemo treatment if CK58 was a dud.'

'I didn't say that,' said Steve, 'just that in the last twelve months, our tests show its efficacy has been greatly reduced. I don't understand how you can be unaware of the change. It's like there's less of the active ingredient in there. I'm including my results in a paper I plan to present next week at the ASCO conference in Denver.'

'Excuse me, Mr Paul! You should be careful about badmouthing an industry leader.'

'Is that a threat, Mr Schwartz?'

'You take it any way you like, son. I got nothing more to say to you.' Lenny hung up and immediately called Big Mac.

'Hold it,' said Kelton. 'I can't talk now. I'm in a meeting here. Meet me for a beer tomorrow night.'

Lenny banged down the receiver in frustration. He prayed it wouldn't be like before, when Freeman and Barclay got on their trail, and MacLeod didn't want to know.

242

As a precaution, he dialled the number of his broker and instructed him to perform a cashless exercise of all his vested stock options. Yes, Lenny confirmed, he was aware the market had dipped slightly but the sale had to go through today. Whatever the stocks were worth, he would take the money and run. He went through his filing cabinets, piling up stacks of papers on his sofa. By the end of the afternoon he had gathered every scrap pertaining to his dealings with Xiang Yang Chemical.

Once his secretary had left for the night, he carried the first armload of documents through to the shredder in the front office. An hour later, his task was almost done. He would leave by the back door, to avoid passing Dan or Walter at the front desk. No point in arousing suspicion. Awkwardly gripping two massive black plastic bags in each hand, Lenny staggered along the hall to the stairwell door, bumping against the walls with each step he took. Reaching his car, he heaved the heavy sacks into the rear seat.

At an office construction site a mile along the road, he pulled in and turned off his headlights. In less than two minutes he was rid of the bags and back on the road. Every last shred of evidence was gone. Details of his business with Xiang Yang lay buried in a massive, half-full dumpster. If any investigation came, nobody was going to pin anything on him this time, not if he could help it.

Chapter 38

'All my misfortunes come of having thought too well of my fellows.' – Jean-Jacques Rousseau

'YOU STUPID ASSHOLE!' hissed Kelton, once the drinks had been served the following night. 'Didn't the last thirty years teach you anything?'

Lenny sat jiggling his right leg, mad at Big Mac, and even more mad at himself. After the Devanacorp fiasco, he should have avoided MacLeod like the plague! 'So what would *you* have said to this Steve Paul guy, huh?'

'Some bastard comes along with conflicting results, you *never* go hostile! You could say our own monthly bio-assays were okay. You sure as hell don't get ratty with a half-assed techie in a college lab!'

'You don't think I should have tried to steer him away from blowing the lid off our scheme? If this prick Paul presents at the ASCO meeting, we'll get the FDA on our top. Then we're dead meat.'

'Cool it, will you? He's entitled to publish his results from commercial products. But trying to scare him off, that's plain dumb.'

'So should I set up a face-to-face with him? Is that your angle?'

Kelton shook his head. 'You know what, Lenny? I don't *have* an angle because it's your job to deal with shit like this. If I'd realised you were this spineless, I wouldn't have brought you on board.'

'I'm on my own with this one, huh?' Lenny tried to quell the rage that rose in him.

'Gotta go. Just deal with it.' Throwing down enough to cover their bill and a tip, Kelton nodded curtly and headed outside. Within seconds there was a *VRROOOOM!* as he gunned his new Corvette out of the parking lot.

*

'Regulatory affairs. Jeremy Bryant here.'

'Jeremy! How are you? I'm returning your call.' said Lenny.

'Yeah. Listen, I'd a guy from the FDA on the phone, asking about CK58. Mentioned reduced efficacy or something of the kind?'

Lenny's worst nightmare was becoming reality; this was what he had feared. 'What did you say to him?'

'I told him it's your baby, and you'd give him the lowdown. I won't tread on your toes.'

Briefly Lenny considered talking again to Kelton, but dismissed the idea. Things had been dry between them since their meeting about Steve Paul. He would do his best. And if that wasn't enough, it was just too bad.

*

The FDA inspectors were pleasant, and congratulated Lenny on the market success of his product. Then one said, 'We expected you to call us. What happened?'

Lenny looked blank. 'Why would I call you?'

'Several months ago you were informed that CK58 was underperforming, were you not?'

'I wouldn't put it that strongly. There was a query from Washington University in St Louis, but they'd screwed up the protocol. It was nothing to do with our product.'

'How would you know that?'

He fought to keep his voice steady. 'Because their sample was fine. I checked with our supplier in Shanghai, reviewed the bio-assays for the most recent batch and for the three preceding ones to make sure everything was okay at our end. Every result was in line with your requirements. No red flags.'

245

'You can show us these reports?'

'They'd have to come from China.'

'So production, packaging and testing are all done off-site. How sure are you that the CK58 tested in the bio-assay is identical to the stuff they actually ship here?'

Lenny's attempt at a laugh came out as a nervous little giggle. 'Guys! Is the Pope Polish? The Chinese lab is fully certified under GLP – good laboratory practices – same as we are.'

The younger of the two men leaned forward. 'I don't think you appreciate how serious this situation is. Your company and *you personally* are in violation of federal law. Number one, you neglected to report the Washington University result, which you are obliged to do the minute you become aware of any adverse effect, or variance in performance, efficacy or safety of your product. Number two, you have no documentation proving that your product has been regularly tested and meets FDA standards. You may be liable for criminal prosecution. Should I continue?'

Lenny swallowed. Fear churned in his gut.

'So when exactly was the potency of the drug reduced?'

He shook his head. 'It wasn't.'

'According to our information, there was a very sudden dip in the efficacy of CK58 not long after Braid went public. How do you account for that?'

'I can't. Wish I could, but I can't. Feedback was all positive,' Lenny stammered.

'You changed suppliers?'

'Changed nothing. Same supplier, same formulation, same everything as before.'

'But not the same result for thousands of people at the end of their lives, it seems! Can we see your records, supply agreements, memos, stuff like that?'

Lenny got up and slid open two drawers filled with empty file holders. 'Ain't much here, but be my guest. You might have more luck with the supply chain guys.'

His invitation was ignored.

'We don't need to tell you that your marketing authorisation for CK58 is suspended and your product is under immediate recall. Until you can prove the efficacy of every sample falls within the 80 to 125 percent window, your FDA approval is withdrawn.'

From being pale at the start of the interview, Lenny's complexion had become an unusual shade of green.

Incoherently he babbled, 'You can't be serious! That St Louis fella, he's a wacko ... wants to sabotage Braid ... come on, guys, you got nothing on me!'

The inspectors looked at one other. 'We won't take up more of your time right now, Mr Schwartz. We'll be in touch.'

Lenny watched them leave. The top of his head felt abnormally hot, water gathered in his mouth and he only just reached the bathroom as the retching began.

*

Arriving home, Tiffany heard a noise coming from the bedroom. She froze, imagining for a horrible moment that an intruder was ransacking the place.

'Oh, it's you!' she cried in relief, as Lenny met her in the foyer. 'You gave me a scare! Why are you back this early? Are you sick?'

'Yeah, sick as a dog. Sit down.'

'Let me get my coat off at least.'

Impatiently she shrugged past him to the hall cloakroom, and locked the door. Had he found out about Kelton and her? Never! The idea wouldn't occur to him: he was too absorbed in that job of his. Lenny couldn't walk and chew gum at the same time! She brushed her hair, put on fresh lipstick, and went through to the living room where he hovered by the window.

'All right, let's hear what's so important.'

'We're in trouble.'

'*We?*'

'Me and MacLeod. A huge can of worms has opened up at work. It could sink the company.' He sat down and hung his head, a picture of despair.

Tiffany waited ... and waited. After about twenty seconds, she reached out. With her bony knuckles she knocked viciously on his skull. '*Hello*? Is anybody home? I'm not a mind reader.'

'Hey, cut it out! Remember the pet project that was going to make us all rich, CK58? It's turned into a crock of shit. We already have the FDA on our tail. It'll be the FBI next.'

She sighed. 'Your cup's always half-empty, isn't it? I don't understand you, really I don't! Everything was done in China: if something's wrong, they should look at the source. Who can prove exactly what you did or didn't do? Your hands are clean, so wise up, for goodness sake!'

'What do you know about anything?' he snarled. 'It's my project. That makes me responsible.'

'Calm yourself down. You need a drink. What does Big Mac say?'

'Nothing. Told me to deal with it. The problem's all mine. If a miracle happens and I come through this in one piece, we're outta here. Otherwise we're screwed. I'll never talk to that double-crossing son of a bitch again! I wish I'd never cast eyes on the bastard.'

'At least Kelton's got guts, doesn't collapse in a heap at the first sign of trouble!' sneered Tiffany. 'You should take a leaf out of his book, instead of whining when you mess up.'

Lenny looked up. 'Mess up, my ass! I warned him from the beginning we were skating on thin ice. But he knew best, insisted on going ahead.'

'And you were scared to stand up to him, right? You're a follower, the one caught holding the bag. You're not half the man he is, Lenny, and never will be!'

'Oh yeah? You don't know him.'

'*But I do*!' she cried. 'This would be funny if it wasn't so sad.'

'Your point being ...?'

'Did you honestly imagine I sat at home alone every night for the last couple of years, while you jetted off all over the world?'

'Shut up! I don't want to hear this.'

'I'm telling you anyhow. It was because of *him* that I stayed on in Chicago.'

'I thought you had more sense, more self-respect than fall for that jerk. These weren't vacation trips, you know!' he yelled. 'I was working my butt off for you.'

Tiffany sighed. 'Yeah, and that was all you had to offer. You think you're young because your hair is dyed and your teeth are capped, but really you're a waste of space, Lenny! Big Mac's the only fun I've had since I met you.'

'Don't fool yourself that you mean anything to him. He'll use you for a while, then you'll be thrown on the scrapheap, beside all the others!'

She went to the bedroom, and slammed the door behind her. When she emerged, lugging a heavy suitcase, Lenny remained where she'd left him on the sofa. She made her way to the foyer, snatched her car keys from the bowl on the side table, and stormed out without a word.

*

Kelton wished he could stop the constant pounding in his head. He lay back on the sofa, TV remote in his hand, and closed his eyes to plan his next move. His first instinct was to run, to get as far away from Chicago as he possibly could. Mexico, or Argentina, maybe?

But it was too late to cash in his company options, with CK58 already under recall: the papers would be full of it in the morning, and Braid's stock price would plummet. His predicament was all down to the incompetence of Lenny

249

Schwartz. But he'd ride out the storm, pin everything on his second-in-command, and salvage what he could from the wreckage.

The intercom buzzed and he ignored it. His phone rang, the answering machine kicked in, and he heard Tiffany's voice.

'Kelton? It's me. I'm in the lobby.'

Lifting the receiver, he growled, 'Go away.'

'Can I come up?'

'What do you want?'

'Please, just let me in.'

He opened his door, and she threw herself on him, sobbing.

'I'm sorry if I'm being a nuisance, but I had to see you!'

Roughly he disengaged himself, and led her to an armchair. Positioning himself on the opposite sofa, he glared steadily at her, his eyebrows raised. 'So?'

'I've left Lenny.'

Betraying no reaction, he continued to study her. 'And?'

'I said I've left Lenny.' Why was he treating her with such surly insolence?

'I heard you the first time. What's it to me?'

'I told him about us.'

She had a certain dimness about her expression, and her teeth really were quite rabbity, he was thinking. On this of all nights, when all he'd worked for might disappear down the tubes, why bother him with this crap?

'Told him what? Don't flatter yourself. There is no *us*.'

'Kelton, don't wind me up.'

Pointedly he ignored the manicured hand reaching out across the coffee table. 'You got the wrong end of the stick, Tiffany. Sure, we had fun, a laugh or two, but that was all. Nobody ever asked you to leave Lenny.'

'I'll divorce him, so we can be together. I love you!'

'Give me a break,' he replied scathingly. 'Is that all you came to say?'

It would have been less painful if he'd socked her in the jaw. Furious, she reached for her purse and jumped to her feet. With stumbling humiliation she made it to the door, and fumbled her way along the corridor to the elevator. Even as she drove off, she imagined his mocking eyes were following her.

All the way to St Louis, she fumed and fretted. Lenny's words came back to her. What he said was true: she had been used. What the hell was she thinking, going to Kelton's apartment in that state, vainly deluding herself that he'd want her? Never had she been made to feel so cheap. He'd looked at her like a piece of dog shit on the sidewalk. If it was the last thing she did, she'd get her revenge on that bastard MacLeod!

Kelton began to feel better after Tiffany's departure. It was strange, he thought, how women were like kiwi fruit: exotic and sweetly delicious when they first appeared on the market, yet humdrum and slightly bitter once freely available.

*

He had barely drunk his first cup of coffee next morning when there was a knock at his office door.

His secretary was distraught. 'I'm sorry, Dr MacLeod, they wouldn't take no for an answer,' she apologised. Beside her stood two FBI agents.

'I'll take it from here, Susan.' He led them in and closed his door.

'I think you know why we've come,' said one.

'Let me guess, CK58?'

Both guys nodded.

'Look, if there's a cock-up, Lenny Schwartz is your man. He was running the show.'

'Under your leadership. You gave him the job, brought him in specifically to handle this product, right?'

'Sure. I knew him for years at Devanacorp – at one time, I even worked for the guy! I needed someone with a successful track record, to manage a product with the potential of CK58.

251

Schwartz seemed like a no-brainer, someone I could trust.'

'Why hire someone you knew was caught skimming expenses? Doesn't sound too trustworthy to me.'

With a jolt of panic, Kelton realised that they'd already been sniffing around.

'I did it out of pity. I was sorry to see him sidelined for something so trivial. It seemed a waste.'

'Presumed he'd be easily persuaded into a bigger scam at Braid, did you?'

Kelton looked indignant. 'Excuse me? To my knowledge, there was no scam. Schwartz was appointed in good faith, and had complete control over his product. That project was his baby, no one else's. Like any CEO worth his salt, I *delegated*. My job is to present results that please the shareholders.'

'Even if it means resorting to criminal action?'

'Absolutely not. My directors have a lot of freedom, but Braid sticks scrupulously to the letter of the law. I don't micromanage, don't demand an explanation for every step my employees take. I oversee the company as a whole, not its individual projects.'

'But the ultimate responsibility for ethical business practice lies with you.'

'Look, Schwartz did a great job, worked his ass off to make our product the number one chemo treatment. As far as I'm concerned, he delivered. How he pulled it off, I don't know. I didn't ask. By your logic, is the Salvation Army guilty of a crime if they unwittingly accept a thief's donation? I don't think so!'

The agents stood up to leave. 'We'll be back.'

No sooner were they gone than Kelton loosened his tie and lifted the phone to call his lawyer.

*

They were in Lenny's office once more.

'We'd like you to come with us for further questioning.'

What had they got from Mac? 'Can I call my lawyer first?'
'Sure. Go right ahead.'

Minutes later, Lenny stood up and put on his suit jacket. His heart was thumping, his knees like jelly. Fondly he looked around him, at the polished wood desk with its framed photograph of a smiling Tiffany, the soft leather sofa by the window, his books and plants and porcelain lamps, the paintings on the walls and the plush carpet beneath his feet. All the trappings of success that he might never again enjoy, because he'd lacked the courage to take a stand.

It was like before, but now the big guns were after him. He'd no chance of coming out of this with a slap on the wrist like at Devanacorp. But one thing was different. This time, he'd have no hesitation in ratting out Big Mac. If he was going down, he'd make damned sure MacLeod went with him.

On his way out, he gave his secretary a sickly grin, and said, 'See you tomorrow.'

If only! Lenny muttered to himself.

*

Tiffany filed a chipped nail while two feet away her mother watched television. Boring! Back to geezer city, where not a damned thing ever changed. It was still the same routine from years ago, in the trailer her mother called home. At six o'clock, a TV dinner was eaten from a tray while they listened to the local network news with Karen Foss. One item made both of them sit up and listen.

'In Chicago, the FDA has ordered the recall of a popular chemotherapy drug made by Braid Pharma. A former St Louis man, Leonard Schwartz, the director in charge of the project, is being questioned regarding a possible scam. As many as four thousand patients in hospitals all over the U.S. may be affected. No charges have yet been filed, but Braid stock took a nosedive today at the start of trading.'

'Geez!' said Tiffany, pushing her half-eaten dinner aside. 'I

253

don't believe it!'

'Nice company you kept up in the Windy City, huh? Maybe that big shot husband of yours is headed for the slammer.' The mother scraped the last of her meal from its plastic container.

'Shaddup, Ma,' replied Tiffany, in no mood to discuss anything. All she wanted was peace and quiet. Was that so much to ask for?

*

'There's no way we can pull off a deal as long as it's just your word against his,' said the lawyer. 'Are you sure you've nothing that would incriminate MacLeod?'

'Like what, a printed plan? How often do I have to tell you? *He* came up with the scheme, demanded that I bust my butt flying back and forth to China to make it all happen. Things were stitched up so I was the sole contact for Xiang Yang Chemical. I was gone half the time. Left him free to begin laying my wife.'

'Let's talk about your wife.'

Lenny winced. It hurt, the memory of his last conversation with Tiffany. It was bad enough that Kelton had been instrumental in landing him in this dilemma, but never would he forgive the sheer cunning with which Tiffany had been lured away from him. The two of them were probably laughing so hard their sides hurt, to know he was languishing in police custody while they lived in luxury!

'Like I said, she left me. I assume she's with him.'

'I'll check it out. I'd like to talk to her.'

'Good luck.'

'I'll tell you, pal, we need it.' The lawyer gathered up his papers. 'I'll keep you posted.'

*

Finding Tiffany was easier than Ken Marshall had expected. It was a favourable sign that she was not still with MacLeod. By ten the next day, he'd unearthed her mother's address and phone

254

number in St Louis.

'Yeah?' said Tiffany, lifting the receiver.

'I'm trying to trace a Tiffany Schwartz.'

'Who wants her?'

'My name's Ken Marshall. I'm her husband's lawyer.'

'So what do you want with me?'

'You're the only one who can help us.'

Ready for battle, she chewed down hard on her bubble gum. 'If this is about the car, my jewellery or whatever, you can forget it. I'm giving nothing back. They're mine.'

Marshall laughed. 'Absolutely. That's not the issue. I want to speak to you in person. Any chance you'll be coming back to Chicago in the next day or two?'

She looked up at the stained styrene ceiling tiles that seemed to close in on her a little more each day, and breathed in the stale smokiness of the air. Why shouldn't she go back north? It was plain stupid to hang around this shithole, when she could have the apartment to herself. Fifteen bucks' worth of gas would take her there.

'I'll think about it,' she said. 'Give me your number. I'll call you.'

*

'I think we've got him!' said Marshall three days afterwards.

Lenny tried to smile. 'Wish I could believe you.'

'Your wife's agreed to testify. MacLeod got carried away one night during one of their trysts, described himself and you as the Lone Ranger and Tonto. She's prepared to say under oath that he told her *his* little scheme worked.'

'Yeah, well something's not right. She's playing games. I told you, they were together, that's where she was headed that night she left me. She won't turn against him, no way!'

'Except they had a bust-up, and she's mad as hell. You know what they say about a woman scorned ...'

Lenny snorted. 'Maybe there is a God after all, huh?'

'Hang tough, Lenny, we're close to a deal here. You come clean, cooperate as fully as possible, and you might get off with five years that would become two with good behaviour. MacLeod could be put away for a lot longer. When he's released, he'll meet such a barrage of civil suits that he'll never get back on his feet again, not in this lifetime.'

Chapter 39

'Once we are destined to live out our lives in the prison of our mind, our duty is to furnish it well.' – Peter Ustinov

IT WAS A BRUTAL WORLD of clanking metal and cold concrete, an alternative universe filled with ugliness and the stench of humanity. Kelton quietly ate the lunch that never varied: a baloney sandwich, a styrofoam cup of water and a bag of potato chips. Food he formerly would have spurned was now one of his few comforts, a bright spot in a tunnel of darkness. He always made a beeline for the end of the steel bench at mealtimes, to minimise the chance of a minor altercation with another inmate.

Naïve enough to believe he was smarter than the bozos he'd be locked up with, he had counted on his intelligence and imagination to deliver him from the festering coarseness of his environment. But such illusions were quickly shattered. Far from providing an escape into another world, his self-absorption blinded him to the crude etiquette of prison life. One day as he sat lost in thought during the recreation hour, he inadvertently allowed his eyes to linger on another offender for a mere second longer than was deemed acceptable. A ferocious beating in the showers followed. It took weeks for the bruises to fade. The memory never would.

With subtle body language constantly in play, his survival hinged on constant awareness of his surroundings. The simplest of glances or movements could incite attack: the unrelenting need to remain vigilant during every waking minute was Kelton's true punishment. Only by learning the code of the caged beasts all around would he make it through. Like carrion thrown into a den of coyotes, he was theirs to do with as they pleased.

He looked forward to the weekly sermons in chapel, not for any religious inspiration, more for the calming change of scene that broke the monotony of the daily grind. One Sunday as they were filing out at the end of the service, a grubby piece of paper was thrust into his hand.

A suspicious officer yelled out, 'Hey! You! Keep movin' along there!'

Unconcerned, Kelton kept walking in line and shoved the scrap into his pocket. He took a couple of paces and briefly glanced at the weaselly, grey-haired schmuck behind him. It was only much later, when his cellmate lay reading, that he risked looking at the note, on which was scrawled some biblical gibberish. Great! Now a religious nutter was trying to latch onto him!

All the same, Kelton approached Nick Duncan next day in the exercise yard.

'So what's up?' he asked.

'I've got a proposition for you. The Feds shut down my last church in Texas. My face has gotten over-exposed, makes it hard to get sponsors to advertise on my broadcasts. I'd go it alone if I could, but I need a new pitch man. That's maybe where you'll come in.'

Kelton grunted. 'Not my scene.'

'Nobody said you have to be a believer. It's a money-spinner. You're smart, you've time to become a fuckin' expert on the scriptures before you leave here! You preached the dogma of pharmaceuticals for years, sold crap to suckers who had faith that you could cure their ills, so what's your problem? Religion's the opium of the people.'

'No thanks, buddy. I'm not interested.'

Duncan was no higher than himself in the pecking order. He could safely be ignored.

*

After lights-out, a voice above him growled, 'You sleepin'?'

Kelton opened one eye. 'What d'ya want?'

'I got a message.'

'Fuck off.'

There was a rustling of paper, then a hand reached down from the upper bunk. 'You'll take it if you know what's good for you. It's from Eddie.'

'Eddie Sloane?'

Reading the note at daylight Kelton muttered under his breath.

> *Your sister wants to see you.*
> *Add her name to your list of approved visitors.*

Involvement with Eddie and his gang was the last thing Kelton needed. Quickly he scribbled a reply:

> *You got the wrong guy. I don't have a sister.*

Back came the answer:

> *You do now.*

Survival at the Joliet Correctional Center hinged on keeping on the right side of the bad-asses. Non-compliance with their demands incurred a beating, or worse: their speciality was planting contraband, which would easily scupper Kelton's upcoming parole hearing. Eddie's tentacles had a long reach.

*

From a distance, she was nice-looking, a breath of fresh air with her shiny hair and bright lipstick. Many times these last few years he'd have given his right arm for a visit from *any* piece of tail like her! Kelton felt stirrings of excitement. Not till he got nearer did he see her smoker's teeth and the crow's feet round her eyes.

She smiled, hoping her nervousness didn't show. It was a mistake to agree to this, foolish to allow herself to be pressured. But the money was good and Eddie's guys were very persuasive.

'Hey, how are ya?' she said. 'It's been a while.'

'I'm okay,' replied Kelton. From the corner of his eye, he saw Eddie watching. 'You?'

'Same old, same old, 'cept I moved to Prospect Heights. Nothing fancy, but at least I have a yard, with room for the dogs to run around.'

'That's great.' He strove to think of something to say, to maintain the charade. 'I can't wait to see it.'

'Yeah, and the best thing is, we got decent restaurants close by – there's a Papa John's Pizza on our block, and the Golden Chopsticks is only five minutes away.'

Kelton tried to look enthusiastic. 'Wow! How about the kids?'

'They call, off and on. Usually when they want money. That's the way it goes ...'

'I guess.'

Silence hung between them, then she asked, 'You been watchin' much TV?'

'Sure, comedies mostly. Don't get that many laughs in here, you know?' He looked up at the big clock on the wall. Ten more minutes until the bell would sound. 'I see you changed your hair; it's lighter than I remembered.'

Inconsequential though it was, Kelton enjoyed the chat as they eased into the roles Eddie had decreed they would play. At the end they smiled at each other.

'It's great to see you again.'

'Same here. I've missed you.'

She left to retrieve her personal items from the secure reception area. In her car she checked her padded jacket: the package sewn into the lining of the left sleeve was gone. Mission accomplished. She exhaled and put the key in the ignition.

That same night, Kelton discovered a handful of little white pills wrapped in crumpled paper beneath his pillow. *Good job,* Eddie had written. *Enjoy.*

More powerful than books or meditation, the Ecstasy provided a blissful escape into a more pleasant world. Kelton dreamed of countries he'd visited, and of women he'd dated. He imagined the perfumed silkiness of their skin against his, instead of the rough scratchiness of his prison blanket. Temporary respite was better than none at all.

Three more months was all he'd to do, before release. Three more visits from his 'sister', then he'd leave this place forever.

*

Out of the blue one day, Carol's phone rang.

'Hi, Mom, how are things?'

'Will! This is a surprise, is everything all right?' There had to be an important reason for him to call from Scotland.

'We just wanted you to be the first to hear ... it's about Fiona and me. We got married today.'

'That's wonderful!'

'And we're having a baby.'

'I couldn't be happier for you, son,' she said, swallowing her disappointment.

It was what she'd been afraid of. Her best boy was lost. Never would he return to live in America now. But he was no longer a boy. He had a wife – and a child on the way. How ironic, that he would abandon his roots for what she had rejected! This was the same pain she had unwittingly inflicted on her own parents: oblivious to the hurt it would cause, she had left them, and gone to settle four thousand miles away. But her freedom of choice had been respected, and her own offspring deserved no less. The greatest irony of all was that Will had married a Murray. Though she had jilted Alex twenty-odd years earlier, they would be eternally linked by a common grandchild.

*

'Where would I find granite sealant?'

'Aisle fifteen, ma'am.' The shelf-stacker barely gave Laura a glance.

A supervisor came heading purposefully in his direction, pointed an index finger at him, at an empty shelf and then back

261

at him. He nodded and shuffled off to the storeroom for another load of light bulbs.

Passing him again on her way out, Laura stopped. Where on earth had she seen that geezer before? Perhaps he'd been a greeter at Wal-Mart, she thought ... yet behind his gaunt greyness was something familiar.

'Kel?' she said, tentatively.

He looked up. 'Something else I can help you with?'

She peered at the name tag on his orange apron, unable to make it out. It had to be him – she'd recognise those eyes anywhere, though their flashy confidence was gone. Instead of focusing on her, they darted around nervously: the eyes of a hunted animal, suspicious of anyone who tried to get too close.

'Excuse me,' she said. 'Didn't we once know each other, a long time ago?'

'I don't think so.'

You can gloat, but I won't be this way much longer, he wanted to tell her. *I'll be back. Bigger, badder and better than ever!*

Like Huey Lewis & The News, he was working towards his *Perfect World*.

All it took was faith in himself, and Kelton had that in spades.

Chapter 40

'Though the mills of God grind slowly,
yet they grind exceeding small;
Though with patience He stands waiting,
with exactness grinds He all.'
– Henry Wadsworth Longfellow

H E HAD SURVIVED THE HUMILIATIONS of the half-way house, had exercised enough restraint to stay clean during his parole, and had kept his temper while doing his assigned duties, difficult though it had often been. Now things were looking up. His re-entry process was complete. No more supervision, no visits to the Day Reporting Center, nor restrictions on his mobility. Kelton was ready to pick up the threads of his life. Eddie Sloane's decision to invest some Ecstasy in him during their time in jail had paid off handsomely.

His new career was risky but lucrative, the product he sold of the highest purity. Brought by freighters that had crossed the Atlantic, sailing via the St Lawrence Seaway into the Great Lakes – Ontario to Erie to Huron to Michigan – the precious shipments were offloaded in Chicago by longshoremen in Eddie's network.

To serve his distribution area that stretched from Chicago to St Louis, Kelton drove a 'company' car. The Porsche was one of the many perks of his job, like his lake-front apartment, one block from where he'd previously lived.

Eddie was a demanding boss and in his turn, Kelton took no bullshit from his clients. Cash on delivery was the rule. On a good trip he might net $10,000. He'd had a few minor skirmishes, supplying dealers in the insalubrious parts of town, but there was no free lunch. It came with the territory and he knew how to take care of himself.

Inevitably a situation arose in St Louis one night, when he *really* had to cut up rough. The punk who tried to double-cross him was left bleeding in an alleyway. They rushed him to the local ER, but he died later.

*

Homicide victim in drugs deal gone wrong

Sergeant Joe Jasko read and reread the item in the *St Louis Post-Dispatch*, and took off his glasses. 'Strange!' he remarked.

'What's up? Aren't you hungry?' asked his wife.

'Not really. This case,' he replied, pointing at the page, 'it rings a bell. I'm trying to think why.'

'Forget it, let somebody else worry. You're just months from retirement. You should be winding down on your day off, not worrying about work.'

'Yeah, yeah, I know. I'm not worried – I'm interested. The missing ear thing, it bothers me.'

'Sweetheart. How many homicides did you deal with in your career? I'll tell you: hundreds. And how much thanks did you get for the sleepless nights you wasted on them? None. So give yourself a break and eat your meal already!'

Donna gave a sigh of despair.

Joe smiled. With other things on his mind, food was an unwelcome distraction. Two dozen years in the squad had gained him a reputation for dogged perseverance. Never one to give up, he wasn't about to start now. His wife went to answer the phone, and he scooped the remains of his meal into the dish of his pet bull terrier.

Not till 4 am did Joe remember: 1968 – that was when he'd seen a similar case. In Ladue Road. He lay listening to Donna's steady breathing, then crept out of bed and went to shower. As the water rained down on him, he pictured the scene of the crash, and the body they'd stumbled upon nearby. He'd been keen to pursue things further, but was ordered by his boss to let it be. The jerk who'd been driving the Mustang got off scot-free. It was doubtful the official file had survived, but Joe had a backup. In his attic lay a collection of old diaries that spanned his whole career, and nothing had been too trivial to be entered in his meticulous records.

*

The house looked pretty much the same as before: same colour of paintwork, same blinds on the windows, same trees in the front garden though they'd grown a lot. Despite all *he'd* been through, nothing for Carol had changed! Or so it seemed to Kelton, until one night as he lurked in her street after dark, he saw a figure moving around in the lighted dining-room. Soundlessly he got out of the car and darted from one tree to another. In the bushes by the window, he crouched low to watch as she replaced some dishes in the cabinet. He could scarcely believe he was seeing his ex-wife. She had definitely lost weight, and her hair was blonder than before. Though now middle-aged, she was as slender as the girl he'd known in Aberdeen. There was no denying she looked great – in fact she had become a beautiful woman.

When the light was turned off, Kelton returned to his car, his mind in turmoil. Bitterness at what he'd given up curdled with an unexpected surge of jealousy. Stretching across for the polythene bag he kept in the glove compartment, he licked one finger, stuck it into the white powder and rubbed it along his gums. His taut facial muscles relaxed. Snorting a line or two back in his hotel would help him forget Carol for a while.

On his next foray into her street, he watched a Lexus pull up in her driveway, with a middle-aged guy at the wheel. The garage door slid up at his approach. She must have found herself a boyfriend ... or had she perhaps married again? Whatever, the guy acted as if he owned the place. A light went on in the master bedroom and movement at the window caught his eye. One blind was snapped shut, then the other. How comfortable they were, Carol and her fancy-man, cavorting around in the house *he* had bought and paid for! The very idea made his blood boil.

*

It was back. In the last few months, it had regularly appeared near her house, always late at night. Each time Carol peeped out from the darkness of the spare bedroom and saw the Porsche, a shudder went through her. Someone was hunched low in the driver's seat. Was it paranoia, to think it was Kelton?

Finally she confessed her fears to Mike.

'Next time, I'll go out and take a look. I hate to see you upset like this,' he soothed, making her feel better.

*

Despite Joe Jasko's best efforts, the police had made little progress with the homicide case: the killer had covered his tracks pretty well.

Kelton was riding on the crest of the wave. The incident had enhanced his reputation in the underworld and provided a welcome addition to his macabre trophy collection. He was Big Mac again! Business was brisk, and he was more upbeat than he'd been in years. Except for one thing.

Since seeing that guy in Carol's house – his house! – a corrosive discontent gnawed at him like indigestion, one that no antacid would cure. He had to get even with this woman who had cheated him out of what was rightfully his! Fury distorted his reason and matters came to a head one night while he sat in the shadows.

The front door opened, and Carol stepped outside, followed by Mike. By the glow of the porch lights, Kelton watched them stroll hand-in-hand down the path to the sidewalk. Parked just thirty feet away, he turned the key in the ignition and headed in their direction, quickly picking up speed. For a split second, his eyes met Carol's. She froze, and Kelton saw her panic as the

Porsche mounted the kerb. Next thing he knew, there was a satisfying thump, and the front wing of his car came in contact with something. Dammit, he thought as he sped off, he'd only skimmed one of them! Still, the warning would bring her down to earth with a bump.

*

The commotion brought a neighbour running out. Another called the emergency services. Minutes later an ambulance and the police were at the scene, and someone helped Carol to her feet. A mighty shove had sent her flying on to the grass, out of the path of the oncoming vehicle. Mike's action had saved her, while he himself had taken the impact of the Porsche's wing. Now he was the focus of the ambulance crew's attention.

'Ma'am, did you see the driver of the car?' Sergeant Jasko asked.

'It was my ex-husband, Kelton.' Carol struggled to stop her teeth from chattering.

Joe could not believe his ears, and wondered if he had heard her correctly. Hadn't he come across that name once before? 'And what's his surname?'

'MacLeod. *Kelton MacLeod.*'

'How about the car? Do you know what make it was?'

'A Porsche, I think,' said Carol. 'With an Illinois registration.'

Seeing the paramedics lay Mike on a stretcher, she began to sob and cried out, 'Wait, I'm coming with you to the hospital!' She felt a restraining hand on her arm.

'You'll see him in a while.'

'But I need to be with him. We just got married last month.'

Joe's voice was firm and reassuring. 'And now what he most needs is a doctor. He's gonna be fine. They'll take good care of him, I promise.'

Mike gave her a feeble wave, and mouthed 'I love you' to her.

'I love you, too,' Carol called back. Reluctantly she allowed herself to be led back home by a female officer.

The sergeant got back in his squad car and spoke into his radio. A general alert went out for a dark, late-model Porsche with Illinois plates.

It all fitted! At last the pieces of the puzzle that had eluded him for so long were connected. He was going to nail that bastard! Joe had struck gold, he was on a roll. It had taken a while, but MacLeod would not escape this time.

*

Bombing east along Highway 40 towards the Poplar Street Bridge, Kelton jerked his head back and fore to the thumping beat of the car stereo. Only a Scottish duo could provide such an appropriate soundtrack for his rekindled interest in Carol! Adrenalin pumped through his system to see the speedometer touch one-ten. In triumph he sang along with The Proclaimers:

> *But I would walk five hundred miles*
> *And I would walk five hundred more*
> *Just to be the man who walked a thousand miles*
> *To fall down at your door.*

Seldom had Kelton been this high. The cocaine was good, but the real kick had been her look of terror when he caught her in the headlights. Now she knew the score, he thought with pride. She'd had it easy while he was out of circulation, but not any longer. He was back and she'd never feel safe again!

Gleefully he saw flashing blue lights about half a mile behind him. This was like the old days with Amy. His car could still outrun any other. After he crossed the bridge into Illinois, he'd be beyond their reach.

On the other side of the Mississippi, he dropped his speed and cruised past East St Louis. He had to cool it: he was safe from these dumb-ass cops. He relaxed, his breathing quieter as the tempo of the music changed. Roger Miller lulled him into a gentler, calmer place:

Suddenly, out of nowhere, a Missouri squad car appeared in Kelton's rear-view mirror, roaring up behind him until it was right on his tail. *Fuck!* Was it a myth, that the law could not pursue a suspect outside their jurisdiction? In the same instant, he became aware of a second police car to his left, parallel with the Porsche. Now it was actually overtaking him! Kelton blasted his horn and flashed his lights from dip to full beam, but the slowpoke in front kept puttering along at a steady fifty-five and refused to speed up. *Shit and damnation!* He was cornered, forced to slow down and pull into the side of the road. A loudhailer sounded, ordering him to turn off his engine and wait in the driver's seat.

But Kelton had other plans. For sure he would not go quietly. Violently he flung open his driver's door and went lurching straight out on to the carriageway, determined to escape if he could. He would not see the inside of Joliet again, not in this life!

The police helplessly watched his gaunt silhouette dodge and weave in the headlights of the oncoming traffic. Cars swerved to avoid him, and collided in a scrunch of metal on metal, a slamming of brakes, and a squealing of tyres. Then Kelton MacLeod's shadowy figure went airborne before landing in the path of an eighteen-wheeler barrelling along at sixty miles an hour.

Back in the Porsche, Roger Miller had reached his final chorus:

And this time no one sang along.

ACKNOWLEDGEMENTS

I would like to thank the entire editing, design and publishing team at Kinord Books for their wonderful support, patience and encouragement in bringing this project to completion.

Also by Elinor Hunter:

A Bad Woman

*It takes **a bad woman** to make a bad man*, the saying goes. Though Queen Victoria's affair with John Brown raises barely an eyebrow, it's a different story for her working-class subjects.

In Scotland, Bella and Isa each discover the harsh realities of loss and single parenthood. Like Victoria, the supposed moral compass of the nation, they risk their reputations to survive tragedy and retain their sanity, only their efforts are met with public censure and humiliation.

The fates of all three share uncanny parallels, yet posterity will brand one of them **a bad woman**. But then nothing is ever as it seems ...

By Jim Forbes:

Taran's Wheel (*Incomers*: Book 1)

What has become of the ancient talisman known as **Taran's Wheel**? A riddle from beyond the grave sets Delia on a hunt. Her search, which takes her from Chicago to the 'Pleasant Vale' of Cromar in Scotland, reveals the dramatic story of the Vale and its people.

But can this story lead Delia to Taran's Wheel, or will sinister forces deny her the prize, even threaten her life?

Scotch and Water (*Incomers*: Book 2)

The 2014 referendum is history, but it's a time of drama for Edinburgh and the ancient land of Lothian.

A metal detector hobbyist is murdered just as he strikes gold. The discovery of cryptic writings sheds new light on a celebrated 19th-century Edinburgh family. A ruthless businesswoman exploits council corruption. Controversially, huge volumes of water are to be pumped to southern England. A violent ultra-nationalist cell plots mayhem in the wake of Scotland's 'no' to independence.

Like scotch and water, these apparently unconnected goings-on make a potent mix: a web of political, criminal and terrorist intrigue linked to a mysterious relic of some of Lothian's earliest incomers.

www.kinordbooks.com